THE NEW YORK BOOK OF MUSIC

THE NEW YORK BOOK OF MUSIC
IRA ROSENBLUM

WITH ILLUSTRATIONS BY EMILY LISKER
CITY & COMPANY · NEW YORK

City & Company
22 West 23rd Street
New York, N.Y. 10010

Printed in the United States of America
Design by Tyler Smith and Leah Lococo with Jillian Blume

Library of Congress Cataloging-in-Publication Data is available
upon request.

ISBN 1-885492-21-9
First Edition

Publisher's Note: Neither City & Company nor the author
has any interest, financial or personal, in the venues listed in this
book. No fees were paid or services rendered in exchange
for inclusion in these pages.

Please also note that every effort was made to ensure that information
regarding addresses, phone numbers, hours, and transportation
was accurate and up-to-date at the time of publication. Unless otherwise
noted, the area code is 212.

ACKNOWLEDGMENTS

It's been said many times before: a book is never the creation of the author alone. So many people helped me write this one that it would be impossible to thank them all. But there are some I would like to single out.

Working in the music business, I've met lots of people whose insights have been invaluable. To everyone who gave me leads or suggestions, thank you. (The list is too long. You know who you are!) Particular thanks are due Gloria Gottschalk for keeping her eyes and ears open; Allan Kozinn, who let me bug him with endless questions; Jon Pareles, Peter Watrous, and Stephen Holden, who shared their rock, jazz, and cabaret expertise; Douglas Drake for filling me in on church music, and Helene Browning for her help with world music.

Special gratitude to Helene Silver and the folks at City & Company for giving me the chance. Also to Lynn Rosenbaum for the initial tip, Kathryn Barrett for interpreting the legalese, and Jamal Rayyis for checking the facts.

Loving thanks to my parents for buying a piano when I was a kid, thereby introducing me to the joys of music; to my closest friends for their understanding during all those times that I went into seclusion while working on this project; to Carol Coburn for the acknowledgment; to Marlene Abel, Barbara Fischer, Barbara Cohen, and the Tuesday night group for seeing me through this often crazy process; and to Mollie, for keeping me company while I worked.

Finally, to Kenneth, who stood by me with the utmost patience, listening to me kvetch, proofreading my copy, and generally being there for me, as he has for the past 20 years. This book is lovingly dedicated to him, and to Gary, whose spirit lives on in the music.

CONTENTS

Introduction 1

How to Use This Guide 3

I'LL TAKE MANHATTAN 7
Manhattan's major and minor concert halls

THE BRONX AND STATEN ISLAND, TOO 26
The same, but for the other boroughs

THE BEST THINGS IN LIFE ARE FREE 36
Buying tickets; free or inexpensive concerts

I HEAR A SYMPHONY 53
Orchestras and chamber groups

A FINE ROMANCE 69
*Organizations and concert series for
singles; romantic places to hear live music*

A NIGHT AT THE OPERA 78
Opera companies, from large to small

VOCAL CHORDS 93
Professional choral groups

GET ME TO THE CHURCH 102
*Churches and synagogues with prominent
concert series*

IT'S CHRISTMASTIME IN THE CITY 113
*Christmas music, Chanukkah,
Winter Solstice, and Kwanzaa celebrations*

IN THE GOOD OLD SUMMERTIME 122
Summer music series and festivals

ALL THAT JAZZ...AND ROCK AND POP 134
Jazz and cabarets; rock, pop, and blues clubs

AROUND THE WORLD 152
Ethnic and folk music

YEAH, BUT IS IT MUSIC? 164
Avant garde, experimental, and performance art

CHILDREN'S CORNER 182
Concerts, events, and organizations for children

MAMA, I WANT TO SING 191
How to find a teacher; neighborhood music schools

AMATEUR NIGHT 203
Amateur choruses and orchestras; summer sings

THE SHOP AROUND THE CORNER 219
*Record shops; sheet music and books, gifts,
and unusual items*

CODA 231
Tours; museums and other attractions

Appendix A 237
Radio stations and music formats

Appendix B 238
*Addresses and phone numbers of major
concert venues*

Index 239

INTRODUCTION

If you are a seasoned New York music lover, you can probably find your way to Carnegie Hall. (Yes, you can practice, practice, practice . . . or you can take the subway.)

But do you know how to get to the Colden Center for the Performing Arts, or the Snug Harbor Cultural Center? (Have you even heard of these places, for that matter?) Did you know that you can enjoy a romantic dinner by candlelight followed by live chamber music—on a floating coffee barge? And hear a jazz concert in the world's largest Gothic cathedral? Do you know where to get great seats for a fully staged, professional performance of "La Traviata"—for less than $25?

Maybe you're a single man or woman who loves music, and you'd like to meet someone who shares your passion. Perhaps your two year old is showing signs of budding musical genius, and you want a teacher for your Mozart-to-be. Say you have a good voice, and you'd like to sing in a chorus, on a real stage, in front of a live audience. Where do you go?

In this city, considered by most to be the arts capital of the world, music is just about everywhere. On any given day, at any time of the year, you can hear an opera, an orchestra, a rock group, chamber music, jazz, avant garde . . . If there's a name for it, and if someone's doing it, you'll find it here—if you know where to look.

That is the aim of this guide—to steer you, quickly and easily, to the concert halls, performing groups and organizations, schools and shops that keep New York humming. You'll find basic information about the city's major—and some of the minor—concert venues and performing groups, including box office phone numbers and the nearest subway stops (it's 57th Street on the B, N, Q or R trains for Carnegie Hall, by the way). You'll discover where affordable tickets are available and which groups offer inexpensive or free concerts; where to find romantic spots and special events for singles; the best opera groups, children's activities, seasonal music, and jazz and rock clubs; and where you can make music in the Big Apple, whether you are looking for a teacher or want to perform in an amateur chorus or orchestra. You'll also find the best shops for recordings, sheet music, and other related merchandise.

Naturally, a book this size cannot be all-inclusive, so apologies to anyone who was omitted. And because this is a New York City guidebook, we did not include the many wonderful concert halls and organizations in the nearby suburban areas. This is also a subjecive guide, so you may not agree with all the opinions expressed in these pages. But we do hope you will find this book an easy-to-read map to the vast treasure that is music in the Big Apple.

HOW TO USE THIS GUIDE

With a few exceptions, entries within chapters are listed alphabetically. Places named after people are listed under their first names, for example, Alice Tully Hall under Alice, Florence Gould Hall under Florence, etc.

Many venues and groups fit neatly into one category, but others were not so tidy. For example, Bargemusic, which appears in the chapter "A Fine Romance," might have worked as well in "The Bronx and Staten Island, Too" or "I Hear a Symphony." You'll find cross-references scattered throughout, directing you to the proper chapter. They are self-explanatory.

For those organizations that are mentioned in more than one chapter, the name is followed by (see p.), where you'll find the main entry for that hall or group. Some places (Carnegie Hall, Avery Fisher Hall, etc.) cropped up so often that, rather than refer you to another page each time, they are grouped together in Appendix B. Whenever a venue is printed in **bold** typeface, its address and phone number can be found in that appendix along with the page reference for the main entry in the book.

For groups whose performances are always at the same venue, that place is specified. Otherwise, only the number of concerts in its series is listed.

You'll notice that some addresses are listed only as a street number with the nearest cross street, while others include the full mailing address, but no cross streets. The former are venues where performances actually take place, and for these, the nearest subway stops (and bus information, for places not reachable by subway alone), have been indicated. The latter are addresses of offices, places you would be more likely to write to or call than actually visit, so no travel information is given. (A useful phone number for anyone using public transportation in the Big Apple is the N.Y.C. Transit Authority information line: 718-330-1234.)

Unless otherwise indicated, the area code for all phone numbers is 212.

Box office hours vary from place to place, so if you plan on buying tickets in person, call ahead for the schedule. Before purchasing tickets by phone, it's helpful to become familiar with the layout of the hall. Stubbs, available in many bookstores, is a thorough compilation of seating plans for New York's theaters and auditoriums. Also, the Manhattan Yellow Pages includes seating plans for the borough's larger halls.

In chapters 1 and 2, which discuss the major halls around the city, you'll see symbols about wheelchair accessibility, food and drink availability, and more. Here is what they mean:

B = Bar on premises
H = Hearing devices available
P = Parking, either on the premises or in a nearby garage giving discounts to concertgoers
PW = Partial wheelchair accessibility (call for further information)
R = Full-service restaurant on the premises
S = Food concession or snacks available
W = Fully wheelchair accessible

The music world is not immune to inflation—ticket prices change from year to year. In view of this, rather than specific numbers which would quickly become outdated, prices have been broken down into three categories: inexpensive (free to $15), moderate ($15 to $40) and expensive ($40 and above). Call for exact prices. (When specific numbers are given, they reflect 1994–95 prices.) Keep in mind that most organizations offer student and senior discounts, as well as a variety of subscription plans.

Finally, this book is not intended to be a list of current performance dates. For those, check the listings in the local newspapers and magazines. In the chapter "The Best Things in Life Are Free" you'll find several phone numbers to call for up-to-date concert information. While these services are not always complete, they do give a good indication of what's happening, when, and where.

I'LL TAKE MANHATTAN

I've lived in Manhattan for the past 20 years, and I still marvel at the abundance of music this small island sustains. Uptown and downtown, East Side and West, concert halls of all sizes vibrate with the sounds of the world's greatest orchestras and conductors, opera singers and instrumentalists, rock groups and jazz players.

Just walk around the city and you get a sense of its unique connection to the art we call the universal language. Streets like Leonard Bernstein Place and Duke Ellington Boulevard pay homage to the legendary artists who made musical history here. Others, like Tin Pan Alley and Swing Street, remind us of New York's indelible link to the worlds of pop and jazz. Year after year, thousands of students flock to our great conservatories, and day and night the strains of pianos, violins, and other instruments drift from practice rooms all over town.

Twenty years ago I didn't know about the many smaller auditoriums scattered around the city, or the profusion of unique orchestras, chamber groups, and opera companies that call this musical wonderland home. I'm still discovering the jazz clubs and experimental music lofts where the latest trends in the avant garde are being shaped. And with each discovery it becomes clearer and clearer why Manhattan is called the musical center of the world.

This chapter lists the major Manhattan venues, and a few of the larger performance organizations (like the New York Philharmonic, the Metropolitan Opera, and the Chamber Music Society of Lincoln Center). If you are looking for a specific place or group and don't see it here, chances are it's in another chapter. Check the index.

AARON DAVIS HALL AT THE CITY COLLEGE OF NEW YORK
Convent Ave. at 135th St. **Subway:** 1 or 9 to 137th St.
Box off. tel.: 650-7100 **Seats:** Marian Anderson Theater, 750; Black Box Theater, 268; Studio Theater, 50 **Tickets:** Inexpensive to moderate
H P S W

The premier theater serving the uptown community, Aaron Davis Hall is the Harlem home of Opera Ebony (see p. 88), the Boys Choir of Harlem (see p. 183), and several major dance companies. In 1994 the main auditorium was renamed the Marian Anderson Theater, an appropriate choice, since it occupies the site of the now defunct Lewisohn Stadium, where Miss Anderson (who was the first black diva to sing at the Metropolitan Opera) appeared with the New York Philharmonic. Performances at Davis Hall focus on music of particular interest to the African-American community, though by no means exclusively. Jazz Institute of Harlem, a 3-concert series featuring Max Roach and others, is designed to reflect the cultural and musical makeup of the neighborhood, while the New Faces/New Voices/New Visions performance series presents familiar and emerging musicians, dancers, writers, and poets.

ALICE TULLY HALL AT LINCOLN CENTER
Broadway at 65th St. **Subway:** 1 or 9 to 66th St.
Box off. tel.: 875-5050 (or CenterCharge: 721-6500)
Seats: 1,096 **Tickets:** Inexpensive to expensive

| H P S W |

Alice Tully Hall, named for the late philanthropist, opened in 1969
as the home of the Chamber Music Society of Lincoln Center (see p.
12). While it may seem unlikely that a hall this size is well suited to
chamber music, Tully somehow feels smaller than it actually is,
making it a wonderful chamber-music venue. It's also popular for
solo recitals and orchestral concerts as well as jazz, avant-garde, and
an occasional opera-in-concert. The Juilliard School often presents
free concerts here (see p. 44).

One of the auditorium's distinctive features is its layout.
Although it was designed with continental seating—meaning no
center aisle (a nuisance if you have to make a quick escape)—just
about any seat in the house provides ample leg room and splendid
sight lines. The acoustics are also quite good.

APOLLO THEATRE
253 W. 125th St., at Lenox Ave. **Subway:** 2 or 3 to 125th St.
Box off. tel.: 864-0372 or 749-5838 (recorded information)
Seats: 1,474 **Tickets:** Moderate

| P W |

This Harlem landmark was built in 1913 as a burlesque house but
was turned into a music hall in 1934. Since then, it's left a lasting
mark on pop culture, introducing some major talents to the world.
Ella Fitzgerald, Sarah Vaughan, and James Brown, among other
illustrious stars, first got their big breaks at the Apollo's legendary
Amateur Night.

Wednesdays are still Amateur Nights, where the audience isn't
shy about letting performers know what it thinks. If you want to

take a stab at it, send an audio or video tape to the Apollo Theatre Amateur Night. (There are also open auditions about four times a year.) On other nights of the week you might catch acts like Ice Cube, Queen Latifah or B.B. King. Don't let the neighborhood scare you away; it's worth the trip uptown.

AVERY FISHER HALL AT LINCOLN CENTER
Broadway at 65th St. **Subway:** 1 or 9 to 66th St.
Box off. tel.: 875-5030 (or CenterCharge: 721-6500)
Seats: 2,738 **Tickets:** Moderate to expensive
Home of the New York Philharmonic (see p. 19)

| B | H | P | R | S | W |

Avery Fisher Hall was an acoustic nightmare when it opened in 1962 as Philharmonic Hall, so when the New York Philharmonic abandoned **Carnegie Hall** for its new home, it had a problem on its hands. Despite a series of small acoustic facelifts, the problem remained unsolved. Then Avery Fisher (of stereo equipment fame) gave Lincoln Center a small fortune to remodel the hall. While its acoustics are still not the best in the world, they have improved 100%. Fisher Hall is now one of the city's premier venues, home not only to the Philharmonic, but also to many visiting orchestras, vocalists, and recitalists, and numerous Lincoln Center-sponsored events (see p. 15).

There are two full-service restaurants in the hall, the PaneVino and the Adagio, but they are pricy. You might do better to explore the huge selection of restaurants near Lincoln Center. Do save room, however, for dessert from the Cafe Vienna in the lobby, particularly if you like Viennese pastries.

BEACON THEATRE (see "All That Jazz")

CAMI HALL

165 W. 57th St., near Seventh Ave.
Subway: 1, 9, A, B, C or D to 59th St./Columbus Circle; B, N, Q or R to
57th St.; D or E to Seventh Ave.
Information: 841-9500 (There is no box office per se)
Seats: 200 **Tickets:** Inexpensive to moderate

| W |

This small but functional auditorium directly across from Carnegie
Hall is named for, and owned by, Columbia Artists Management,
one of New York's big music management companies. CAMI, as the
firm is known, used to show off its own artists here, and still uses
the hall to audition potential clients. But now concerts are strictly
rentals, so the quality of the performances is erratic. One group that
regularly meets here is the Gilbert and Sullivan Society of New York
(see p. 83).

CARNEGIE HALL AND WEILL RECITAL HALL

57th St. at Seventh Ave. **Subway:** 1, 9, A, B, C or D to 59th St./Columbus
Circle; B, N, Q or R to 57th St.; D or E to Seventh Ave.
Box off. tel.: 247-7800 **Seats:** Carnegie, 2,804; Weill, 268
Tickets: Inexpensive to expensive

| B H P R S W |

While its not the oldest or the biggest concert hall in the world, it
is definitely one of the best, with acoustics that are the envy of many
a house manager. Since its first concert in 1891, conducted by none
other than Tchaikovsky, its stage has been host to Leonard Bernstein,
the Beatles, Judy Garland, Frank Sinatra, Jascha Heifetz, Ella
Fitzgerald, and Jessye Norman, among others, not to mention all the
great orchestras and conductors of the world. Primarily a classical
venue, Carnegie also hosts the finest jazz, folk, and pop artists.

Hats off to violinist Isaac Stern, the president of Carnegie Hall,
who led the fight to keep the grand old lady of 57th Street from the
wrecker's ball in 1960. After closing for some badly needed

renovations in 1986, the hall reopened later that year, more elegant and majestic than ever, and with ample room in the formerly claustrophobic lobby. The Carnegie East Room, a fine art deco dining room, is available to ticket holders for buffet dinners two hours before any Carnegie Hall-sponsored events in the main hall. Reservations are necessary. (Not all events in the hall are Carnegie sponsored, so call ahead to confirm.)

A separate entrance at 154 W. 57th St. will lead you to Weill Recital Hall, a small, comfortable auditorium formerly known as Carnegie Recital Hall, where many instrumentalists and chamber groups perform. Lots of aspiring soloists give their debuts here, and you might hear an unknown, future star. Yo-Yo Ma, John Cage, and the Kronos Quartet made their first New York appearances here.

(See also Carnegie Hall in "All That Jazz"; Carnegie Hall Rose Museum and Tours in "Coda")

CHAMBER MUSIC SOCIETY OF LINCOLN CENTER
70 Lincoln Center Plaza, 10th Fl., New York, N.Y. 10023
Information and subscriptions: 875-5788 **Tickets:** Moderate.
Performs at **Alice Tully Hall** and the Walter Reade Theater (see p. 24)

The Chamber Music Society of Lincoln Center possibly has done more than any other organization in the country to change the image of chamber music. With its big-name artists, such as Ani Kavafian, Fred Sherry, and Ransom Wilson, its well-rounded programs, and community-minded activities, the Society is proof that chamber music is not just for a select few. In its first 25 years (its silver anniversary was in 1994), it has played 1,500 concerts and commissioned 80 new works by some of the most brilliant composers of our time, among them John Corigliano, Joan Tower, and Bright Sheng. To give exposure to the leading contemporary works, in 1993 the Society initiated a 3-concert "Music of Our Time" series at the Walter Reade Theater to augment the new-music offerings at its regular concerts.

Recently the Society launched several new programs, including "Chamber Music 101," a lecture series, and "Behind the Scenes at the Chamber Music Society," that gives an inside view of what is involved in preparing concerts and includes discussions and attending working rehearsals.

(See also Chamber Music Society in "A Fine Romance"; Chamber Music Society in "Children's Corner")

CITY CENTER
131 W. 55th St., near Sixth Ave. **Subway:** B, N, Q or R to 57th St.
Box off. tel.: 581-7907 or 581-1212 **Seats:** 2,684 **Tickets:** Moderate
`B S W`

City Center is one of Manhattan's loveliest performance spaces. Built in 1923 as a meeting hall for the Ancient and Accepted Order of the Mystic Shrine, its Moorish facade and interior details earned it the nickname "Mecca Temple." In 1943 Mayor Fiorello LaGuardia saved it from demolition and declared it City Center, "a temple for the performing arts." Now primarily a dance space, enough music events take place to warrant including it here. (A performance several years ago by the KODO Drummers of Japan was one of the most thrilling musical experiences I can remember.)

THE CLOISTERS (see "A Fine Romance")

FLORENCE GOULD HALL AT THE FRENCH INSTITUTE–ALLIANCE FRANÇAISE
55 E. 59th St., between Madison and Park Aves. **Subway:** N or R to Fifth Ave.; 4, 5 or 6 to 59th St.; B or Q to Lexington Ave.
Box off. tel.: 355-6160 **Seats:** 400 **Tickets:** Inexpensive to moderate
`H P S W`

Built in 1988, Gould Hall is a welcome addition to Manhattan's long list of performance spaces. It is the home of the Florence Gould

Hall Chamber Players, the resident ensemble from France that specializes in—you guessed it—French music. At their four Sunday afternoon concerts a year, they play an eclectic repertoire of mostly 19th- and 20th-century composers. Subscriptions for all four concerts include a French brunch with wine, food, and the chance to mingle with other Francophiles. The hall is also regularly used by many other groups, including Concert Royal (see p. 57) and the Little Orchestra Society (see p. 60).

GRACE RAINEY ROGERS AUDITORIUM (see Metropolitan Museum of Art)

JUILLIARD THEATER (see Juilliard School in "The Best Things in Life Are Free")

KATHRYN BACHE MILLER THEATRE AT COLUMBIA UNIVERSITY
Broadway at 116th St. **Subway:** 1 or 9 to 116th St.
Box off. tel.: 854-7799 **Seats:** 684 **Tickets:** Inexpensive to moderate
☐ **W** ☐

Given its affiliation with Columbia University, it's not surprising that the Miller Theatre puts on such a wide variety of affordable and exciting programs. Of particular note are the excellent contemporary series, such as Sonic Boom (see p. 176) and the Consortium (see p. 167). The hall was completely renovated in the late 80's, and now several fine orchestras tune up on Miller's stage, including the Riverside Symphony (see p. 68), the New York Virtuoso Chamber Symphony (see p. 65), and the Columbia University Orchestra (see p. 208). Many accomplished solo recitalists, chamber ensembles, and jazz groups perform here, too. Most events are around $15, making Miller a great place for those who are watching their budgets.

KAYE PLAYHOUSE AT HUNTER COLLEGE

68th St., between Park and Lexington Aves.
Subway: 6 to 68th St./Hunter College **Box off. tel.:** 772-4448
Seats: 664 **Tickets:** Inexpensive to moderate
| H S (at some events) W |

With the help of Sylvia and Danny Kaye, who donated $1 million toward its renovation, the former Hunter College Playhouse reopened in 1993 with a new name (officially the Sylvia and Danny Kaye Playhouse) and a new image. Now the biggest name performers appear at this wonderful hall just cross-town from Lincoln Center, reestablishing Hunter as a major force in the arts. (Back in the 1950's and 60's, superstars like Horowitz and Heifetz appeared there regularly). It's a state-of-the-art auditorium, acoustically appealing and comfortable (with mahogany-backed seats).

Also new to Hunter is the 145-seat Ida K. Lang Recital Hall, a well-equipped space located in the North Building (695 Park Ave., entrance on 68th St., between Park and Lex. Aves.) where the college's music, communications, theater, and film departments are housed. Named for a Hunter alumna whose children donated a sizable sum to help build it and inaugurated in the spring of 1995, the hall will be used for concerts by soloists, chamber groups, and small choral ensembles.

LINCOLN CENTER FOR THE PERFORMING ARTS

Subway: 1 or 9 to 66th St.

See separate listings in this chapter for **Alice Tully Hall**; **Avery Fisher Hall**; Chamber Music Society of Lincoln Center; Metropolitan Opera; New York City Opera; and Walter Reade Theater.

(See also N.Y. Public Library-Bruno Walter Auditorium in "The Best Things in Life Are Free"; Lincoln Center Festival, Lincoln Center Out-of-Doors, Midsummer Night Swing, and Mostly Mozart Festival in "In the Good Old Summertime," and Jazz at Lincoln Center in "All That Jazz")

MADISON SQUARE GARDEN AND THE PARAMOUNT

Seventh Ave. at 33d St. **Subway:** 1, 2, 3, 9, A, C, E to 34th St./Penn Station
Box off. tel.: 465-MSG1 (6741) or Ticketmaster 307-7171
Seats: Garden, 17,000-20,000 (depending on the event); Paramount, 5,600
Tickets: Moderate to expensive

B H P (you must reserve in advance) S W

So what if it's primarily a sports arena? It's the Garden, and when
superstars like Paul Simon or Barbra Streisand show up, you can bet
it's the place to be, although you might need to break the bank—the
1994 Streisand concert saw ticket prices reach an all-time high of
$350! You would also do well to bring binoculars because, unless
you're up close to the stage, you're going to need them.

The Paramount, which opened in 1991 on the site of the old Felt
Forum, presents pop stars like James Taylor, Patti LaBelle, and
Michael Bolton. Compared to the Garden, the 5,600-seat Paramount
is downright cozy.

(See also Tours in "Coda")

MERKIN CONCERT HALL AND ANN GOODMAN RECITAL HALL

129 W. 67th St., between Broadway and Amsterdam Ave.
Subway: 1 or 9 to 66th St.; 2 or 3 to 72d St. **Box off. tel.:** 362-8719
Seats: Merkin, 457; Ann Goodman, 115 **Tickets:** Moderate

H S W

Merkin is one of the best halls in Manhattan. It has good acoustics,
and it's big enough to feel grand yet small enough to lend a feeling
of intimacy to solo recitals or chamber music. Because it's part of the
Elaine Kaufman Cultural Center, some events that take place here
are related to Jewish culture. (The hall is dark on Friday evenings
and all Jewish holidays; in the summer, when the Jewish Sabbath
ends late, concerts do not begin until 9 P.M.)

In addition to being a favorite rental space, Merkin produces many
of its own innovative series, like "New Sounds Live," which features
ethnic, jazz, and avant-garde music broadcast on WNYC radio (93.9

FM); "The Listening Room," conversations with artists and their protégés, hosted by radio personality Robert Sherman, and "Heritage Concerts," a series devoted to Jewish music, culture, and life.

(See also Cocktail Concerts in "A Fine Romance"; Interpretations Series in "Yeah, But Is It Music?")

METROPOLITAN MUSEUM OF ART

Grace Rainey Rogers Auditorium
Fifth Ave. at 82d St. **Subway:** 4, 5 or 6 to 86th St.
Box off. tel.: 570-3949 **Seats:** 708 **Tickets:** Moderate
B (on weekends) H P R W

Follow a long corridor of Egyptian art and you're at the Grace Rainey Rogers Auditorium, one of the city's best mid-sized halls, with excellent acoustics and comfortable seats. Chamber groups like the Juilliard String Quartet and Musicians from Marlboro are regulars here, as are recitals by artists like Emanuel Ax, Richard Stoltzman, and Jean-Pierre Rampal, and jazz by the Billy Taylor Trio. Best of all, you are in one of the world's great museums, with all that incredible art at hand. Occasionally, there are concerts in the Temple of Dendur and the Garden Court. Note that single tickets are hard to come by since subscribers account for most of the seats.

(See also Metropolitan Museum in "A Fine Romance" and "Children's Corner")

METROPOLITAN OPERA, AT LINCOLN CENTER

Broadway at 64th St. **Subway:** 1 or 9 to 66th St.
Box off. tel.: 362-6000 **Tickets:** Moderate to expensive; many subscription plans available **Seats:** 3,949
B H P R S W

Some consider the Met Lincoln Center's pièce de résistance, others think it's a gaudy imposter. Whatever your views about the building itself, there's no denying that the singing that goes on inside the world's largest opera house is often the best you'll hear anywhere. (And artistic director James Levine's orchestra isn't bad, either!) The Met is the standard against which all other opera companies are judged.

The tried and true war-horses ("Aïda," "La Bohème," "Tosca," etc.) make up the bulk of the repertory, but the company also presents many unusual and rarely heard works, such as Dvorak's "Rusalka" and Shostakovich's "Lady Macbeth of Mtsensk," and in the last few years has mounted several important premieres (Corigliano's "The Ghosts of Versailles" and Glass's "The Voyage" come to mind).

In the "If-You-Can't-Beat-'Em, Outdo 'Em" category, the house was recently equipped with a brand new "Met Titles" system, individual screens attached to the back of each seat, providing simultaneous computerized translations (used even for English operas). You do have the option of turning it off at any time.

I still get a kick out of watching the chandeliers disappear into the ceiling, heralding the beginning of the performance. As you approach the house from the plaza, be sure to notice the spectacular Chagall murals in the lobby. Of course, a night at the Met, if you want to sit where you can actually see what's happening on stage, can end up costing a bundle, as the top tickets are now more than $125, but there are less expensive seats available. And if you don't mind being on your feet for three or more hours, standing room is also available. It goes on sale every Saturday morning for the coming week at $14 for the Orchestra section, $10 for Family Circle, cash only.

(See also Metropolitan Opera Guild in "A Night at the Opera"; Metropolitan Opera in the Parks in "In the Good Old Summertime"; Metropoltian Opera Shops in "The Shop Around the Corner")

MILLER THEATRE (see Kathryn Bache Miller Theatre)

NEW YORK CITY OPERA
Performs at the New York State Theater, Lincoln Center
Broadway at 64th St. **Subway:** 1 or 9 to 66th St.
Box off. tel.: 870-5570 **Seats:** 2,737
Tickets: Moderate to expensive; many subscription plans available
B H P S W

City Opera was founded in 1944 to give New Yorkers high-quality,
affordable opera performed mostly by Americans. Since then it has
served as a training ground for countless singers who have catapulted
to major international careers. One of them, Beverly Sills, later
became the company's artistic director and helped establish it as one
of America's most visible and respected opera groups.

Located diagonally across the plaza from the Met, City Opera is in
residence at the New York State Theater, which, while adequate for
dance (New York City Ballet's home is also here), was not designed
with opera at heart. Nevertheless, NYCO manages to put on first-
rate, imaginatively staged, and well-sung productions. And the best
seats in the house are still about half the price of the Met's.

The company maintains an interesting repertory, with the best-
loved classics interspersed with rare or completely new operas. During
its 50th-anniversary season in 1993–94, in the span of a single week it
presented three major premieres by Lukas Foss, Ezra Laderman, and
Hugo Weisgall. All operas are presented with supertitles, which, for
my money, is a real plus. They also mount delightful productions of
operettas and musicals like "The Mikado" and "Brigadoon."

NEW YORK PHILHARMONIC
10 Lincoln Center Plaza, New York, N.Y. 10023
Performs at **Avery Fisher Hall**
Information: 875-5656 (audience services); 875-5709 (24-hour concert
hotline) **Tickets:** Moderate to expensive

It's the oldest professional orchestra in the country, the one critics
love to hate, and when it's at the top of its form, it's as good as an

orchestra can get. And under its latest music director, Kurt Masur, the Phil has been in tip-top shape.

Since its inception in 1842, the Phiharmonic has played an astounding 12,000+ concerts, been led by virtually every great conductor, accompanied all the megastar soloists, and presented the world or American premieres of major symphonies including Beethoven's Ninth, Dvorak's "New World," and Mahler's Sixth. It has commissioned and premiered dozens of pieces from the best-known composers. Generations of kids have been introduced to classical music courtesy of the orchestra's Young People's Concerts (see p. 189), and millions of New Yorkers have relaxed under the summer stars at its free parks concerts (see p. 130)

In addition to the regular subscription concerts, some rehearsals are open to the public for only $10, and the orchestra plays a free concert every Memorial Day weekend at the **Cathedral of St. John the Divine**.

(See also NYP Ensembles in "I Hear a Symphony"; NYP Young People's Concerts in "Children's Corner"; NYP Parks Concerts in "The Good Old Summertime"; NYP Rush Hour Concerts, Casual Saturdays, and Young Subscribers Club in "A Fine Romance")

NEW YORK STATE THEATER (see New York City Opera)

92D STREET Y–TISCH CENTER FOR THE ARTS (KAUFMANN CONCERT HALL)
1395 Lexington Ave., at 92d St. **Subway:** 6 to 96th St.
Box off. tel.: 415-5440, or Y-Charge, 996-1100
Seats: 916 **Tickets:** Moderate to expensive
| H P S W |

The Y has been an oasis of culture on the Upper East Side since 1874, bringing quality music to audiences who come from all over the metropolitan area to enjoy its varied offerings. Kaufmann Concert Hall is an acoustically superior auditorium where many a career has been launched, and over the years Claudio Arrau, the

Budapest Quartet, Mischa Elman, Wanda Landowska, and numerous other legendary musicians have graced the stage.

Central to the Y's musical nervous system is the New York Chamber Symphony, a 17-year-old ensemble that, under its music director Gerard Schwarz, has made many significant contributions to the New York music scene. If the Chamber Symphony is the Y's brain, then its heart must be Chamber Music at the Y, a wonderful series directed by Jaime Laredo that features the Kalichstein-Laredo-Robinson Trio, Isaac Stern, and others performing the great works from the chamber repertoire. Among the remaining organs that complete this metaphorical body are Keyboard Conversations with Jeffrey Siegel, a lecture–recital series with each program focusing on a particular composer; the Young Concert Artists debut presentations of its winners, who in the past have included Dawn Upshaw and Richard Goode, and the off-again, on-again Schubertiade, a ten-year, in-depth study of most of Franz Schubert's works.

The Y also presents the best in folk, pop, and jazz. "Cabaret Nights" features the finest singers from the club circuit, like Steve Ross and Karen Akers; "Lyrics and Lyricists," which celebrated its silver anniversary in 1994, is a delightful perusal of songs by the great American songwriters; jazz is duly represented by Jazz Piano at the Y and the Jazz in July festival.

(See also 92d St. Y School of Music in "Mama, I Want to Sing"; Family Musik in "Children's Corner")

PACE DOWNTOWN THEATER AT THE SCHIMMEL CENTER FOR THE ARTS

3 Spruce St., between Park Row and Gold St.
Subway: 2 or 3 to Park Place; 4, 5 or 6 to Brooklyn Bridge; N or R to City Hall. **Box off.:** 346-1715 **Seats:** 659 **Tickets:** Inexpensive to moderate
H P W

The Pace Downtown Theater, along with the Tribeca Performing Arts Center, provides a compelling reason to head to lower Manhattan to hear a concert. Part of Pace University, this large auditorium (which is mainly used for theater), also hosts operas, orchestras, and recitals. Its jazz series, "Highlights in Jazz," is the longest running—and one of the best—in the city, with artists like Dick Hyman, Marian McPartland and Doc Cheatham rocking the stage.

THE PARAMOUNT (see Madison Square Garden)

RADIO CITY MUSIC HALL
Sixth Ave. at 50th St. **Subway:** B, D, Q or F to Rockefeller Center; N or R to 49th St. **Information:** 247-4777 (There is no phone to the box office; all tickets can be purchased through Ticketmaster, 307-7171)
Seats: 5,874 **Tickets:** Moderate to expensive
 B H P S W

One of my most vivid childhood memories is going to Radio City Music Hall. It was magic for me then and it still is now. It's one of the finest examples of art deco design you'll find anywhere, and with two Wurlitzer organs and one of the best technically equipped stages in the world, shows here can be real dazzlers. Now the focus is mostly on concerts by the biggest name pop stars. And, of course, there are those Rockettes . . .

(See also Radio City Christmas Spectacular in "It's Christmastime in the City"; Tours in "Coda")

RENEE WEILER CONCERT HALL (see Greenwich House Music School in "Mama, I Want to Sing")

SYMPHONY SPACE
2537 Broadway, at 95th St. **Subway:** 1, 2, 3 or 9 to 96th St.
Box off. tel.: 864-5400 **Seats:** 884 **Tickets:** Inexpensive to moderate
 H S W

Symphony Space was born in 1978, from an crumbling old Upper

West Side movie house, and with its recently refurbished interior, it is still thriving. Its annual free "Wall-to-Wall" concerts (12 hours of music by a single composer, performed by a myriad of artists) is one of the most popular events in town. Another, newer series, "Face the Music and Dance," features performances by, and conversations with, contemporary composers and choreographers. Symphony Space also has several highly successful nonmusical events, like "Selected Shorts," readings by authors, and the annual "Bloomsday on Broadway," a James Joyce tribute. Many local groups, including the Mannes College of Music Orchestra (see p. 46) and the New York Gilbert and Sullivan Players (see p. 88), rent the space for their performances.

TAIPEI THEATER IN THE MCGRAW-HILL BUILDING

1221 Sixth Ave., near 49th St. **Subway:** B, D, F or Q to Rockefeller Center
Box off. tel.: 373-1850 **Seats:** 234 **Tickets:** Moderate
`P W`

One of the newest arrivals on the scene, the Taipei is a pleasant space where traditional Chinese music, theater, and dance are presented by Asian as well as some Western artists. Operas here are particularly dazzling, with colorful costumes and exotic props, and the English supertitles let non-Chinese speaking people in on the plots. There are also chamber and choral concerts, and even puppet shows. This is a wonderful little theater presenting high-quality, fascinating performances at affordable prices.

TOWN HALL

123 W. 43d St., between Broadway and Sixth Ave. **Subway:** 1, 2, 3, 7, 9, N, R or shuttle to Times Square; B, D, F or Q to 42d St.
Box off. tel.: 840-2824 **Seats:** 1,495 **Tickets:** Moderate
`B P (must get coupons in advance) W`

Now three-quarters of a century old, Town Hall was originally built by a group of suffragettes as a forum for political debates. Its excellent acoustics began attracting musicians from around the world, and it soon rivaled Carnegie as the place to perform in New York. It hasn't carried that kind of clout for some time, but it is still used regularly by visiting orchestras, chamber groups, and the like. Town Hall has also jumped on the concert production bandwagon and now presents several series of its own. One, "Century of Change," looks chronologically at the 20th century, decade by decade, through music and other arts. (It's about halfway through this century.) Another, "Not Just Jazz," is a blend of poetry, film, dance, and jazz, and explores everything from ethnic music to radical swing.

TRIBECA PERFORMING ARTS CENTER

199 Chambers St., near Greenwich St. **Subway:** 1, 2, 3, 9, A, C, E, J or M to Chambers St. **Box off. tel.:** 346-8510 **Seats:** 925 (main auditorium) **Tickets:** Inexpensive to moderate

| W |

Formerly known as the Triplex, Tribeca PAC is part of the Borough of Manhattan Community College, and is still the biggest performing arts presenter in lower Manhattan. Mainly used for theater, with three well-designed stages for that purpose, the well-equipped main auditorium is the home of the BMCC/Downtown Symphony (see p. 206). It also hosts concerts by other orchestras, jazz groups, and visiting opera troupes, is convenient to public transportation, and at night offers a dazzling view of lower Manhattan.

WALTER READE THEATER AT LINCOLN CENTER

165 W. 65th St., on the upper plaza **Subway:** 1 or 9 to 66th St. **Box off. tel.:** 875-5601 or 5600 (recorded information) **Seats:** 268 **Tickets:** Moderate

| H P S W |

The Walter Reade Theater opened in 1991 as the home of the Film Society of Lincoln Center, but Lincoln Center Productions also uses it for concerts, including the Chamber Music Society's new "Music of Our Times" series. It's one of the best chamber-music spaces in the whole Lincoln Center complex. Because it's a movie theater, it's steeply raked, so you can see the stage from anywhere in the house. It's small, so you're never far from the performers. And the acoustics are marvelous. A new Sunday morning series lets you start the day with a piano trio or string quartet, and then it's off to brunch on Columbus Avenue.

WEILL RECITAL HALL (see Carnegie Hall)

WINTER GARDEN
World Financial Center at Battery Park City
West St., between Liberty and Vesey Sts.
Subway: 1, N or R to Cortlandt St./World Trade Center; A, C or E to Chambers St. **Information:** 945-0505 (There is no box office.)
Seats: 2,000+ **Tickets:** All events are free
 B R W

A magnificent five-story glassed atrium looking out at the Hudson River, the Winter Garden offers an eclectic array of free musical events, from well-known chamber groups and choruses to jazz and pop singers. The view is spectacular and there are several decent restaurants on site. Many of the events take place in the early evening hours, making for a pleasant way to relax after a hard day at the office.

THE BRONX AND STATEN ISLAND, TOO

While it might be difficult for many Manhattanites to believe, civilization as we know it does not begin and end on our tiny island. Never to venture from Manhattan is to miss out on a world of choice music tucked away in all corners of the city.

The outer boroughs offer opportunties to catch the same big-name artists who regularly appear in Manhattan, but at a fraction of the cost one would pay at Lincoln Center or Carnegie Hall. Not to mention the unique events that take place nowhere else: for instance, the inventive Next Wave Festival at the Brooklyn Academy of Music.

Each borough has its own orchestra, and you'll find resident opera companies and chamber music ensembles calling the Bronx, Brooklyn, Queens, or Staten Island home. There's great jazz and pop music, too, like the Jazz Live series at Flushing Town Hall or the Jazz/Pop Series at the Colden Center. Spots like Snug Harbor on

Staten Island, Wave Hill in the Bronx, and Brooklyn's Bargemusic enhance the concert-going experience with spectacular settings and views not to be found at any of Manhattan's halls.

So, by all means, explore all the musical nooks and crannies of Manhattan. But remember, New York is a five-borough symphony: to appreciate the entire work, you must hear all the movements.

BARGEMUSIC (see "A Fine Romance")

BRONX ARTS ENSEMBLE
Van Cortlandt Park Golf House, the Bronx, N.Y. 10471   718-601-7399
Tickets: Inexpensive to moderate

The resident ensemble at Fordham University's Bronx Rose Hill Campus, the BAE presents excellent orchestral and chamber concerts, for adults and children, at locations throughout the borough (and occasionally in Manhattan). If you've ever wondered what the interiors of those magnificent mansions in Riverdale look like, BAE has a series just for you: "Chamber Music in Great Homes," where the music can be heard as it was meant to be, in someone's living room.

BAE has a slew of exciting children's programs that they bring to the concert stage and into the schools. Among them are "Babar the Elephant," told to the music of Poulenc, with masks and props; "Introduction to Jazz" and "Sing On! The Gospel Tradition," a rousing hour of spirituals with the Ebony Ecumenical Choir.

During the summer, BAE presents Summermusic, a series of free concerts, including chamber and orchestral, classical and pop, at two venues each Sunday: a 2 P.M. performance at Rockwood Drive Circle in Van Cortlandt Park, repeated at 4 P.M. at Fordham University.

BRONX SYMPHONY ORCHESTRA (see Lehman Center for the Performing Arts)

BROOKLYN ACADEMY OF MUSIC
AND BROOKLYN PHILHARMONIC ORCHESTRA

30 Lafayette Ave., at Ashland Pl. **Subway:** 2, 3, 4, 5, D, Q or LIRR to Atlantic Ave.; B, N or R to Pacific St.; A or C to Lafayette Ave.; G to Fulton St. There is also a bus, courtesy of BAM, from Lexington Ave. and 51st St. in Manhattan to the Academy, leaving one hour before curtain; it returns to points on the East Side, from the Village to 86th St., and the West Side, from 60th to 86th Sts. Cost is $4 each way; $3 to subscribers; reservations required. **Box off. tel.:** 718-636-4100

Seats: There are four theaters at BAM. Three are at the Lafayette Ave. address: the Opera House, 2,086; Carey Playhouse, 1,007; Lepercq Space, 550. Three blocks away is the 893-seat Majestic Theatre, at 651 Fulton St., near Ashland Pl. **Tickets:** Moderate to expensive

H (Opera House only) P S W

Any tourist—or native New Yorker, for that matter—who never gets to BAM (as the Academy is affectionately called) is missing one of New York's real gems. The oldest performing arts center in the country, it opened in 1861, and has since brought some of the most innovative music to New York audiences. BAM's annual Next Wave Festival, which takes place in the fall, is the acme of avant-garde, offering the finest in experimental music, opera, theater, and dance. Since its inception in 1983, it has showcased artists like Philip Glass, Tom Waits, Martha Graham, and countless others, and has introduced many prominent international arts groups to American audiences.

BAM is the home of the Brooklyn Philharmonic, now under the direction of Dennis Russell Davies, who will pass the baton to Robert Spano in 1996. The orchestra is known for its creative programming, like the "Soundwave" series—weekend-long mini-festivals exploring themes such as "The Russian Stravinsky" or "The European Mystics" by mixing orchestral and chamber programs with discussions, visual presentations, readings, and even dance. The Academy is also the venue of choice for some of the best international companies, including the Kirov Opera from Russia and the French Baroque ensemble Les Arts Florissants.

Just three blocks away is the Majestic Theatre, an abandoned movie house that was restored to resemble a decaying ruin. Used mostly for theatrical productions, the Majestic also houses an occasional opera, chamber, jazz, or pop concert. (Majestic information: 718-361-3216.)

BROOKLYN CENTER FOR THE PERFORMING ARTS AT BROOKLYN COLLEGE
1 block east of the intersection of Flatbush and Nostrand Aves.
Subway: 2 to Flatbush Ave./Brooklyn College **Box off. tel.:** 718-951-4500
Seats: Walt Whitman Hall, 2,500; Gershwin Theater, 504; Levenson
Recital Hall, 165 **Tickets:** Inexpensive to moderate

`P PW S`

Eclectic programming is one of Brooklyn Center's strongest suits. One week you might hear a touring opera company doing "Don Giovanni" and the next a Broadway superstar like Rita Moreno, a klezmer band, or a string quartet. Most of the performances take place in the larger Whitman Hall, but in some ways the Gershwin is the better theater (it's smaller, has better sight lines and acoustics). In the Gershwin's basement is the Levenson Recital Hall, where many music students and faculty members from the College's Music Conservatory play free recitals. For kids, there's a Sunday afternoon Family Time series with theater, circus, puppet shows, and other events suitable for children ages four and up.

BROOKLYN MUSEUM
200 Eastern Parkway, at Prospect Park **Subway:** 2 or 3 to Eastern
Parkway/Brooklyn Museum **Information:** 718-638-5000
Seats: Iris B. and Gerald Cantor Auditorium, 460
Tickets: Inexpensive

`H P R W`

Housed in a 19th-century neoclassical building, the Brooklyn Museum is New York State's second largest art museum, with more than one and a half million artworks. Musically, it's an active venue, particularly in the summertime, when a fine jazz series, featuring leading artists like Cyrus Chestnut and Julius Hemphill, is offered on Sunday afternoons in August in the sculpture garden for under $10.

The museum also hosts some interesting world music performances, including the annual Mahrajan al-Fan, a day-long festival of Arabic culture featuring music, dance, lectures, and demonstrations on traditional instruments, as well as films and videos, poetry readings, and of course, delectable foods.

BROOKLYN PHILHARMONIC ORCHESTRA (see Brooklyn Academy of Music)

CENTRAL QUEENS Y PERFORMANCE SPACE
67-09 108th St., Forest Hills, N.Y. 11375   718-268-5011
Tickets: Moderate

Formerly known as the Forest Hills Performance Space, the name recently changed to reveal its affiliation with the YM-YWHA. Programs reflect the Jewish connection: Israeli and Jewish music and performers form the bulk of the Y's presentations, though from time to time you'll find something totally unrelated. Almost all performances take place at the 475-seat Queens Theatre in the Park, in nearby Flushing Meadows–Corona Park.

COLDEN CENTER FOR THE PERFORMING ARTS AT QUEENS COLLEGE
Kissena Blvd. at the Long Island Expressway
Subway: 7 to Main St.; from there, take the Q17 or Q25-34 buses.
Box off. tel.: 718-793-8080; Queens College Arts Hotline:
718-997-ARTS (2787) Seats: Colden Auditorium, 2,143; LeFrak Concert
Hall, 489 Tickets: Inexpensive to moderate
  P S W

Colden Center is the oldest performing arts presenter in Queens. Home of the Queens Symphony Orchestra (see p. 34), it brings the same big-name artists who play the major venues in Manhattan (Itzhak Perlman, Luciano Pavarotti, Tony Bennett, Wynton Marsalis), but for considerably less money. The large, comfortable auditorium is easy to reach and only minutes from Manhattan.

The LeFrak Concert Hall, at the college's Copland School of Music, is the latest addition to the complex. It opened in 1992 to rave reviews as a mid-sized recital hall with superior acoustics. Top-name recitalists play here, and Copland School students and faculty members give free performances.

(See also KidsClassics in "Children's Corner.")

COLLEGE OF STATEN ISLAND CENTER FOR THE ARTS

2800 Victory Blvd. **Transportation:** From Staten Island Ferry terminal, take the S62 bus to the college. **Information:** 718-982-2330
Tickets: Inexpensive to moderate

H P W

Located in a recently constructed area of the Willowbrook Campus, the brand-new Center for the Arts at the College of Staten Island encompasses four theaters and a conference center featuring state-of-the-art technology. Two large halls, the 900-seat Auditorium and 450-seat Williamson Theater, are versatile facilities that can accommodate orchestras, theater, and even operatic presentations, while two smaller auditoriums, a recital hall and a lecture hall, with 150 seats each, are more intimate forums for solo recitals and chamber music.

FLUSHING TOWN HALL

137-35 Northern Blvd., at Linden Blvd., Queens **Subway:** 7 to Main St.
Box off. tel.: 718-463-7700 **Seats:** Café, 96; Chamber Music Hall, 150
Tickets: Inexpensive

P R (for jazz series only) W

Flushing Town Hall was designated a landmark in 1967 as the last remaining example of a small town hall in the city. Built in 1864, it fell into disrepair in the late 1970's, but with the help of the Flushing Council on Culture and the Arts, it was subsequently restored and turned into a vital multi-cultural arts center.

Jazz Live! is the pride and joy of programming here. On Thursday nights, at 8 P.M. and again at 10 P.M., some of the biggest names in jazz (Barry Harris, Ray Barretto, and Abbey Lincoln, to name a few) show up in the hall's café, along with catered international cuisine. Admission is $15 ($10 for students and seniors).

The latest addition to Flushing Town Hall's music calendar is the "Chamber Music Through the Ages" series, six Sunday afternoon concerts, each focusing on a particular historical period. Performances are preceded by a lecture which in the inaugural season was hosted by Robert Sherman, executive producer of the classical music radio station WQXR.

HISTORIC RICHMOND TOWN (see "Around the World")

HOSTOS CENTER FOR THE ARTS AT HOSTOS COMMUNITY COLLEGE
450 Grand Concourse, at 149th St., the Bronx **Subway:** 2, 4 or 5 to 149th St.
Box off. tel.: 718-518-4455 **Seats:** Main Theater, 907; Repertory Theater,
367 **Tickets:** Inexpensive to moderate

P S W

With a Hispanic population of roughly two million, it's surprising that it took New York City so long to produce a performing arts center specifically dedicated to Latin and Caribbean culture. It wasn't until 1994 that the Hostos Center for the Arts opened in the South Bronx, filling the gap. The 58 million dollar cultural complex houses all kinds of musical events, from classical to jazz, salsa, and merengue. It's a welcome addition to New York's diverse musical community. A professional art gallery here is open to the public before and during intermissions of all scheduled shows.

KINGSBOROUGH COMMUNITY COLLEGE THEATER

2001 Oriental Blvd., at Oxford St., Brooklyn **Subway:** D or Q to Brighton
Beach, then the B-1 bus to the college **Box off. tel.:** 718-368-5596
Seats: 700 **Tickets:** Moderate

`P  W`

For residents of Manhattan Beach and other neighboring
communities at the far reaches of Brooklyn, KCC's Cultural Affairs
Program offers the chance for some bona fide New York City culture
without having to travel far from home. A wide variety of events
takes place here, from pop singers and big bands to chamber music
and choral groups. Music is only one facet of the performance series,
which also includes theater, dance, and children's events.

LEHMAN CENTER FOR THE PERFORMING ARTS AT LEHMAN COLLEGE

250 Bedford Park Blvd. West, at Golden Ave., the Bronx
Subway: 4 or D to Bedford Park Blvd. **Box off. tel.:** 718-960-8833
Seats: Concert Hall, 2,310; Lovinger Theater, 500 **Tickets:** Inexpensive to
moderate

`H  P  PW`

Musically, Lehman is like a shining beacon in the Bronx, offering a
wide variety of quality performances at affordable prices. From high-
brow orchestra and opera to jazz and Broadway, Lehman has
something to suit every taste. Its international series imports groups
like the BBC Philharmonic and the Bulgarian Women's Choir, while
the Sunday matinee series features such performers as Barbara Cook
and the Newport Jazz Festival. The concert hall is also the home of
the Bronx Opera Company (see p. 81) and the Bronx Symphony
Orchestra, a hybrid amateur–professional orchestra that presents five
free concerts a year. The Lovinger Theater hosts well-produced plays
and musicals. There is plenty of free attended parking at Lehman,
and it's also easily reached by public transportation.

MAJESTIC THEATER (see Brooklyn Academy of Music)

QUEENS SYMPHONY ORCHESTRA
31-00 47th Ave., Long Island City, N.Y. 11101   718-786-8880
Performs at the Colden Center and occasionally at York College or
LaGuardia Community College. **Tickets:** Moderate

This is the only fully professional orchestra in Queens and is among
the top regional orchestras in the country, with big-name soloists
like Vladimir Feltsman and Itzhak Perlman enhancing the programs.
Music director Arthur Fagen draws a polished, focused sound from
his players, and his concerts are always well received. In addition to
the regular series, the Queens Symphony has an in-school education
program, free outdoor parks concerts, a youth Gospel choir, and a
competition for young soloists.

QUEENSBOROUGH COMMUNITY COLLEGE THEATER
56th Ave. at Springfield Blvd., Bayside **Subway:** 7 to Main St., then Q27
bus to Springfield Blvd. and 56th Ave.; E or F to 169th St., then Q30 to
Springfield Blvd. **Box off. tel.:** 718-631-6311 **Seats:** 875
Tickets: Inexpensive to moderate
| P W |

Used mainly for college-related performances, this theater is the
home of the Queensborough Orchestra and the After Dinner Opera
Company (see p. 79). The college also has a professional performing
arts series that brings in some respectable music, dance, and theater,
and on rare occasions, a big international group will make its
American debut here, as did the Vienna Academy in 1995.

REGINA HALL (see Regina Opera Company in "A Night at the Opera")

SNUG HARBOR CULTURAL CENTER
1000 Richmond Terrace, at Fillmore St., Staten Island
Transportation: Staten Island Ferry to terminal, then the S40 bus
Box off. tel.: 718-448-2500 **Tickets:** Inexpensive to moderate
P PW S

Overlooking New York harbor, Snug Harbor is one of the most picturesque spots in the city (the Staten Island Botanical Gardens are located here). This 83-acre former home for aging seamen is fast becoming a prominent cultural center. There are currently two main performance areas: the indoor 210-seat Veterans Memorial Hall, and the outdoor South Meadow, which can accommodate about 5,000 and where many free summer concerts are held featuring both well-established and emerging artists. Plans to renovate the 800-seat Music Hall are on the board. Snug Harbor also has two fine museums, the Newhouse Center for Contemporary Arts and the Staten Island Children's Museum. If you go, leave time to take the self-guided tour, which begins at the visitor's center.

STATEN ISLAND SYMPHONY
631 Howard Ave., Staten Island, N.Y. 10301   718-390-3426
Tickets: Inexpensive to moderate

The Staten Island Symphony is a professional orchestra that doesn't venture far from home: all concerts take place on the island, often at the College of Staten Island (see p. 31). There are four per season, with programming that doesn't stray far off the beaten path of classical and light classical standards.

WAVE HILL (see "A Fine Romance")

WILLIAMSON THEATER (see College of Staten Island)

THE BEST THINGS IN LIFE ARE FREE

You don't have to be a millionaire to enjoy great music in New York City. There are myriad events that are free or close to it—you just have to know where to find them. If you're savvy, you can attend a concert every day of the week and not have to shell out more than the subway or bus fare it takes to get there and home again.

Inexpensive doesn't necessarily mean mediocre. Some series, the People's Symphony Concerts, for example, present major-league performers for incredibly low prices. The New York Philharmonic opens a few of its dress rehearsals to the public for only $10. If you don't mind being on your feet for a few hours, you can take advantage of low-priced standing room tickets available at many places, including the Metropolitan Opera.

Here are a few tips on buying tickets, which can be applied to all concerts, inexpensive and high-priced alike.

If you're willing to sit in the uppermost reaches of the larger halls, you can save a bundle. Some auditoriums have acoustics good enough that you can hear from any part of the house. You just might not be able to see, so it's a good idea to bring binoculars.

Often you can buy seats for a "sold out" performance on the day of the concert because of cancellations or exchanges. So even if the ads say it's sold out, do call at the last minute. You might be pleasantly surprised. If all else fails, stand outside the hall for 30 minutes or so before curtain time. You'll probably find somebody trying to unload a ticket. And if they're desperate enough, you can probably bargain.

If you're looking to save some money, following are some suggestions:

BRYANT PARK HALF PRICE TICKET BOOTH
Sixth Ave. at 42d St.   382-2323
Subway: B, D, F or Q to 42d St.; 7 to 5th Ave.

Located at the northwest corner of the park, this service for music and dance works just like the popular TKTS booths for theater tickets. Just show up on any given day and take your chances as to which shows are posted; tickets are sold for half their face value, plus a small service charge. You can also purchase full-price tickets in advance here. Unlike the TKTS booths, the Bryant Park Booth rarely has long lines. Open every day except Monday from noon to 7 P.M. (closed from 2–3 P.M.).

THEATER DEVELOPMENT FUND
221-0013

For an annual membership fee of $14 you receive a monthly mailing offering discounted tickets for specific theater, music, and dance events all around the city. You can also purchase vouchers, sold in packs of five for $20, which can be used as full or partial admission to certain designated events. (That's what the ads means when they say "TDF vouchers accepted.") To qualify for membership you must be a student or a teacher, a retiree, a professional in the arts, or a member of the armed forces, the clergy, or a labor union. To apply, write to Theater Development Fund, 1501 Broadway, 21st floor, New York, N.Y. 10036. Include a self-addressed stamped envelope, and proof of qualification.

TDF also has a phone service called New York City On Stage, from which, by navigating around a series of menus, you can get concert information for specific days of the week: 768-1818. Another similar service is the Arts and Festivals Information Line: 765-2787.

NORMAN J. SEAMAN ENTERTAINMENT CLUB

322 W. 52nd St. Box 693, New York, N.Y. 10101 718-855-9293

For almost half a century Norman Seaman has been providing New Yorkers with an alternative to paying exorbitant box office prices. For an annual membership fee (first year, $29.95 for two subscribers; lower for renewals), you get a monthly listing of music and theater events available to members at nominal costs. You can also call for daily updates, since Seaman adds many shows at the last minute.

MUSICIANS CLUB OF NEW YORK

20 W. 64th St. Suite 19G, New York, N.Y. 10023   799-4448

Members of the Musicians Club are both professional musicians and lay music lovers. The club sponsors a series of concerts at several venues around the city, including the Bruno Walter Auditorium (see p. 49), the Kosciuszko Foundation (see p. 60) and Steinway Hall (see p. 52). Special gala evenings also take place in private homes. A single membership is $50 a year; all events are free for members and their guests.

Those are the generalities. Now on to specifics. If you're looking for inexpensive, high-quality performances, there are a number of institutions you should get to know.

The New York Public Library offers a vast number of free cultural events at many of its branches in Manhattan, the Bronx, and Staten Island. A monthly calendar that, in addition to music, lists lectures, films, readings, and exhibitions is available at any branch (not by mail). It's worth stopping by to pick one up. Also ask for a calendar of special children's events—there are many interesting, free activities for kids. Information: 869-8089. Brooklyn and Queens have their own library systems, which also sponsor free concerts; check with any of the local branches.

The City University of New York is a marvelous source of music, with concerts at affiliated colleges and junior colleges in all five boroughs. CUNY-TV publishes a quarterly calendar of events that includes its own television programming. Write to CUNY-TV, 25 W. 43d St., New York, N.Y. 10036. Information: 719-9128.

Many other local colleges and universities also offer inexpensive concerts. A few that come to mind (which are not detailed in this chapter) are Columbia University (854-7799), New York University (998-5252 or 5441), and Marymount Manhattan (517-0475).

Finally, New York's three internationally acclaimed music conservatories, the Juilliard School, the Manhattan School of Music, and the Mannes College of Music, all have high-quality orchestral, chamber, solo, and opera performances open to the public, most of them free. (Details for each are in individual entries in this chapter. For information on their Preparatory and Extension divisions, see "Mama, I Want to Sing.")

Following is a sampling of organizations that present concerts for a maximum of $10 a ticket. (Contemporary and experimental music groups, whose performances are usually quite inexpensive, are listed in "Yeah, But Is It Music?"; for free summer events, see "In the Good Old Summertime"; for concerts at the neighborhood music schools, see "Mama, I Want to Sing.")

ABSOLUTE ENSEMBLE
30 W. 60th St. Suite 4S, New York, N.Y. 10023   262-0312
4-concert season at Christ and St. Stephen's Church (see p. 104)

This chamber orchestra of 18 string players (plus winds and brass as needed) is a newcomer on the scene, but already has shown promise. Its aim is to change the way people view traditional "classical" concerts, and it refuses to be boxed into any particular category. Hence, programs might include anything from Gregorian chant to Mozart to jazz.

AMERICAN LANDMARK FESTIVALS AT FEDERAL HALL
26 Wall St., at Nassau St.   866-2086 **Subway:** J, M, or Z to Broad St.; 2, 3, 4 or 5 to Wall St.; N or R to Rector St.

American Landmarks presents weekly classical music concerts, including vocal and instrumental soloists and ensembles, by professional artists, some with well-established careers, others just beginning. It also maintains its own opera company, American Landmark Festivals Opera, which produces concert (and on rare occasions, staged) versions of works from many periods. Most performances are at Federal Hall or the Theodore Roosevelt Birthplace (28 E. 20th St.). All are free (but entrance to the Roosevelt Birthplace is $2).

AMSTERDAM ROOM AT DOROT
171 W. 85th St., near Amsterdam Ave.   769-2850
Subway: 1 or 9 to 86th St.

The Amsterdam Room used to be the chapel of a funeral parlor, but don't let that scare you away! The building was renovated in 1987 and taken over by Dorot, a social services agency that rents out the concert space. It's a pretty room with stained glass windows that can comfortably accommodate 100 people, though they often squeeze in more. Some surprisingly decent performers show up here.

AN DIE MUSIK
1060 Fifth Ave., New York, N.Y. 10128   831-8331
2-concert series at **Merkin Concert Hall**

This top-notch group, whose name comes from a Schubert song meaning "in praise of music," is a uniquely configured quintet consisting of oboe, string trio, and piano. Programs run the gamut from Bach to Brubeck, and just about everyone in between.

ARTISTS-IN-RADIO   333-5200
Concert Artists Guild, an organization devoted to up-and-coming classical musicians, and WQXR-radio sponsor this series of eight free concerts, which are recorded live for later broadcast on the radio. The concerts take place at venues in all five boroughs and feature some exceptionally fine chamber music players.

BRONX SYMPHONY ORCHESTRA (see Lehman Center for the Performing Arts in "The Bronx and Staten Island, Too")

CARNEGIE HALL NEIGHBORHOOD CONCERTS
903-9715

Since 1976, Carnegie Hall and the New York City Department of
Cultural Affairs have sponsored free concerts of all kinds of music, at
libraries, senior centers, churches, and other community gathering
places in all five boroughs. (They also bring music into the city's
shelters.) This is an extremely broad series, offering classical, Latin,
jazz, country music, and more. Wherever you live, one of these
events is probably happening not too far away. Call for a schedule.

CENTERFOLD COFFEEHOUSE
Church of St. Paul and St. Andrew
263 W. 86th St., at West End Ave.   866-4454   **Subway:** 1 or 9 to 86th St.

A popular Upper West Side gathering spot for music and theater
fans since 1973, Centerfold is open Fridays and Saturdays at 8 P.M.
When they're not presenting plays or poetry readings, they're
holding concerts of one variety or another. You might catch a
classical chamber music ensemble, a folk group, or a pop singer
(Suzanne Vega's first professional performance was here). The shows
take place in a comfortable, circular room seating 75.

CITY ISLAND CHAMBER ENSEMBLE (see "A Fine Romance")

FRICK COLLECTION
1 E. 70th St., at Fifth Ave.   288-0700   **Subway:** 6 to 68th St.
The good news is that this fine little museum—once the home of
steel magnate Henry Clay Frick—offers free concerts by
internationally acclaimed artists. The bad news is that its system for
obtaining tickets is so complicated it might scare even the most
steadfast away. Don't let it! These are excellent programs by
noteworthy performers, many of whose only New York appearances
take place here. If you're lucky, you might get in at the last minute,

as all unclaimed seats are released five minutes before the performance; if not, you can sit in the garden court right outside the 175-seat concert hall, where the music is piped in.

GRAMERCY BRASS

18 Gramercy Park South, Box 1620, New York, N.Y. 10003 229-7607

The Gramercy Brass was founded in 1982, and by 1985 had already twice won first prize in the North American Brass Band Championships. The group draws on New York's top professional brass players as its members, who present, in various configurations, a concert series at the Brotherhood Synagogue (28 Gramercy Park South), where they are in residence, and other local venues. In the summertime Gramercy Brass plays free concerts in Union Square Park.

GUITAR AMONG OTHERS

225 13th St., 5D, Brooklyn, N.Y. 11215   718-788-1988
Performs at the Church of St. Luke in the Fields (487 Hudson St., near Grove St., in Greenwich Village)

As implied by its name, this series explores chamber works for the guitar with other instruments. Sometimes it's with strings, sometimes winds, sometimes piano . . . you get the picture. Concerts also include well-informed commentary on the composers and their music.

GUITAR STAGE

250 W. 54th St., between Broadway and Eighth Ave. 757-3255
Subway: A, B, C, D, 1 or 9 to 59th St./Columbus Circle

A boon for guitar enthusiasts, this informal 70-seat performance space is run by the American Institute for Guitar, which presents equal doses of classical, jazz, Latin, flameco, Brazilian, and any other type of guitar music you can think of. The Institute also offers lessons.

HOTEL WALES CHAMBER MUSIC SOIRÉES
1295 Madison Ave., at 92d St. 876-6000 **Subway:** 6 to 96th St.

Free Sunday evening concerts, at 6 P.M. and again at 8 P.M., are
organized and sometimes performed by pianist Ilan Rechtman.
Programs are mainly the standard fare, but the music-making is of
high quality. The series has become so popular that a second show
had to be added. Reservations are required; without them you'll have
trouble getting in.

THE JUILLIARD SCHOOL
Broadway at 65th St. **Subway:** 1 or 9 to 66th St.
General information: 799-5000; Concert Office: 769-7406

Juilliard attracts the world's most talented young musicians, and
many of its faculty members are big-name performers. With that as a
given, you can bet that performances here are of the highest quality.

Juilliard maintains three orchestras—the Juilliard, Symphony,
and Chamber—which equal some of the finest professional orchestras
in the country. Top-calibre students, chosen by contest, appear as
soloists in concertos. Orchestral concerts are usually free, or never
more than $10. Opera lovers are well acquainted with the semi-
annual productions by the Juilliard Opera Center, often excellent
renderings of unusual or rarely performed works.

The Daniel Saidenberg Faculty Recital Series presents free
concerts by faculty members, many of whom play elsewhere for top
prices. The quartet-in-residence, the Juilliard String Quartet, has
long been considered one of the world's foremost chamber
ensembles. Juilliard presents two regular student chamber music
series at Alice Tully Hall, and student ensembles also play in parks
and indoor atriums around the city. For contemporary music buffs,
the school's annual Focus! Festival is one of the highlights of the
season, and the recently formed New Juilliard Ensemble presents
skillfully played new-music programs.

Tickets are required for most Juilliard concerts, even the free ones. Call the concert office for more information. One way to keep track of the multitude of events that take place here is by subscribing to the Juilliard Journal ($15 a year). It prints a detailed monthly calendar of school-related events.

LAURA SPELLMAN ROCKEFELLER MEMORIAL CARILLON (see "Coda")

MANHATTAN SCHOOL OF MUSIC
120 Claremont Ave. (Broadway at 122d St.)   749-2802
Subway: 1 or 9 to 125th St.

The Manhattan School of Music presents more than 400 public (and mostly free) concerts a year. Its two main orchestras, the MSM Symphony and the Philharmonia, perform dozens of programs each season, with student soloists selected by competition. A third orchestra, the Manhattan Chamber Sinfonia, is a high-quality ensemble whose members include students in the school's unique Orchestral Performance degree program.

Opera occupies a prominent spot on Manhattan's calendar, with two productions a year by the school's Brownlee Opera Theater and one in conjunction with the new Handel Project, an intensive study of that composer's vocal masterpieces.

A Faculty Recital Series was recently established and includes performances by many of the school's acclaimed teachers. Several chamber groups present regular concert series, among them the resident American String Quartet and the newly formed New York Wind Soloists. Contemporary music is represented by the New Music Consort, one of the city's premier contemporary music groups, also in residence. The top-notch jazz program features concerts by the MSM Jazz Orchestra and the Jazz Lab Band, and some of the world's finest guitarists appear in the school's Augustine Guitar Series.

MANNES COLLEGE OF MUSIC
150 W. 85th St. 580-0210 or 496-8524 **Subway:** 1, 9, B or C to 86th St.

Mannes completes the triumverate of New York's professional music schools, and with its move a decade or so ago from the Upper East to the Upper West Side, the stretch along Broadway from Lincoln Center to 122d Street might well be called "Conservatory Corridor." Like those of its two neighbors, the school's symphony, the Mannes Orchestra, gives free performances (usually at **Symphony Space**), with student soloists chosen by contest.

The opera department presents opera scenes and excerpts throughout the year, with a full production mounted in the spring. Mannes also has a superb historical performance program, with its shining star, the Mannes Camerata, specializing in theatrical works from the Middle Ages through the Baroque period. It presents two ambitious and highly acclaimed productions a year.

A number of fine chamber groups are in residence at the college, including the Orion String Quartet and the Yajima-Ni-McDonald Piano Trio, and they play free concerts. New Music Mannes, a contemporary ensemble, is a strong presence on the new music scene, and one of the prime voices in the annual Mannes Contemporary Festival. Finally, choral music lovers should watch for the fine performances by the Mannes Chorus and Mannes Chamber Singers.

THE MUSIC PROJECT
825 West End Ave., 2C, New York, N.Y. 10025   222-9190
4-concert season at **Weill Recital Hall**

In 1976 a group of young performers decided to form an ensemble to play chamber works of various intrumental combinations without having to invite guest artists. The result was the Music Project, a 10-member ensemble of winds, strings, and piano. Since then, the group has presented concerts covering a broad repertoire, from the old war-horses to seldom-heard music of many periods and styles.

MUSIC UNDER NEW YORK
204 W. 80th St., New York, N.Y. 10024   362-3830

There are dozens of places to hear great music in New York. But, the subway? Well, sure. Street performers throughout the ages have taken to the public thoroughfares, and some entertainers today are no different. Music Under New York, under the auspices of the Metropolitan Transit Authority, regularly presents more than 75 individual musicians and ensembles playing everything from classical chamber music to Cajun, bluegrass, African, jazz, and more, in some 20 stations (not on platforms) throughout the subway and commuter rail system. Special events include day-long marathons with special themes and holiday concerts.

NEW SCHOOL CONCERTS
66 W. 12th St., between Fifth and Sixth Aves.   229-5689
Subway: 1, 2, 3, 9 or F to 14th St.

The New School has had a long and strong connection to American music. John Cage, Aaron Copland, and Henry Cowell are but a few of the composers who were associated with the college. New School Concerts was founded in 1957 by the late violinist Alexander Schneider and has since presented the New York debuts of the Guarneri and Cleveland String Quartets, and the pianist Peter Serkin. Which all goes to say that the series offers high-quality music, by major artists, at very minor prices. It takes place on seven Sundays at 2 P.M. in the school's Tishman Auditorium.

   (See also New School in "All That Jazz")

NEW YORK CITY HOUSING AUTHORITY SYMPHONY ORCHESTRA
250 Broadway, Room 2101, New York, N.Y. 10007   306-3746/47

Its name may not conjure up the sweet sounds of violins, but this group, which has been around for a quarter of a century, serves a noble purpose: it brings classical music to residents of the city's housing projects while giving minority musicians the chance to play in an orchestra (and get paid for it). Its members—mostly blacks and Hispanics—include public housing tenants and workers as well as music students and freelancers trying to eke out a living. Most of the concerts are free and take place in the summer at parks, community centers, and even prisons. During the winter the orchestra raises money for itself by playing at **Alice Tully Hall** or **Weill Recital Hall**. Tickets for these benefits range from $25 to $50.

NEW-YORK HISTORICAL SOCIETY
Central Park West at 77th St.   873-3400   **Subway:** B or C to 81st St.

After being closed for renovations, the Historical Society reopened in the spring of 1995 with festivities that included a concert series, "The Pulse of the City"—popular and classical performances paying homage to New York's musical history. A fitting celebration for the city's oldest museum, which, before it was closed, presented many wonderful, affordable concerts. Now that it's open again, let the music resume!

NEW YORK PUBLIC LIBRARY
Concerts take place at many of the library's branches, but three in particular are worth mention:

•THE CENTRAL RESEARCH LIBRARY
Fifth Ave. at 42d St.   930-057
Subway: 7 to 5th Ave.; B, D, F or Q to 42d St.

More commonly known as the main branch, the Central Research Library (the one with the lions guarding the entrance) presents a variety of musical events, among them a 3-concert series at the Celeste Bartos Forum by the flutist Eugenia Zukerman and the keyboardist Anthony Newman in which the artists explore a specific historical theme, not only through music, but documents and letters as well.

•DONNELL LIBRARY CENTER
20 W. 53d St., between 5th and 6th Aves.   621-0618 **Subway:** E or F to
5th Ave.; B, D, F or Q to 47th–50th St./Rockefeller Center

Donnell has its own theater, where on any given day you might hear
anything from a piano recital and a Broadway singer to a jazz band
and even a fully staged opera.

•BRUNO WALTER AUDITORIUM AT THE LIBRARY FOR THE PERFORMING ARTS AT LINCOLN CENTER
111 Amsterdam Ave., at 65th St. 870-1630 **Subway:** 1 or 9 to 66th St.

At the Bruno Walter Auditorium you might hear recitals and
chamber music concerts that would not be out of place on the stages
of the surrounding Lincoln Center venues. The library's
programmers have also caught the "concerts-with-themes" fever and
regularly present series such as "Four Centuries of French Music" and
"Performing Arts of Asia."
   (See also N.Y. Public Library for the Performing Arts in "Coda")

NEW YORK SOCIETY FOR ETHICAL CULTURE
2 W. 64th St., at Central Park West   874-5210
Subway: A, B, C, D, 1 or 9 to 59th St./Columbus Circle

This handsome West Side institution boasts an 870-seat oak-paneled
auditorium with Tiffany windows. Most concerts here are free, and
many young recitalists like to play in this space. (Harpsichordist
Gerald Ranck is in the midst of traversing the complete keyboard
sonatas of Scarlatti.)

NICHOLAS ROERICH MUSEUM
319 W. 107th St., near Riverside Drive   864-7752
Subway: 1 or 9 to 110th St.

This small museum-in-a-brownstone exhibits the paintings of
Nicholas Roerich, a Russian-born artist, philosopher, and writer.

Among these works are Roerich's set designs for operas by Rimsky-Korsakov and Stravinsky. The museum also holds free concerts, featuring recitals by soloists, singers, and small chamber groups. The gallery seats about 70, and is one of the neighborhood's little gems.

NOONDAY CONCERTS

c/o Trinity Church Concert Office, 74 Trinity Place, New York, N.Y. 10006
602-0747 or 0873

If you work in the financial district, then you're in luck, because you can't be too far from historic old St. Paul's Chapel (Broadway at Fulton St.), where twice a week, on Mondays and Thursdays, Noonday Concerts hosts a series of lunchtime recitals. The programs, which last between 45 minutes to an hour, are by established local performers and admission is practically nothing (suggested donation is $2). Noonday Concerts also sponsors Opera at Noon, abridged versions of the old standards held together by a narrator, and "Concerts to Go," which sends performers to nursing homes and community centers in all five boroughs.

OMEGA ENSEMBLE

315 W. 86th St., Suite 15B, New York, N.Y. 10024   362-2723

A violin, cello, clarinet, and piano ensemble, Omega's Gifts to the City concerts is a free series of standard chamber works at the Fifth Avenue Presbyterian Church (at 55th St.), three Sundays at 2 P.M., each followed by a meet-the-artist reception and musical dialogue. Omega also plays at **Merkin Concert Hall**, but you'll have to pay to hear them there.

PEOPLE'S SYMPHONY CONCERTS

201 W. 54th St., New York, N.Y. 10019   586-4680

People's Symphony is one of the bargains of the century. For as little as $2.50 a ticket (if you subscribe) or $7 (if you don't) you can hear some of the biggest name soloists in recitals or chamber concerts. The roster for one recent season included the Cleveland String Quartet, the Orpheus Chamber Orchestra (see p. 66), Christopher O'Riley, and Joseph Kalichstein. Often performers will try out a program here before taking it to Carnegie Hall or Lincoln Center. The concerts take place at Washington Irving High School (Irving Pl. at 16th St.), or at **Town Hall**.

POSITIVE MUSIC

165 W. 46th St., Suite 1309, New York, N.Y. 10036   840-2959

This is entertainment with a social mission, started in 1993 by bass player Charles Tomlinson, who wanted to create a high-quality chamber music series that would raise AIDS awareness and explore the role of the creative arts in health and healing. The performers (gay and straight) present six free concerts a year at the Lesbian and Gay Community Services Center (208 W. 13th St. in Greenwich Village).

ROSEWOOD CHAMBER ENSEMBLE

43-31 39th St., Long Island City, N.Y. 11104   718-729-4614

Rosewood was organized in 1978 when a woodwind quintet decided it was high time Queens had a quality chamber ensemble of its own. A few years later, strings and piano were added to form the group that exists today. Rosewood offers a concert series, music education programs, and outreach activities in local Queens neighborhoods.

SHOWBOAT BARGE AT THE HUDSON WATERFRONT MUSEUM

Pier 45, Conover and Beard Sts. Red Hook, Brooklyn   718-624-4719

Transportation: A, C or F to Jay St./Borough Hall; then the B61 bus to the last stop. There is also free shuttle bus service from Brooklyn Heights and Park Slope for all shows.

Skipper David Sharps discovered this 1914 Lehigh Valley Railroad barge submerged in six feet of mud on the Hudson River shore, spent several years fixing it up and, voilà! New York got a new performance space. On 14 weekends from May to December, music, theater, film, and other events are presented free (Mr. Sharps even does some juggling). Performances—focused heavily on singer/songwriters and bands—take place at sunset on Saturdays or on Sunday afternoons on the 100-seat wooden barge; seating is also available on the pier (chairs provided) and patrons are invited to bring a picnic.

STEINWAY HALL

109 W. 57th St., near Sixth Ave.   246-1100
Subway: N, R, B or Q to 57th St.

The folks who sell the illustrious pianos sponsor about ten concerts a year in their posh showroom near Carnegie Hall. The spotlight, naturally, is on pianists, though other instrumentalists and singers occasionally give recitals here too. Steinway is fairly meticulous about their chosen artists, so you can generally expect solid performances. Concerts are free, but reservations are suggested since the room can only accommodate about 100 people.

(See also Steinway Factory Tour in "Coda")

WINTER GARDEN (see "I'll Take Manhattan")

I HEAR A SYMPHONY

While most American cities have an orchestra and a resident chamber ensemble or two, New York has a host of full-time, professional orchestras and chamber groups that offer an extraordinary variety of music.

Heading the clan of our city's diverse family of orchestras and chamber groups is the venerable New York Philharmonic, the country's oldest and one of its finest orchestras. Next come its younger siblings, the Brooklyn Philharmonic and the Queens, Bronx, and Staten Island symphonies, each residing in its own borough.

There are the American Symphony and the St. Luke's Orchestra and Chamber Ensemble, keeping busy with their own concert series and accompanying choruses and singers all around town. Concert Royal and the Early Music Foundation both gaze back in time, while the American Composers Orchestra looks to the 20th century for inspiration.

Concordia and the New York Pops play in a lighter vein, while ensembles like LonGar Ebony and the New York City Housing Authority Symphony give voice to African-American works and performers. The Jupiter Symphony has been led through highs and lows by one faithful conductor (Jens Nygaard), while the Orpheus Chamber Orchestra has no conductor at all.

These represent just a small portion of the vast family. There are many others who will welcome you into their homes and share their music with you. If you are a truly appreciative guest, you might be treated to an encore!

This family of music-makers has scores of distant cousins, too, including the various amateur orchestras and contemporary-music ensembles; you'll find their portraits in separate chapters. When a group performs in one venue only, it is indicated; if it plays in many places, none are listed. For purposes of brevity, we've limited our discussion of chamber groups to those with five or more members—with one or two exceptions, as usual!

AMERICAN COMPOSERS ORCHESTRA

1775 Broadway, Suite 525, New York, N.Y. 10019   977-8495
Tickets: Inexpensive to moderate
5-concert season at **Carnegie Hall** with preconcert discussions

This orchestra specializes in 20th-century American music, and its director, Dennis Russell Davies, is no stranger to the genre. (He is also at the helm of the Brooklyn Philharmonic (see p. 28), another champion of new music.) ACO's programs are highly eclectic and representative of a myriad of styles. Audiences seem to love them. Especially noteworthy is the orchestra's annual week-long festival of Latin-American music, "Sonidos de las Americas," which each season focuses on a different country.

AMERICAN SYMPHONY ORCHESTRA
850 Seventh Ave., Suite 1202, New York, N.Y. 10019   581-1365
Tickets: Moderate
6-concert series at **Avery Fisher Hall**

"Theme" concerts are all the rage nowadays, and Leon Botstein, the American Symphony's Music Director, is one of the movement's most stalwart devotees. In past seasons the orchestra has explored everything from Italian influences on 19th-century German culture to American music in the 1980's. Sometimes these themes are stretched thin just a bit, but the orchestra always delivers lively, well-played performances.

AN DIE MUSIK (see "The Best Things In Life Are Free")

ARTEK
170 W. 73d St., 3C, New York, N.Y. 10023 873-0473
Tickets: Moderate

One of the finest period-instrument ensembles in the country, Artek offers a mixture of staged theatrical productions, oratorios, and chamber music concerts. The core group is made up of lutes, gambas, and keyboards, with singers, winds, and other strings often swelling the ranks. Artek's virtuoso early-music performances are impeccably played, with close attention paid to historical detail, without sacrificing imagination.

BARGEMUSIC (see "A Fine Romance")

BRIDGEHAMPTON CHAMBER MUSIC IN NEW YORK
767 Fifth Ave., 43d Fl., New York, N.Y. 10153   750-5776
Tickets: Moderate

The Long Island summer festival shakes off the beach sand and moves to the city for the rest of the year. It presents four pairs of concerts on Sundays and Mondays, in the Jewish Museum's recently renovated concert hall (see p. 157). Bridghampton's roster of performers is impressive, with renowned artists like Fred Sherry, Ani Kavafian, and André-Michel Schub. Before the Sunday afternoon performances, ticketholders may attend a rehearsal and witness the nitty-gritty of music-making. Concert tickets also gain you admission to the museum.

BRONX ARTS ENSEMBLE (see "The Bronx and Staten Island, Too")

BRONX SYMPHONY ORCHESTRA (see Lehman Center for the Performing Arts in "The Bronx and Staten Island, Too")

BROOKLYN NEIGHBORHOOD CHAMBER ORCHESTRA
1344 E. 22d St., Brooklyn, N.Y. 11210   718-252-6162
Tickets: Inexpensive

When this local group started in the basement of its music director Ruth Slade two decades ago, it was a small chamber group scrambling for places to play. Now it's a 45-member orchestra that performs six or seven concerts a year, mostly at the Flatbush-Tompkins Building on Dorchester Road in its home borough. It also presents an annual chamber music concert at **Alice Tully Hall** or **Weill Recital Hall**.

CHAMBER MUSIC SOCIETY OF LINCOLN CENTER (see "I'll Take Manhattan")

CHAMBER MUSIC THROUGH THE AGES (see Flushing Town Hall in "The Bronx and Staten Island, Too")

CITY ISLAND CHAMBER ENSEMBLE (see "A Fine Romance")

CLARION MUSIC SOCIETY

123 W. 3d St., New York, N.Y. 10012   477-3663
Tickets: Inexpensive to moderate
4-concert season at the **Kaye Playhouse**

Newell Jenkins, Clarion's artistic director, is a sort of musical archaeologist known for unearthing obscure works by famous 17th- and 18th-century composers like Handel and Vivaldi, most of them as yet unpublished. He then transcribes the music, bringing it to the concert stage for what is most likely its first modern hearing. Clarion delivers solid, worthwhile performances, often on historic instruments.

CONCERT ROYAL

235 W. 102d St., Suite 3D, New York, N.Y. 10025   662-8829
Tickets: Moderate
2 series, at **Merkin Concert Hall** and **Florence Gould Hall**

One of the city's prominent original-instrument orchestras since 1974, Concert Royal presents excellent performances of Baroque and early classical operas, vocal and orchestral music, and sponsors soloists in recitals. The "Soirées Baroques" series at Florence Gould Hall is especially engaging, focusing on French music, sometimes with guest dancers, and always preceded by an informal concert talk and champagne. Concert Royal is in residence at St. Thomas Church (see p. 110) and performs in the annual "Messiah" and Easter concerts there.

CONCORDIA ORCHESTRA

850 Seventh Ave., Suite 1202, New York, N.Y. 10019   581-2392
Tickets: Moderate
3- or 4-concert series at **Alice Tully Hall**

Not a classical orchestra, not a jazz orchestra, and not a pops orchestra, Concordia is a sort of hybrid of all three, dedicated to breaking down the barriers between jazz and classical music. Since its founding in 1984, music director Marin Alsop has led the group in programs with themes like "Country Meets Classical" or "From Harlem to Hollywood." Concordia's concerts are fun, creative, and accessible. Easy listening, you might say.

(See also Handel's "Messiah" in "It's Christmastime in the City")

COSMOPOLITAN SYMPHONY ORCHESTRA
P.O. Box 1045, Ansonia Station, New York, N.Y. 10023   873-7784
Tickets: Inexpensive

Since 1964 Cosmopolitan has provided opportunities for many distinguished conductors and soloists to be heard. Notable debuts made with the orchestra have included the conductor Gerard Schwarz and the violinist Nadja Salerno-Sonnenberg. The related Cosmopolitan Chamber Players performs chamber music concerts at **Weill Recital Hall** and various other venues around the city, often for free.

EARLY MUSIC FOUNDATION
217 W. 71st St., New York, N.Y. 10023   749-6600
Tickets: Moderate

The Early Music Foundation is the overseeing organization for three of New York's best early-music groups, the Ensemble for Early Music and Grande Bande, both in residence at the **Cathedral of St. John the Divine**, and Parthenia, a consort of viols. Each is a leading exponent of the authentic-instrument movement, paying great respect to historical performance practice. While the Ensemble focuses on medieval and Renaissance music and music drama, the Bande is more modern, venturing way into the Baroque and early Classical!

(See also Ensemble for Early Music in "It's Christmastime in the City")

FESTIVAL CHAMBER MUSIC SOCIETY (see "A Fine Romance")

FLORENCE GOULD HALL CHAMBER PLAYERS (see Florence Gould Hall in"I'll Take Manhattan")

FOUR NATIONS ENSEMBLE
39 Plaza St., 4C, Brooklyn, N.Y. 11217   518-537-5379
Tickets: Inexpensive
3-concert series at the **Miller Theatre**

A highly acclaimed period-instrument group made up of harpsichord/fortepiano, cello, and violin, Four Nations is one of New York's notable early-music ensembles. Its members, Andrew Appel, Loretta O'Sullivan, and Ryan Brown, are polished performers, and their concerts of music from the late Renaissance through the Viennese classical composers (Haydn, Mozart, Beethoven) are sensitively played, often with exceptional guest artists. The trio is also dedicated to arts education and works with public school students in the city's poorer neighborhoods.

GOLIARD CONCERTS
21-65 41 St., Astoria, N.Y. 11105   718-728-8927   **Tickets:** Inexpensive
From a small community-based chamber ensemble started in 1983, Goliard has become a group with a presence all around town. In addition to a regular instrumental and choral music series at Steinway Reformed Church in Astoria and at **Merkin Concert Hall** in Manhattan, Goliard presents outdoor summer concerts and Christmastime events, and offers a children's series at the Colden Center (see KidsClassics in "Children's Corner')

JULIUS GROSSMAN ORCHESTRA (see "In the Good Old Summertime")

JUPITER SYMPHONY

155 W. 68th St., New York, N.Y. 10023   799-1259
Tickets: Inexpensive to moderate

The Jupiter Symphony has faced oblivion several times over the years
and has somehow managed to pull itself back from the brink. Lucky
for us! After many seasons at **Alice Tully Hall**, this remarkable
group, led by Jens Nygaard, now performs at the Good Shepherd
Presbyterian Church (152 W. 66th St.), a small church with fine
acoustics. Nygaard presents high-quality concerts with well-known
soloists. He is most at home in the classical period (Mozart, Haydn,
etc.) but is not afraid to venture into unknown territory, offering
premieres and rarely played musical curiosities.

KOSCIUSZKO FOUNDATION

15 E. 65th St.   734-2130   **Subway:** B or Q to Lex. Ave.; 6 to 68th St.
Tickets: Inexpensive

A well-established center for Polish culture, the Kosciuszko
Foundation, in conjunction with Hunter College, presents a monthly
chamber music series at its East Side town house. Concerts take place
in a pleasant room decorated with striking 19th- and 20th-century
Polish art. The music-making is splendid, and each concert is
followed by a meet-the-artist reception with some interesting food.

LITTLE ORCHESTRA SOCIETY

220 W. 42d St., 18th Fl., New York, N.Y. 10036   704-2100
Tickets: Moderate

Despite its name, there's nothing little about the Little Orchestra
Society. It's been around since the 1940's and has presented an
impressive array of artists, many of whom have gone on to
international acclaim. Under Dino Anagnost, its music director and
conductor of many years, the orchestra's Masterworks Series, devoted
to 20th-century music that is easy on the ears, includes the familiar

and not so familiar, with more than familiar (even well-known) soloists. Two children's series, "Lollipops" and "Happy Concerts," are among the best kid's shows in town (see p. 187).

(See also Amahl and the Night Visitors and Annual Candlelight Concerts in "It's Christmastime in the City"; Metropolitan Singers/the Greek Choral Society in "Amateur Night")

LONGAR EBONY ENSEMBLE

P.O. Box 1208, Cathedral Station, New York, N.Y. 10025   749-5500
Tickets: Inexpensive

LonGar is a true family enterprise, the brainchild of soprano Roberta Long and her daughters, percussionist Yvonne Garner and violist Crystal Garner. Focusing primarily on the works of black composers, the group performs all around the city, but enjoys a particularly strong association with the Harlem School of the Arts (see p. 196). LonGar has expanded its horizons considerably since its 1980 debut, both in the scope of its repertoire and in the size of its performing forces, which now generally include guest artists.

MANHATTAN CHAMBER ORCHESTRA

282 West End Ave., 1R, New York, N.Y. 10023   787-6134
Tickets: Inexpensive to moderate

The Manhattan Chamber Orchestra was founded in 1985 by Richard Auldon Clark, an enterprising conductor with an almost fanatic love of 20th-century American music. His programs are heavily weighted toward that end of the musical spectrum (works by Cowell, Hanson, Copland, and David Amram crop up frequently), but the orchestra also plays some of the contemporary Europeans like Milhaud and Varèse, as well as Verdi, Mozart, and composers from just about every period.

MIDAMERICA PRODUCTIONS
70 W. 36th St., Suite 305, New York, N.Y. 10018   239-0205
Tickets: Moderate to expensive
Performances at **Carnegie Hall** and **Avery Fisher Hall**

MidAmerica provides opportunities for orchestras and choral groups from high schools and colleges across the country to perform in New York. It regularly presents orchestras like the New England Symphonic Ensemble, and has even introduced some fine groups from Europe, including the Martinu Philharmonic from the Czech Republic, and the State Philharmonic of Bialystok, Poland. MidAmerica's concerts—often featuring large choral works—are enjoyable, as long as you remember that these are for the most part student performers and adjust your expectations accordingly.

MUSIC BEFORE 1800 (see Corpus Christi Church in "Get Me to the Church")

THE MUSIC PROJECT (see "The Best Things in Life Are Free")

MUSICIANS' ACCORD (see "Yeah, But Is It Music?")

MUSICIANS FROM MARLBORO
201 W. 54th St., Suite 1C, New York, N.Y. 10019
581-5197 (information); 570-3949 (tickets)
Tickets: Moderate

This traveling band of players from the famed summer school and festival in Marlboro, Vt., presents the best chamber concerts you can expect to hear anywhere. The school was started in 1951 by Adolf Busch and Rudolf Serkin, who put the tiny Vermont town on the international musical map, and their rigorous standards have been consistently upheld. Performers include pianist Murray Perahia, violinist Jaime Laredo, and soprano Benita Valente. The group travels all around the country, but in New York their venue of choice is the **Metropolitan Museum of Art**.

THE NEW AMERICAN CHAMBER ORCHESTRA
NYANA Cultural Arts Department
17 Battery Pl., New York, N.Y. 10004   248-4100
Tickets: Moderate

Members of this string orchestra are 20 refugees from the former Soviet Union who were among the finest orchestral musicians in that country before emigrating to the United States. (They played in the Moscow Philharmonic, the Moscow Radio Symphony, and the St. Petersburg Symphony, among others.) The orchestra presents about four concerts a year, sponsored by NYANA, a refugee assistance organization. Although currently made up of Russian Jews, the orchestra is open to qualified immigrants from any country or of any faith.

NEW AMSTERDAM SYMPHONY ORCHESTRA (see "Amateur Night")

NEW SCHOOL CONCERTS (see "The Best Things in Life Are Free")

NEW YORK CHAMBER ENSEMBLE
475 Riverside Drive, New York, N.Y. 10115   870-2439
Tickets: Moderate
Ensemble-in-residence at the **Kaye Playhouse**

From performances of the old masters to contemporary multi-media programs, the New York Chamber Ensemble consistently gives its audiences inventive, well-played concerts. Directed by Stephen Rogers Radcliffe, the 15-member ensemble combines the big sonority of a full orchestra with the intimacy of a chamber ensemble. In the early summer the group heads for the beach, where it takes up residence at the Cape May Music Festival in New Jersey.

NEW YORK CHAMBER SYMPHONY (see 92d Street Y-Tisch Center in "I'll Take Manhattan")

NEW YORK FESTIVAL OF SONG (see "Vocal Chords")

NEW YORK PHILHARMONIC (see "I'll Take Manhattan")

NEW YORK PHILHARMONIC ENSEMBLES
(see p. 19 for service information)
Tickets: Inexpensive

You've seen them at Avery Fisher Hall in the orchestra, now catch them at **Merkin Concert Hall** in smaller ensembles. Members of the New York Philharmonic, that is. Six times a season they get together, in various groupings, for all varieties of chamber music. The programs are thoughtfully designed, and performances are top notch.

NEW YORK PHILOMUSICA CHAMBER ENSEMBLE
105 W. 73d St., New York, N.Y. 10023   580-9933
Tickets: Moderate
5-concert series at **Merkin Concert Hall**

The New York Philomusica Chamber Ensemble, a mix of winds, strings and piano, is about to celebrate its silver anniversary, and it continues to delve into the realm of unusual repertory. Its members are accomplished musicians who understand the art of ensemble playing, making for intelligent and enjoyable concerts.

NEW YORK POPS ORCHESTRA
881 Seventh Ave., Suite 903, New York, N.Y. 10019   765-7677
Tickets: Inexpensive to expensive
Performs at **Carnegie Hall**

Skitch Henderson (remember him from The Tonight Show?) founded the Pops in 1983, and it's since become the largest independent pops orchestra in the country. While it may not be as universally loved as the legendary Boston Pops, the New York Pops has attracted a loyal following for its highly entertaining programs. (See also "It's Christmastime in the City")

NEW YORK PRO ARTE CHAMBER ORCHESTRA

P.O. Box 652, Gracie Station, New York, N.Y. 10028   876-1084
Tickets: Inexpensive

This highly acclaimed 12-member string ensemble, founded by its music director Raffael Adler, recently celebrated its silver anniversary season. In 1978, it was the first American string orchestra to be invited to the Soviet Union, where it made a five-week, nine-city tour. The group's vast repertoire encompasses music from the 17th century to the present, and it often plays commissioned American works or dusts off long-forgotten compositions. It presents three to five concerts a year, mostly at the Church of the Heavenly Rest (see p. 105).

NEW YORK VIRTUOSI CHAMBER SYMPHONY

C.W. Post Campus, Box 361, Greenvale, N.Y. 11548   516-797-9166
Tickets: Inexpensive to moderate
In residence at the **Miller Theatre** and Long Island University's C.W. Post College

A 35-piece ensemble composed of leading New York musicians, some of whom are New York Philharmonic members, the New York Virtuosi Chamber Symphony is a solid orchestra that presents well-balanced programs mixing the old masters with contemporary American works. Founder and music director Kenneth Klein draws a refined sound from his group, and manages to attract some big-name guest soloists, like Emanuel Ax, Shura Cherkassky, and Ransom Wilson.

NEW YORK YOUTH SYMPHONY (see "Children's Corner")

ORCHESTRA OF ST. LUKE'S AND THE ST. LUKE'S CHAMBER ENSEMBLE
130 W. 42d St., Suite 804, New York, N.Y. 10036   840-7470
Tickets: Inexpensive to expensive

One of the most ubiquitous groups in town, the St. Luke's Orchestra
has a subscription series at **Carnegie Hall**, and the well-rounded
programs and first-rate soloists make listening a joy. It also often
appears at other venues as the accompanying orchestra for singers
and choruses. The Chamber Ensemble, a core group from the
orchestra, plays two series, one at **Weill Recital Hall**, the other at
the Brooklyn Museum (see p. 29). St. Luke's has an active
commissioning program, which has produced many interesting new
chamber works from well-known composers.

(See also St. Luke's Chamber Ensemble in "Children's Corner";
Guggenheim Museum SoHo in "Yeah, But Is It Music?")

ORPHEUS CHAMBER ORCHESTRA
490 Riverside Drive, New York, N.Y. 10027   678-1704
Tickets: Moderate to expensive
3- or 4-concert series at **Carnegie Hall**

The next time someone claims an orchestra can't play without a
conductor, tell them about Orpheus. This remarkable ensemble
delivers magnificent music, without a conductor, season after season.
Its vast repertoire ranges from the old to the new, and the finest
soloists, like Alicia de Larrocha and Dawn Upshaw, are engaged by
the group.

PARNASSUS (see "Yeah, But Is It Music?")

PHILHARMONIA VIRTUOSI
145 Palisade St., Dobbs Ferry, N.Y. 10522   914-693-5595
Tickets: Moderate
4-concert series at the **Metropolitan Museum of Art** (it also has a
Westchester County series)

This Westchester-based chamber orchestra is led by founder Richard
Kapp, who likes to personalize each concert with his informative
chats before—and sometimes during—the performances. The
orchestra presents pleasing programs, attracts good soloists, and has
a series of "Cushion Concerts" for kids three to nine, in three
Westchester locations.

PIERPONT MORGAN LIBRARY
29 E. 36th St., at Madison Ave.   685-0008 or 685-0610
Subway: 6 to 33d St.; B, D, F, N, Q or R to 34th St.   **Tickets:** Moderate

On display in this wonderful small museum are the rare books,
manuscripts, and drawings that belonged to financier J. Pierpont
Morgan. The illustrious collection includes some important musical
manuscripts, like Mozart's handwritten score of the "Haffner"
Symphony and works by Beethoven, Berlioz, and Mahler. These
manuscripts are sometimes featured in a series called "The Collection
in Concert," where they are given first-rate performances by some of
New York's finest musicians. Also appearing in the Morgan's music
series are medieval and Renaissance music groups like the Ensemble
for Early Music (see p. 58) and Pomerium (see p. 100).

QUEENSBOROUGH ORCHESTRA (see Queensborough Community
College in "The Bronx and Staten Island, Too")

QUEENS SYMPHONY ORCHESTRA (see "The Bronx and Staten Island,
Too")

RIVERSIDE SYMPHONY
258 Riverside Drive, 7C, New York, N.Y. 10025   864-4197
Performs at **Alice Tully Hall** and the **Miller Theatre**
Tickets: Inexpensive to moderate

The Riverside Symphony's focus is on previously undiscovered young artists, unknown works by the masters, and brand-new works. Under its music director George Rothman, the orchestra presents ambitious programs, many of which include premieres by important composers. These are solid, if not always inspired, performances. Riverside also holds a new-music reading series at the **Miller Theatre**.

STATEN ISLAND SYMPHONY (see "The Bronx and Staten Island, Too")

SYLVAN WINDS
P.O. Box 4267, Grand Central Station, New York, N.Y. 10163   249-8835
Tickets: Moderate
3-concert series at **Weill Recital Hall**

An outgrowth of the Sylvan Wind Quintet founded in 1976, the Sylvan Winds offers programs of the standard wind repertory, transcriptions, and 20th-century works, often with prominent guest artists. It has premiered works by Gustav Holst, Gunther Schuller, and other notable composers. The only wind ensemble in the city with an annual subscription series, Sylvan Winds also offers ongoing educational and outreach programs. And if you're wandering about the Lincoln Center Plaza on a summer evening, you're likely to hear their sylvan tones in a Mostly Mozart Festival preconcert serenade (see p. 129).

A FINE ROMANCE

Ah, love!

The songs say it's all you need, it's what makes the world go round, it's a many splendored thing.

If only it were that simple . . .

In New York City, where the tempo of life runs from *allegro* to *molto vivace*, and most people are constantly on the run, it's not often easy to find the time and the place for romance.

In this chapter you'll discover a number of places where the combination of music and setting is conducive to romance, whether you've only recently met your music-loving mate, or you've been together for 50 years.

If you are single, and your dream date is someone whose heart melts at the sound of a Schubert symphony, a jazz trio, or a Puccini aria, this chapter also includes some organizations where you might meet that special someone who shares your passion for music. Not all of the groups or series listed here are exclusively for singles (though some are), and while there's no guarantee any of them can help you find true love, it's worth a try.

After all, if, as Shakespeare wrote, music is the food of love, then New York is a sonic banquet. Why not share the feast?

CAJUN CONNECTION
95 Lexington Ave., 4D, New York, N.Y. 10016
685-7597 or 718-479-4936

Where else but the Big Apple would you find a couple of New York women sponsoring dances with the best authentic Louisiana music? That's just what Laura Selikson and Myrna Wolfe are doing. Once a month, their Cajun Connection holds a Sunday afternoon dance at the Louisiana Community Bar and Grill (622 Broadway, near Houston St.), with music by some of the hottest Cajun and Zydeco bands from the bayou. (They also host a Saturday night dance in Westchester County.) For $12.50—or $15, depending on the band— you get an hour of dance lessons and three hours of live music. There's also Cajun food, served festival-style. It's a friendly crowd, with a comfortable mix of singles and couples.

CENTER CIRCLE (LINCOLN CENTER)
875-5444

For socially conscious professional New Yorkers (single or married), age 40 or under. Membership ($300 annually) provides access to all Center Circle events throughout the year, from performances and rehearsals to private receptions with the artists. You also get discounts at Lincoln Center's garage, Performing Arts Shop and Gallery (see p. 229), and PaneVino Restaurant in Avery Fisher Hall (so you can afford to ask him or her out to dinner).

CHAMBER MUSIC SOCIETY OF LINCOLN CENTER (see p. 12)

The Society has a Chamber Music Club geared toward the 20- and 30-something crowd. It hosts preconcert champagne and hors d'oeuvres receptions in **Alice Tully Hall** three times a season. Also offered are occasional preconcert wine tastings. A subscription is $95.

CLASSICAL MUSIC LOVERS' EXCHANGE
P.O. Box 31, Pelham, N.Y. 10803   800-233-CMLS (2657)

A dating service for highbrows, CMLE matches members who share interests as designated on biographical profiles. It costs $65 to join for half a year, which buys you a monthly mailing featuring other members' bios; if one strikes your fancy, you may request the longer version (for a $2 fee). The rest is in the stars.

FESTIVAL CHAMBER MUSIC SOCIETY
750 Third Ave., Suite 2400, New York, N.Y. 10017   678-6970

Performs at **Merkin Concert Hall**. Single tickets, $15 ($18 at door, $12 for four or more)

In addition to high-quality chamber music, Festival also offers a preconcert buffet for $15 in Merkin's art gallery, and a champagne and strawberry reception after each of their five concerts, where you can meet the artists (and who knows who else?).

GILBERT AND SULLIVAN SOCIETY OF NEW YORK (see "A Night at the Opera")

LINCOLN CENTER OFF STAGE
Kaplan Penthouse, 10th Fl., 70 Lincoln Center Plaza   875-5440

Four behind-the-scenes conversations with some of Lincoln Center's visiting artists, followed by wine and cheese receptions for mingling. $14 per event.

MERKIN CONCERT HALL

Merkin has a Twilight Concert Series, three one hour-long lecture–concerts at 7 P.M., preceded by a cocktail reception at 6:30. These are presented in conjunction with the New York chapter of Hadassah, so the themes are predominantly Jewish. Tickets are $15; series of three, $36.

MIDSUMMER NIGHT SWING (see "In the Good Old Summertime")

MUSIC AND ART LOVERS CLUB FOR SINGLES
1401 Ocean Ave., Brooklyn, N.Y. 11230   718-252-LOVE (5683)

This club, which has more than 500 members (ages 21 to 70 and split fairly evenly among the sexes), puts out a quarterly newsletter that includes a partial list of members and short bios, as well as an advice column and other articles. If you find a bio you like, you can send away for a longer version plus a photo for $5. The club also publishes a fun-seekers guide of events and sponsors activities like dinner dances on a luxury yacht or a night at the opera. Annual membership is $82.

NEW YORK PHILHARMONIC (see p. 19)
The Philharmonic offers three innovative series that, while not specifically for singles, provide good opportunities for meeting and mingling.

•Rush Hour Concerts: Hour-long programs beginning at 6:45 P.M. on weeknights, with post-concert receptions. Tickets range from $10 to $35.

•Casual Saturdays: Full-length concerts featuring chamber and orchestral music, and post-concert discussions with the orchestra's musicians. Tickets range from $12 to $50.

•Young Subscribers Club (875-5732): A relatively new idea from the Philharmonic's marketing mavens, the Young Subscribers Club, for 18- to 30-year-olds, offers $15 tickets for second-tier box seats, for three Friday evening concerts, with a special event—a lecture or a reception, for example—before or after the concert. May be purchased individually or as a subscription.

WESTCHESTER PHILHARMONIC
111 North Central Ave., Hartsdale, N.Y. 10530   914-682-3707
The orchestra's Symphony Singles series, which originally included a party after special designated performances, was discontinued in 1994 because of financial problems. But so many people clamored about it that the orchestra's administrators reinstated this popular series. This time around they're offering wine tastings before three concerts during the season, for $25 per event.

ROMANTIC SPOTS

Sure, a quiet, candlelit dinner for two in an elegant restaurant with live music in the background is romantic, but add an enchanted garden, or a breathtaking view of the Manhattan skyline, and it's even more so. Following is a variety of places that offer fine music in settings sure to help put you in the mood for love.

THE ALGONQUIN HOTEL OAK ROOM

59 W. 44th St., between Fifth and Sixth Aves. 840-6800
Subway: 7 to 5th Ave.; B, D, F or Q to 42d St.
Cover: Weekdays, $30; weekends, $35. Minimum: $15.

This, along with the Carlyle (see p. 137) and Rainbow and Stars (see
p. 76), is the crème de la crème of the cabaret world. The Oak Room
is a sophisticated club with oak-paneled walls and enough
atmosphere to last you for days. The best-known—and best—
performers play here, which is why it can be difficult getting a
reservation. If you go, spend a moment or two in the hotel lobby
stargazing (lots of actors and writers hang out here), or ghost
hunting—this is, after all, where Dorothy Parker and George S.
Kaufman and company had their legendary roundtable.

BARGEMUSIC

Furman St. at Fulton Ferry Landing, under the Brooklyn Bridge, Brooklyn
718-624-4061 **Subway:** A to High St./Brooklyn Bridge; 2 or 3 to Clark St.
Tickets: Moderate

Olga Bloom, a feisty, outspoken, and totally lovable character,
almost singlehandedly transformed this old coffee barge into a
magnificent floating concert hall. Moored in the East River, the
wood-paneled barge offers breathtaking views of lower Manhattan
and the Brooklyn Bridge. Every Thursday evening and Sunday
afternoon there are wonderful chamber music concerts by highly
accomplished performers. About once a month, Bargemusic hosts a
candlelight dinner and concert. For $100 (a big chunk of which is
tax-deductible) you get cocktails at an open bar and a delicious
dinner with wine, followed by a concert, with dessert at
intermission. This is one of the most romantic spots in the city, so
don't miss it.

CITY ISLAND CHAMBER ENSEMBLE

at Le Refuge Inn, 620 City Island Ave., the Bronx   718-885-2478
Subway: 6 to Pelham Bay Park; then the Bx12 bus to City Island

Every Sunday at noon, a group of musicians meet at this charming
bed and breakfast on City Island to play chamber music. It's a lovely
setting in an area of the city that has the feeling of a quaint New
England fishing village. Admission ($10) is on a first-come, first-
serve basis, and includes wine, coffee, and a reception with the artists
after the concert. A nice idea for a Sunday afternoon outing.

THE CLOISTERS

Fort Tryon Park   923-3700 **Subway:** A to 190th St.

This is one of New York's magnificent jewels that not many people
seem to know about. An arm of the Metropolitan Museum of Art, the
Cloisters houses a breathtaking collection of medieval art, including
tapestries from the collection of John D. Rockefeller Jr. and some
exquisite illuminated manuscripts and stained-glass windows. In the
spring when the lilacs are in bloom, the bouquet is intoxicating.
Some wonderful concerts are given here by early-music groups all
year long, but particularly recommended is the annual performance
by the Waverly Consort of "The Christmas Story" (see p. 121).

GUGGENHEIM MUSEUM

1070 Fifth Ave., at 89th St.   360-3503 **Subway:** 4, 5 or 6 to 86th St.

Relax with a glass of wine or enjoy a cappuccino and pastry while
hearing some fine live jazz and Brazilian music. Every Friday and
Saturday evening, from 5 P.M. to 8 P.M., the famous spiral art
museum turns its extraordinary Frank Lloyd Wright rotunda into a
sort of jazz club, free with the $7 admission (and if you go on Friday
after 6 P.M., admission is pay as you wish.)

METROPOLITAN MUSEUM OF ART
535-7710 or 879-5500 **Subway:** 4, 5 or 6 to 86th St.

Live classical music by the Great Hall Balcony Bar Quintet is
presented on Fridays and Saturdays from 5 P.M. to 8 P.M. in the
museum's balcony bar. Admission to the museum is the only fee. It's
a nice, relaxed place to spend some time with your partner, to meet
someone, or to bring a date. And you get to wander about the
museum, which is open until 8:45 P.M. on both nights.

RAINBOW AND STARS
30 Rockefeller Plaza, 49th–50th St.   632-5000
Subway: B, D, F or Q to 47th–50th St./Rockefeller Center

$40 cover with minimums (dinner for the first show, light supper or
dessert for the second)

   This stylish cabaret on the 65th floor of the old RCA (now the
GE) building at Rockefeller Center is romance personified. You
won't find better views of the city anywhere. You won't find better
cabaret singers anywhere else, either, with performers like Rosemary
Clooney and Maureen McGovern, among others, lighting up the
stage for two shows a night. If you go, be sure to peek into the
Rainbow Room next door. It's a glittering art deco restaurant with a
revolving dance floor that will knock your socks off!

RUSSIAN TEA ROOM
150 W. 57th St., between Sixth and Seventh Aves.   265-0947
Subway: 1, 9, A, B, C or D to 59th St./Columbus Circle; B, N, Q or R to
57th St. **Cover:** $25; $10 minimum

Not long ago, the acclaimed restaurant transformed a small upstairs
back room into a weekend cabaret, and although it's only a part-time
venture, it's become one of the most popular cabarets in town. It
may not fit everyone's image of romantic: it's small (seats about 100)
and crowded. But it's also elegantly opulent, and books some terrific

acts. The menu is different from that of the world-renowned main restaurant downstairs, but the food has the same Russian flavor and is just as well prepared.

TAVERN ON THE GREEN CHESTNUT ROOM

Central Park West at 67th St. 873-3200 **Subway:** B or C to 72d St.
Cover: Tues.–Thur., and Sun.: $18.50; Fri.–Sat., $24.50. No minimum.

The trees outside Tavern on the Green sparkle all year round with little white lights, making it seem like Christmas every day. Indoors, there is food and music, and a general feeling of luxury. The cozy Chestnut Room, one of New York's newer clubs, has the same expensive menu as the main dining room and the added attraction of a wonderful German Steinway concert grand piano, and live music by people like Nancy LaMott, Cyrus Chestnut, and the Illinois Jacquet Big Band.

WAVE HILL

675 W. 252d St., at Independence Ave., Riverdale, Bronx   718-549-3200
Subway: A to 207th St., then the #20 bus to 246th St.; 1 to 231st St., then #7, 10 or 20 buses to 246th St.; Metro-North to the Riverdale Station
Tickets: Inexpensive

Wave Hill puts on nine classical and jazz concerts a year, from late fall through early spring, in one of the most stunning settings in New York. (It's hard to believe that this place is really within the confines of the city.) High on a hill overlooking the Hudson River, Wave Hill is a mansion and 28-acre botanical paradise that was once the estate of Mark Twain, Arturo Toscanini, and several other famous residents. The gardens are some of the most beautiful you'll ever see. The concerts take place in the manor, which seats 150, and offer the chance to hear fine music in a magical setting.

A NIGHT AT THE OPERA

Whether you adore opera or you've never given it a chance, New York is *the* American city in which to explore its many facets. With more than 40 companies in the five boroughs, you can experience opera here in almost any shape or form. There are groups that present modern interpretations of the old war-horses, while others do traditional stagings of obscure works. One company mounts nothing but French operas, while others focus solely on contemporary American works. From the Metropolitan Opera, with its superstar roster and lavish stagings, to tiny companies on shoestring budgets, you're almost guaranteed to find a production you will enjoy.

If you're already an opera lover, you know what a powerful experience a great performance can be. If you're a novice, here's some advice before you take the plunge.

First, do a little homework. Listen to the score and read the libretto— or at least a synopsis—in advance, since often the plots are impossibly intricate. If it's your very first time, you may want to consider a production sung in English, or an abridged version that will include the great arias tied together by narration. The New York City Opera and now even the Met use English titles, so you don't have to ponder the meaning of all those words.

Don't buy into the myth that good opera is unaffordable. True, top price seats at the Met will cost you dearly, but you don't have to sit in the front orchestra to enjoy the production, and seats in other parts of the house are reasonable. And there are many other competent companies whose tickets will set you back only slightly more than a movie.

For opera fans, a good all-around resource is Opera America, a not-for-profit service organization that publishes a handy register of member companies nationwide. For information, write to 777 14th St. NW, Suite 520, Washington D.C. 20005. Phone: 202-347-9262.

Here are some local companies that have been on the scene for at least three years. Operas can be expensive to produce, and small companies with noble intentions but empty pocketbooks come and go. At the end of this chapter you'll find a few fledgling groups with respectable beginnings. Let's hope they all make it into their second and third seasons.

AFTER DINNER OPERA COMPANY
23 Stuyvesant St., New York, N.Y. 10003   477-6212
Tickets: Inexpensive

In residence at Queenborough Community College (see p. 34), the company shows up at other venues too—and not only after dinner! Richard Flusser, the troupe's director, specializes in small-scale American operas that you probably won't see mounted in too many other places. He's been at it for almost half a century, so he knows what he's doing, and his solid productions show it.

AMATO OPERA THEATRE
319 Bowery, at Second St.   228-8200
Tickets: Moderate

Anthony and Sally Amato, an indefatigable husband-and-wife team, have been running their mom-and-pop company for almost 50 years, and are living proof that where there are voices, there can be opera. On a shoestring budget, they mount fully staged productions of the world's most beloved works ("Aïda," "Madama Butterfly," "Die Fledermaus" . . . the list is long), on a stage about the size of many living rooms (the theater is only 20 feet wide). The singers can be inconsistent, but when they are good, they are a pleasure.

For children, the company has an "Operas in Brief" series of four Saturday afternoon performances consisting of excerpts from operas with English narration, designed to introduce youngsters (and adults) to the world of opera.

AMERICAN CHAMBER OPERA COMPANY
P.O. Box 909, Ansonia Station, New York, N.Y. 10023   781-0857
Tickets: Moderate

The American Chamber Opera Company performs operas from the 1600's to the present, in English, but its forte is 20th-century American works, which it does extremely well. As chamber operas are usually only one act long, the company often presents double, triple, or even quadruple bills.

AMERICAN LANDMARK FESTIVALS (see "The Best Things in Life Are Free")

AMERICAN OPERA PROJECTS
at SoHo Center for New Opera (formerly the Blue Door Studio)
463 Broome St., near Greene St.   431-8102 **Subway:** N or R to
Prince St.; 6 to Spring St. **Tickets:** Inexpensive

This troupe specializes in contemporary American operas, often
works that they themselves have commissioned. Many performances
are actually readings of works-in-progress, which is an interesting
way to hear new music as it is being created. During the week, the
center is open by appointment as a resource center and archive for
new American opera.

BLUE HILL TROUPE (see "Amateur Night")

BRANDENBURG OPERA (see Liederkranz Opera Theatre)

BRONX OPERA COMPANY
5 Minerva Place, Bronx, N.Y. 10468   718-365-4209
Tickets: Inexpensive to moderate

Since its inception in 1967, the Bronx Opera Company has
established itself as one of the city's best small opera companies. Its
alumni include an impressive number of singers who have gone on
to big careers (Clamma Dale, Joyce Guyer, Neil Rosenshein, and
others). The company presents two productions each year, in January
and May, with full orchestra, and sung in English. Each is presented
one weekend at the Lehman Center for the Performing Arts (see p.
33) and the next at the John Jay College Theatre (10th Ave. and
59th St., in Manhattan).

BROWNLEE OPERA THEATER (see Manhattan School of Music in "The
Best Things in Life Are Free")

CENTER FOR CONTEMPORARY OPERA

P.O. Box 1350, Gracie Station, New York, N.Y. 10028   308-6728
Tickets: Inexpensive to moderate

The Center for Contemporary Opera has the difficult task of
convincing audiences that modern opera can be listener friendly. To
that end, it not only presents major new operas (usually four per
season) but also sponsors recitals of American music, has a program
of operas for children, and gives workshops, readings, and lectures. It
also holds an international competition, and the finals are open to
the public, offering a chance to hear unknown voices on the verge of
discovery.

DICAPO OPERA THEATRE

184 E. 76th St., near Lexington Ave. **Subway:** 6 to 77th St.
Information: 759-7672;   **Box Office:** 288-9438
Tickets: Inexpensive to moderate

DiCapo is a top-notch company that presents the classics as well as
contemporary operas, and it doen't shy away from challenging works.
It also has a resident Shakespeare troupe, which mounts plays by the
Bard, and, for the holidays, puts on a production of Dickens's "A
Christmas Carol" and hosts a carol sing-along.

EMPIRE STATE OPERA

62 Bay Eighth St., Brooklyn, N.Y. 11228   718-837-1176
Tickets: Inexpensive

It's just as well that this company, formerly known as the Brooklyn
Lyric Opera, changed its name to Empire State, since its
performances no longer take place in Brooklyn but at Temple Ansche
Chesed (West End Ave. at 100th St., in Manhattan). It features
young singers aspiring to bigger operatic careers. During
intermissions you might find them mingling with audience
members in the lobby—you'll never get this close to the stars at the

Met! Empire also has an Introduction to Opera program for elementary school kids, many of whom would not otherwise be exposed to the genre.

ENCOMPASS MUSIC THEATRE
484 W. 43d St., Suite 20H, New York, N.Y. 10036   594-7880
Tickets: Moderate

Encompass was founded in 1975 as a home for American opera and new music theater pieces. Since then, it has given the New York, American, and world premieres of groundbreaking works like Robert Moran and Michael John Lachiusa's "Desert of Roses" and Carl Orff's "The Wise Woman," and it continues to offer thoughtful revivals and new productions of innovative operas and music theater creations. The company uses spirited young singers who in the past have gone on to perform with major opera companies.

GILBERT AND SULLIVAN SOCIETY OF NEW YORK CITY
c/o Francis Yasprika
1351 65th St., Brooklyn, N.Y. 11219   (212) 722-1285

Not a performing group per se, the Gilbert and Sullivan Society is a club for people who enjoy the light operas of the venerable Victorian duo. It holds monthly meetings from September to June, at which concert versions of operettas are performed by visiting companies. Meetings might also include a lecture, or book or recording reviews, topped off by a social hour with refreshments. These free evenings (at CAMI Hall, see p. 00) are open to the public, but if you attend more than one, be prepared for a little pressure to join. Membership is $30 a year, which buys you an 8-page newsletter and invitations to theater parties and other special events.

GOLDEN FLEECE LTD.–THE COMPOSERS CHAMBER THEATRE
220 W. 19th St., New York, N.Y. 10011   691-6105
Tickets: Inexpensive

Golden Fleece has probably been responsible for the local premieres
of more new American operas than any other group in town. Since
1975, it has presented the New York debuts of dozens of operas and
music theater works by such composers as Ned Rorem, Jon Deak,
and William Bolcom, among others. Each year Golden Fleece
presents commissioned operas, as well as readings of works-in-
progress and concerts featuring settings by poets, playwrights,
lyricists, and librettists. Shows take place at the Sanford Meisner
Theatre (164 11th Ave., near 23d St.), and at Theatre 22 (54 W. 22d
St., between 5th and 6th Aves.).

I GIULLARI DI PIAZZA
110 Sullivan St., New York, N.Y. 10012   431-7179 Tickets: Inexpensive
In residence at the **Cathedral of St. John the Divine**.

Not so much an opera company as a singing-dancing-acting troupe
dedicated to the theatrical and folk music traditions of Southern
Italy, I Giullari di Piazza (which means "jesters of the square") puts
on some of the most colorful shows in town. Its lively productions
are for the most part re-creations of Renaissance or commedia
dell'arte works, and the annual Christmas pageant, "La Cantata dei
Pastori," has been delighting audiences since 1983 (see "It's
Christmastime in the City").

IL PICCOLO TEATRO DELL'OPERA
118 Pierrepont St., Brooklyn, N.Y. 11201   718-643-7775
Tickets: Inexpensive to moderate

A well-established Brooklyn-based company, Il Piccolo Teatro
Dell'Opera presents concert and fully staged productions of smaller
scaled operas ("The Impresario," "The Rape of Lucretia") or excerpts

from longer ones. Casts feature emerging artists, some of whom are quite good. Renee Fleming, Carl Halvorson, and Camellia Johnson are a few recognizable singers who have appeared with the company. Because many of the shows run only about an hour or so, they are suitable for children. Il Piccolo Teatro also gives free summertime performances in Prospect Park, and has a strong public school outreach program.

JUILLIARD OPERA CENTER (see Juilliard School in "The Best Things in Life Are Free")

LA GRAN SCENA OPERA COMPANY
211 E. 11th St., #9, New York, N.Y. 10003   460-9124   **Tickets:** Moderate

This is not your everyday opera company. It's an all-male troupe whose singers' high C's can rival those of the best sopranos in the business. Gran Scena's productions are outrageously funny, but don't let that fool you: the artistic level is high, and the singers are all well-trained. And they have names you'll never forget, like Sylvia Bills (sorry, Beverly) and Gabriella Tonnoziti-Casseruola, the world's oldest living diva. Do yourself a favor: don't miss them.

LIEDERKRANZ OPERA THEATRE
6 E. 87th St., at Fifth Ave.   534-0880   **Subway:** 4, 5 or 6 to 86th St.
Tickets: Inexpensive

The oldest ethnic singing club in America, Liederkranz was formed in the 19th century by German immigrants to keep their native music alive in this country. The Opera Theatre, the club's performing arm, puts on operas, operettas, and recitals, mainly to showcase the winners of its annual voice competition, which in the past have included Deborah Voigt, Renee Fleming, and others who now have major careers. The winners are also presented in an Alice Tully Hall concert. This is high-quality singing, at more than reasonable prices. Once a season, Liederkranz has a dinner–theater production, with a sit-down dinner and performance.

Liederkranz also has a training company, the Brandenburg Opera, whose members pay for coaching and the chance to perform in public.

L'OPÉRA FRANÇAIS DE NEW YORK
301 W. 108th St., 4E, New York, N.Y. 10025   349-7009
Tickets: Moderate
2 performances a season at **Alice Tully Hall**

L'Opéra Français de New York is devoted exclusively to French opera. It also tackles works by non-French composers who used French texts for operas written for the French stage. Talk about Francophilia! Past seasons have included Offenbach's "Orpheus in the Underworld" and Gluck's "Orphée et Eurydice," and the company continues to offer rarely performed gems, either in concert form or semi-staged.

MANHATTAN OPERA ASSOCIATION
P.O. Box 475, Planetarium Station, New York, N.Y. 10024   769-4217

If you can't travel to the opera, Manhattan Opera Association brings it to you. This almost 20-year-old organization goes to community centers, schools, and homes for the aged, offering standard opera fare accompanied by piano. Productions are costumed and fully staged with MOA's own portable sets. It also puts on full productions with orchestra at William J. O'Shea Junior High School (100 W. 77th St., near Columbus Ave.).

MANHATTAN OPERA THEATRE

Times Square Hotel
255 W. 43d St.
New York, N.Y. 10036   354-7900 ext. 647

On less than a shoestring budget, Allen Charlet, the director of this small but credible company, manages time and again to crank out resourceful, well-sung productions of operas hardly ever performed anywhere else in the city. We're talking Gounod's "Queen of Sheba," Bizet's "Djamileh," and Leoncavallo's "Zaza." The performances are accompanied by a piano.

MANNES OPERA ENSEMBLE (see Mannes College of Music in "The Best Things in Life Are Free")

MEASURED BREATHS THEATRE COMPANY

193 Spring St., 3R, New York, N.Y. 10012 334-8402 **Tickets:** Moderate

One of the most original groups in town, Measured Breaths explores the elusive ties among music, drama, and movement. Founded in 1989, the small company specializes in unusual stagings of old and new works (Lully's "Amadis" set in the Wild West, Handel's "Tamerlano" amid American presidential politics) that move far beyond the realm of traditional opera. Performances are in English, making the works more accessible to unfamiliar audiences.

METROPOLITAN OPERA (see "I'll Take Manhattan")

METROPOLITAN OPERA GUILD

70 Lincoln Center Plaza, New York, N.Y. 10023   769-7028

The fund-raising and educational arm of the Met, the Guild was formed in 1935 to find ways of making opera more accessible to the general public. With more than 100,000 members across the country it is now the largest organization of its kind. The Guild sponsors lectures and publishes the magazine Opera News as well as multimedia educational materials that are distributed to schools nationally. It also runs the gift shops at Lincoln Center (see p. 229).

(See also Growing Up with Opera in "Children's Corner")

NEW YORK CITY OPERA (see "I'll Take Manhattan")

NEW YORK GILBERT AND SULLIVAN PLAYERS
251 W. 91st St., 4C, New York, N.Y. 10024   769-1000
Tickets: Moderate

One of only a few light opera groups left in New York City, the Gilbert and Sullivan Players offers Savoyards the chance to sail the ocean blue on the "H.M.S. Pinafore" or defer to the Lord High Executioner in "The Mikado." And when they are not doing Gilbert and Sullivan, they might be dabbling in an American musical or two. Many of their performances take place at **Symphony Space** around Christmas and New Year's.

NEW YORK GRAND OPERA (see "In the Good Old Summertime")

OPERA AT NOON (see Noonday Concerts in "The Best Things in Life Are Free")

OPERA EBONY
2109 Broadway, #1418, New York, N.Y. 10023   874-7245
Tickets: Moderate

Opera Ebony is a multiracial company that gives special attention to African-American and other minority singers and composers. Founded in the early 70's, the company puts on works from the traditional operatic canon ("Carmen," "The Marriage of Figaro," and the like) as well as more unusual contemporary works, such as Dorothy Rudd Moore's "Frederick Douglass" and Noa Ain's "The

Outcast," which Opera Ebony premiered. Many of the company's performances are at **Aaron Davis Hall**, where it is in residence.

OPERA MANHATTAN

211 W. 56th St., 36M, New York, N.Y. 10019 799-1660
Tickets: Moderate

This little company specializes in neglected masterpieces: Fauré's "Pénélope," Handel's "Amadigi," and Dukas's "Ariane et Barbe-Bleu" are just a few of the productions that have appeared in past years. Half of all ticket proceeds go to AIDS research organizations, so when you attend, you're giving to charity at the same time.

OPERA ORCHESTRA OF NEW YORK

P.O. Box 1226, New York, N.Y. 10023 799-1982
Tickets: Moderate to expensive
Performs at **Carnegie Hall**

Eve Queler, Opera Orchestra's founder and music director, says her mission is to present concert versions of rarely heard masterpieces with the best voices in the lead roles. An ambitious mission, but one in which she's succeeded. Past years have found Grace Bumbry, Aprile Millo, Jennifer Larmore, Paul Plishka, and many other stars on Opera Orchestra's stage, in little known works like Donizetti's "Linda di Chamounix" and Puccini's "Edgar." While none of the works are staged or in costume, these are high-quality performances well worth any opera lover's attention.

OPERA QUOTANNIS

c/o Bart Folse, Eugene Lang College
65 W. 11th St., New York, N.Y. 10011 923-7800 ext. 1604
Tickets: Inexpensive to moderate

Opera Quotannis—Latin for "annual opera"—believes that opera is not realistic. (After all, how many people actually stop to sing an aria before committing murder?) So it shies away from realism in its productions, promoting abstract stagings and new forms of expression instead. Its first opera, Gluck's "Orfeo ed Euridice," was presented in 1991, and since then it has mounted some unusual performances, including a rare staged version of Schoenberg's "Pierrot Lunaire."

OPERASPECTIVES
26-30 30th St., Astoria, N.Y. 11102   718-278-1369
Tickets: Inexpensive to moderate

Aiming to make opera more audience friendly, OperaSpectives presents smaller versions of big works. Arias and ensembles are sung unabridged and in the original language, but English narration fills in the plot. For newcomers to opera, this provides a good introduction to the classics, which, performed in their entirety, might last for three, four, or even more hours.

QUEENS OPERA ASSOCIATION
P.O. Box 1574, Sayreville, N.J. 08872   908-390-9743
Tickets: Inexpensive to moderate

Don't be fooled by the Jersey address. The Queens Opera office has relocated, but the company continues to perform a series in Brooklyn and Queens, as it has for 30-some odd years. Since 1961, the company has put on more than a thousand fully staged productions of popular and lesser-known works. Its "Opera Appreciation" series introduces public school students to the genre, while a "Cameo Productions" program brings concerts and opera excerpts to senior centers, clubs, and other community centers. The Association's annual competition and "New Artists" series have helped launch the careers of many singers and conductors.

REGINA OPERA COMPANY
1251 Tabor Court, Brooklyn, N.Y. 11219   718-232-3555
Tickets: Inexpensive

Brooklyn's only year-round opera company, Regina offers three fully staged operas with a 35-piece orchestra and five vocal–orchestral concerts per year at Regina Hall (65th St. and 12th Ave., in Brooklyn). Located on the border of Borough Park and Bensonhurst, the 23-year-old company is a good training ground for singers aspiring to bigger and better things.

REPERTORIO ESPAÑOL (see "Around the World")

RIVERSIDE OPERA ENSEMBLE
230 Riverside Drive, 1N, New York, N.Y. 10025   662-6843
Tickets: Inexpensive to moderate

Riverside is a showcase company dedicated to presenting young talent to the professional community, as well as providing New York audiences the opportunity to see and hear seldom-performed operas and musical theater works.

SINGERS FORUM
39 W. 19th St., 4th Fl., New York, N.Y. 10011 366-0541
Tickets: Inexpensive

"Singers" in Singers Forum means all kinds of singers, not just opera. So, while opera is produced here, there's also a fair share of jazz, musical theater, and cabaret. More a school than a performing company, this is where singers come for training; audiences are more like innocent bystanders. When full-fledged opera performances do take place, they are generally competent and quite enjoyable.

VILLAGE LIGHT OPERA GROUP (see "Amateur Night")

Some new groups to keep an eye (or ear) on:

ELYSIAN OPERA GROUP

711 West End Ave., 2JS, New York, N.Y. 10025   749-6962

A chamber-opera company founded in 1994, Elysian presents concert versions of small-scale operas and other works from the standard and neglected repertory. Fully staged productions are a future goal.

LYRIC THEATRE, LTD.

1 Astor Place, 4K, New York, N.Y. 260-8797

Lyric's inaugural season (1994-95) included performances in local churches of "La Traviata" and "Luisa Miller" as well as the premiere of Marek Harris's "A Free Man's Worship."

LYRITAS PERFORMERS

216 W. 89th St., New York, N.Y. 10024   362-7439

Lyritas presents operas in English, usually in concert version. In its brief existence, the company has already given a world premiere, Lucas Mason's "The Cask of Amontillado," based on the Edgar Allen Poe story.

NEW YORK VERISMO OPERA, INC.

720 Fort Washington Ave., Suite 3V, New York, N.Y. 10040   781-1920

This young company's mission is to perform nothing but verismo operas, those late 19th-century works about real people expressing real feelings in real life situations (or so they say). Works by Catalani, Giordano, and Cilèa, presented in concert form, highlighted the group's inaugural season in 1994.

VOCAL CHORDS

No one knows exactly when humans started singing in groups, but we do know that the ancient Greeks, who coined the word "chorus," held choral music festivals of sorts. In the Middle Ages, the early liturgical chants (which now top the classical and pop charts) paved the way for the great masses and oratorios written by just about every major composer of the Baroque and Classical periods, and, thanks to Mr. Beethoven, choruses even found their way into symphonies.

I can't imagine anything more rousing than a brilliant performance of the "Ode to Joy" from Beethoven's Ninth or the finale from Mahler's "Resurrection" Symphony, and I often find the most thrilling moments in operas are provided by the chorus. Despite all that, professional choristers are often viewed as low on the musical totem pole, even though they are well-trained singers who study vocal technique, theory, solfège, and all the other musical elements that soloists must master. Conductors expect things from professional choruses—perfect sight reading, rhythmic acuity, and general all-around musical refinement—that they don't necessarily demand from the amateurs. They spend long, grueling hours in rehearsals and don't make much money for their efforts.

So the next time you attend a concert by one of New York's many fine choruses, remember to give the choristers their due. They've earned it.

All the choruses listed here are professional ensembles, but New York also has many fine volunteer choral groups, like the Oratorio Society and the Dessoff Choirs, which you'll find in the chapter "Amateur Night."

AMOR ARTIS CHORUS AND ORCHESTRA
At St. Jean Baptiste Church
184 E. 76th St., at Lexington Ave.   288-5082
Subway: 6 to 77th St. **Tickets:** Inexpensive to moderate

Amor Artis specializes in the music of the Renaissance and lesser known works of the Baroque. At its debut concert in 1962, the group presented the American premiere of Handel's oratorio "Esther." Under the direction of founder Johannes Somary, the chorus gives three concerts a year at St. Jean Baptiste, a splendid landmark Baroque church on the Upper East Side. One of them is an all-Bach concert on New Year's Eve. What better way to ring in the New Year?

ANONYMOUS 4 (see St. Michael's Church in "Get Me to the Church")

ASCENSION MUSIC
At the Church of the Ascension
Fifth Ave. at 10th St.   254-8553 **Subway:** N or R to 8th St.; F to 14th St.
Tickets: Inexpensive to moderate

This beautiful church, with its famous LaFarge murals and sculptures by Saint-Gaudens, is the home of Ascension Music, one of the premier professional choral groups in the country. It evolved from a concert series sponsored by the church but split off in 1990 and became an independent entity, though its concerts still take place at the church. They range from early Renaissance works, which are given thoughtful readings, to 19th- and 20th-century masterpieces. These are outstanding performances, beautifully sung and economically priced.

BOYS CHOIR OF HARLEM (see "Children's Corner")

CANTERBURY CHORAL SOCIETY (see Church of the Heavenly Rest in "Get Me to the Church")

CANTICUM NOVUM SINGERS (see "Amateur Night")

I CANTORI DI NEW YORK (see "Amateur Night")

CHORAL SYMPHONY SOCIETY AND CANTATA SINGERS
945 West End Ave., Suite 1B, New York, N.Y. 10025   864-7541
Tickets: Inexpensive

The Choral Symphony Society is the umbrella organization for several groups, most notably the Cantata Singers, a 16-member professional choir that presents polished performances of masterpieces like Bach's B-minor Mass and more obscure works such as Handel's oratorio "Hercules." Most performances are at Christ and St. Stephen's Church (see p. 104).

COLLEGIATE CHORALE (see "Amateur Night")

DESSOFF CHOIRS (see "Amateur Night")

GREGG SMITH SINGERS
171 W. 71st St., New York, N.Y. 10023   874-2990
Tickets: Moderate
Performs a 3 or 4-concert season at St. Peter's Church (see p. 110).

Gregg Smith is a tireless missionary for contemporary American vocal music, and this impeccable 16-voice ensemble is the vehicle that carries out his mission. Since 1955, the Singers have presented hundreds of premieres, probably more than any other individual American choral group, and with more than 80 albums to their credit, they are among the most recorded choruses in the country. While American music represents about 75% of their programming, the Singers are equally at home with Renaissance music and works from the traditional European literature.

LIONHEART
311 E. 50th St., 12B, New York, N.Y. 10022   663-2402
Tickets: Inexpensive
3-concert season at St. Ignatius of Antioch Church (West End Ave. at 87th St.), where they are in residence.

A male vocal sextet specializing in music of the Middle Ages and the Renaissance, Lionheart made a successful debut in 1993 and has continued to uphold high standards. In addition to early music, which they sing with aplomb, the group is starting to explore the opposite end of the musical spectrum by performing new music written expressly for them.

METROPOLITAN GREEK CHORALE (see "Amateur Night")

MUSICA SACRA CHORUS AND ORCHESTRA
165 W. 86th St., New York, N.Y. 10024   874-3104 **Tickets:** Moderate

This is one of the city's most respected choruses, and no wonder. Richard Westenburg's 35 dedicated singers are a fine-tuned group whose performances are always satisfying. Ever since Musica Sacra was founded in 1968, its **Carnegie Hall** and **Avery Fisher Hall** concerts of the old masterpieces and major new works have been expertly sung and virtuosically played by the orchestra. Its annual "Messiah" performances are among the most popular in town (see p. 114). The organization also has a major educational outreach program, hosts lectures, and even runs an annual Bach vocal competition.

Because of a budget deficit, Musica Sacra had to cancel its 1994-95 **Carnegie Hall** season, and its future is a tad shaky. But at the time of this writing, the chorus's administrators were planning a full schedule of concerts for 1995-96.

MUSICA VIVA CHORUS AND ORCHESTRA
1157 Lexington Ave., at 80th St.   794-3646
Subway: 6 to 77th St. **Tickets:** Inexpensive

Musica Viva is in residence at the Unitarian Church of All Souls (at the above address), an exquisite, barrel-vaulted church on the Upper East Side. Since 1977, the group has put on some of the most interesting choral concerts in the city, with programs combining the sacred and the secular. One of only a handful of choruses with its own professional orchestra, Musica Viva has given the New York premieres of several fascinating choral works, like Jean-Louis Petit's "Gloria" and Vaughan Williams's Fantasia on the "Old 104th," a piano concerto with chorus and orchestra. Each season it presents one concert on period instruments.

(See also "Handel's Messiah" sing-alongs in "It's Christmastime in the City")

MUSICIANS OF MELODIOUS ACCORD
801 West End Ave., New York, N.Y. 10025   663-1165
Tickets: Inexpensive

Composer, teacher, and conductor Alice Parker has been at the helm of this accomplished 16-voice chamber choir since its inception in 1984. The group gives three or four concerts a year, focusing on music of the Renaissance and the 20th century, and specializing in newly set pieces from the folk tradition. An annual concert of spirituals is a highlight of their season. Performances are only part of Melodious Accord's mission; the group also presents community sing-alongs at branches of the N.Y. Public Library (see p. 39), hosts an annual symposium for poets and composers, and sponsors a biennial Composition Search.

NATIONAL CHORALE AND NATIONAL CHORAL COUNCIL
1650 Broadway, Suite 301, New York, N.Y. 10019   333-5333
Tickets: Moderate

The National Chorale is one of the foremost choruses in the country. Led by the indefatigable Martin Josman, its three concerts at **Avery Fisher Hall**—an annual performance of Handel's "Messiah" (see p. 114) and two others of masterpieces like the Mozart Requiem or Bach's "St. John Passion"—are among the best choral presentations in town. In the summer, the Chorale holds its annual "Festival of American Music Theatre," a free concert series featuring the best of Gershwin, Sondheim, Bernstein, and other musical theater greats, in parks around the city and in nearby suburbs.

The National Choral Council, the Chorale's parent organization, is tireless in its efforts to promote choral singing in the schools and the general community. Its two annual Sing-Ins—"Messiah" in December (see p. 115) and a recently established Spring Sing-In—are popular with thousands of Big Apple music lovers. The Council sponsors an artists-in-residence program in metro area high schools and hosts an annual N.Y.C. High School Choral Festival at the **Miller Theatre**.

NEW AMSTERDAM SINGERS (see "Amateur Night")

NEW YORK CITY GAY MEN'S CHORUS (see "Amateur Night")

NEW YORK CHORAL SOCIETY (see "Amateur Night")

NEW YORK CONCERT SINGERS
75 East End Ave., Suite 9L, New York, N.Y. 10028   879-4412
Tickets: Inexpensive
2 concerts at **Merkin Concert Hall**; other performances elsewhere

The N.Y. Concert Singers has a soft spot for contemporary music and
has commissioned and presented world premieres by William
Bolcom, David Diamond, Libby Larsen, and others. But the chorus
is just as comfortable with Schubert, Mozart, and Brahms, and lately
has expanded its reach to include early music. Under its founder and
music director Judith Clurman, the Concert Singers has become a
versatile group that performs as a full chorus, a chamber chorus, an a
cappella ensemble, and even a quartet.

NEW YORK FESTIVAL OF SONG
P.O. Box 1397, Cathedral Station, New York, N.Y. 10025   662-9909
Tickets: Moderate
Performances at the **92d St. Y** and **Weill Recital Hall**

This is the only chamber organization in the city that focuses solely
on the art of the song. Founders Steven Blier and Michael Barrett
have an encyclopedic knowledge of the vocal repertoire and their
programs show it. They include familiar and unknown music from
around the world, spotlighting works by living American composers,
often giving premieres. (They gave the first American performance
of Leonard Bernstein's final composition, "Arias and Barcarolles.")
NYFOS's member artists are accomplished singers who deliver
masterful renditions of interesting music.

NEW YORK MADRIGAL SINGERS
235 W. 102d St., 12B, New York, N.Y. 10025   472-1662
Tickets: Inexpensive

A 12-member a cappella group specializing in chamber music from
the Renaissance and Baroque, the New York Madrigal Singers gives
polished, well-blended performances. Though the repertory is 99%
early music, you will hear an occasional work by, say, Bruckner or
Ned Rorem. Many of their concerts are at the Church of Notre Dame
(114th St. at Morningside Drive). Suggested contribution: $10.

NEW YORK VIRTUOSO SINGERS
2 Cove Road, South Salem, N.Y. 10590   914-763-3453
Tickets: Inexpensive to moderate
3-concert series at **Merkin Concert Hall**

Led by Harold Rosenbaum, one of New York's high-profile choral
conductors, the 16-voice N.Y. Virtuoso Singers performs works from
all periods, with a special emphasis on contemporary music. Its
programming is inventive, with unusual works like Rachmaninoff's
"All-Night Vigil" adding special flavor. In addition to the Merkin
Hall series, the chorus appears with the Orchestra of St. Luke's (see
p. 66), the American Symphony (see p. 55), and other groups.

ORATORIO SOCIETY OF NEW YORK (see "Amateur Night")

POMERIUM
375 Riverside Drive, 10E, New York, N.Y. 10025   316-3953
Tickets: Inexpensive to moderate

Pomerium literally means a garden, and this group produces some
magnificent musical flowers. A 15-voice a cappella ensemble,
Pomerium focuses on the 15th and 16th centuries (its specialty is
the music of Guillaume Du Fay, which it has recorded). The choir
was founded in 1972 and has sung at many venues, including the

Metropolitan Museum of Art, the Cloisters (see p. 75), and in the Music Before 1800 Series (see p. 106), where it holds the record for most appearances by any one group—18, to date.

RUSSIAN CHAMBER CHORUS OF NEW YORK (see "Amateur Night")

RUSSIAN EMIGRÉ CHOIR
145 Fourth Ave., New York, N.Y. 10003   254-1717 **Tickets:** Inexpensive

Like the New American Chamber Orchestra (see p. 63), the 12-voice Russian Emigré Choir—this country's only professional Russian choir—is made up of immigrants who were active performers in their former Soviet homelands. Run by Andrea Goodman, a well-known name in the New York choral world, the choir gives about eight concerts a season at various venues around town, focusing on Russian and Jewish music. It also runs workshops in the city's public schools.

STONEWALL CHORALE (see "Amateur Night")

WEST VILLAGE CHORALE (see "Amateur Night")

GET ME TO THE CHURCH

It used to be that you could rely on churches for liturgical choral music or a decent organ recital, but for music in a more secular vein, you had to look elsewhere. Not so anymore. Churches and synagogues are now playing bigger parts in everyday community life, reclaiming the function enjoyed by the European cathedrals of the Middle Ages, when even worldly daily activity centered on the church.

Today, New York's houses of worship are competing with concert halls for the attention of music lovers. The arts calendars of some churches and synagogues reveal anything from the expected (and welcome) choral concerts and organ recitals to performance art, jazz, rock bands, African tribal folk singers, and even ritual Buddhist chanting. Audiences comprise not only members of the congregations but people from far and wide, who are attracted by the variety and quality of the performances.

And by the value. Since for the most part churches are cheaper to rent than many of the standard concert venues, performers are able to keep the lid on ticket prices. Many concerts are free, or by small donation. The few whose prices rival the big halls equal (or sometimes surpass) them in quality.

Since so many New York churches and synagogues incorporate good music into their services, we've focused—with a few exceptions—on those where music is independent from worship.

ALL SOULS UNITARIAN CHURCH (see Musica Viva in "Vocal Chords")

CATHEDRAL OF ST. JOHN THE DIVINE
Amsterdam Ave. at 112th St.   662-2133 or 307-7171
Subway:1 or 9 to 110th St.

The world's largest Gothic cathedral, this monumental space can seat nearly 3,000 people for concerts. Programmers here believe that all music is sacred, and the many types of concerts they present are testament to that credo. Sacred choral music, jazz, folk, avant-garde: there are so many varieties it would be impossible to describe them all in a short paragraph. Two of my favorites are the Halloween event featuring an old silent horror movie accompanied by the colossal Skinner organ followed by a spectacular procession of ghouls and goblins, and the Paul Winter Consort's winter solstice celebration (see p. 120). The Cathedral also has an exceptional choir, sponsors an annual "Interfaith Concert of Remembrance" in memory of the Holocaust, and hosts a free performance by the New York Philharmonic each Memorial Day weekend (see p. 20). (When you go, be sure to check out the wonderful gift shop, which, among other items, sells extraordinary gargoyles and other cut stone merchandise.)

CHRIST AND ST. STEPHEN'S CHURCH

120 W. 69th St., between Broadway and Columbus Ave.   787-2755
Subway: C, 1, 2, 3 or 9 to 72d St.

God should be pleased to have a cultural organization named after him: the Adonai Arts Foundation (Adonai being the Hebrew word for God) at Christ and St. Stephen's Church, which presents numerous concerts each season. At this small church with the little grassy front yard you might catch anything from a children's piano recital to a choral concert, a string quartet, or an opera by one of the smaller local professional companies.

CHURCH OF ST. ANN AND THE HOLY TRINITY

157 Montague St., at Clinton St., Brooklyn   718-858-2424
Subway: 2, 3, 4 or 5 to Borough Hall; N or R to Court St.

A national landmark, this Gothic revival church was the first in America to use figurative stained-glass windows (some say they equal in beauty those of the great European cathedrals). The church's cultural arm, Arts at St. Ann's, puts on some of the most electrifying programs to be heard anywhere in New York, let alone a church. It was here that the founders of the Velvet Underground, Lou Reed and John Cale, reunited for their tribute to Andy Warhol, "Songs for 'Drella." Here that David Byrne gave the premiere of his first orchestral work, "The Forest." And here that innovative music-theater pieces and even composer Harry Partch's operas played on his homemade instruments are staples. And all for an affordable $15 to $20.

CHURCH OF ST. IGNATIUS LOYOLA

980 Park Ave., at 84th St.   288-2520 **Subway:** 4, 5 or 6 to 86th St.

A few years ago, accompanied by much hoopla, a new mechanical-action organ—the largest in the city—was installed at the Church of St. Ignatius Loyola, rekindling an interest in the grandest of instruments. The church capitalized on this and initiated a series of organ recitals on the much-acclaimed instrument (built by the English firm N.P. Mander to the tune of $1.25 million). But with all the excitement over the organ, let's not forget about the church's excellent choir, which presents choral masterpieces as well as newer works. Tickets for the series, called "Sacred Music Is a Sacred Space," aren't particularly cheap (single tickets go as high as $30), but they're worth every penny.

(See also Tours in "Coda")

CHURCH OF ST. LUKE IN THE FIELDS (see West Village Chorale in "Amateur Night")

CHURCH OF ST. MARY THE VIRGIN
145 W. 46th St., between Sixth and Seventh Aves.   921-2939
Subway: 1, 2, 3, 7, 9, N, R or shuttle to Times Square; B, D, F or Q to 42d St.

Stepping into St. Mary's is like entering a time warp. Suddenly, the surrounding chaos of Times Square seems a million miles away. The landmark Italian Renaissance church, with its rich architecture, superb Aeolian-Skinner organ, and wonderful acoustics, is the perfect place for live performances, particularly of vocal music. St. Mary's concert series is immaculately conceived, with some of the finest choral and instrumental ensembles you'll hear anywhere. At a recent concert by the Tallis Scholars, a splendid early-music choral group, I thought I'd died and gone to musical heaven.

CHURCH OF THE ASCENSION (see Ascension Music in "Vocal Chords")

CHURCH OF THE HEAVENLY REST
2 E. 90th St., at Fifth Ave.   289-3400   **Subway:** 4, 5 or 6 to 86th St.
A lovely little church opposite the Cooper-Hewitt Museum and the Engineer's Gate into Central Park, Heavenly Rest is the home of the

Canterbury Choral Society, a 100-voice chorus whose forte is semi-staged presentations of oratorios, a rarity in the choral world. It also does the big masterpieces like the great Masses of Bach, Mozart, and Beethoven, as well as contemporary works. The church is also home to the New York Pro Arte Chamber Orchestra (see p. 65) and has an ongoing jazz series, Heavenly Jazz—and with performers like Bucky Pizzarelli and Dave McKenna, it really is!

CHURCH OF THE HOLY TRINITY (EPISCOPALIAN)
316 E. 88th St., between First and Second Aves.   289-4100
Subway: 4, 5 or 6 to 86th St.

In 1988 Holy Trinity had an excellent 60-rank Rieger pipe organ installed, and organists from around the world now come to play recitals on it, making the church a haven for organ music lovers. Holy Trinity also presents concerts by its own fine choir and visiting ensembles of note, like the Choir of Trinity Church (of Cambridge, England), and recitals by instrumental and vocal soloists. And at $15 a seat, you might say prices are divine.

CONGREGATION ANSCHE CHESED (see Empire State Opera in "A Night at the Opera")

CORPUS CHRISTI CHURCH
529 W. 121st St., near Broadway   666-9266 Subway: 1 or 9 to 125th St.

Music Before 1800, one of the finest early-music series in the country, is housed at Corpus Christi Church. Established in 1975 when the period-instrument craze was revving into high gear, it presents both well-established and up-and-coming groups. Programs encompass a vast repertory of secular and sacred instrumental and vocal works (or a combination of the two) for larger groups as well as solo performers or duos. Its own ensemble-in-residence, Music Before 1800 Productions, is a group of from six to ten singers with viola da gamba and harpsichord or organ continuo who present music from the 16th through the 18th centuries as well as contemporary works, many of them commissioned.

HEBREW UNION COLLEGE–JEWISH INSTITUTE OF RELIGION
1 West Fourth St., between Broadway and Mercer St.   674-5300
Subway: A, B, C, D, E or F to W. 4th St.; N or R to 8th St.

Hebrew Union College has a fine cantorial school where students sometimes give performances. But the main cultural attraction here is a Sunday afternoon series of lectures, films, and concerts that includes about five live musical performances a year, ranging from sacred vocal music to art songs by Israeli composers. Concerts are $7; students and seniors, $5.

HOLY TRINITY LUTHERAN CHURCH
Central Park West at 65t St.   877-6815
Subway: 1 or 9 to 66th St.; A, B, C or D to 59th St.

As cantor at St. Thomas Church in 18th-century Leipzig, Johann Sebastian Bach wrote a cantata every week to be used in the church service. In 1968, for the first time in America, Holy Trinity Lutheran started presenting these marvelous works weekly on the appropriate days of the liturgical year. This outstanding Bach Vespers series grew into one of the most popular music events in New York, and Bach lovers flock here in droves. The excellent Holy Trinity Bach Choir, and its guest soloists and instrumentalists, are the admirable performers. Admission is by free-will donation.

PARK AVENUE SYNAGOGUE
50 E. 87th St., at Madison Ave.   369-2600
Subway: 4, 5 or 6 to 86th St.

In the late 19th century, the larger European synagogues had resident cantors and choral directors who composed liturgical music for their magnificent choirs. In keeping with this tradition, twice a year (on a Friday evening in the fall and a Saturday morning in the spring) the Park Avenue Synagogue holds "concert services," at which the cantor and choir, accompanied by organ and other instruments, incorporate new choral works into the service. Some are commissioned, others are premieres of older works from obscure manuscripts. Several of this century's best composers, including Kurt Weill and Leonard Bernstein, have written music for these services.

RIVERSIDE CHURCH
Riverside Drive at 120th St.   222-5900 or 870-6722
Subway: 1 or 9 to 116th St. or 125th St.

Riverside has one of the most active music programs of any church in town. A summer series of six organ recitals showcases the superb Aeolian-Skinner organ, and the outstanding choir gives several big-scale concerts throughout the year. Free chamber music by notable singers and instrumentalists is offered every second Sunday afternoon of each month in the church's Romanesque Christ Chapel. Riverside sponsors an annual English handbell festival with 100 ringers from the metropolitan area, and each December holds a "Messiah" sing-along (see p. 115). There are occasional concerts by visiting orchestras and choirs, and neighborhood residents are treated to free recitals on the world's largest carillon every Sunday (see Laura Spellman Rockefeller Memorial Carillon in "Coda").

ST. BARTHOLOMEW'S CHURCH
Park Ave. at 51st St.   751-1616 ext. 226 or 248
Subway: E or F to Lexington Ave.; 6 to 51st St.

A magnificent domed Romanesque church, St. Bartholomew's has a rich musical history. In 1905 an organist named Leopold Stokowski (yes, the very one) came from England to be choirmaster at the church. Fond of orchestral transcriptions, he would include parts of oratorios in the service, and so the practice of presenting big choral works with organ accompaniment was firmly established. Stokowski went on to become one of the great conductors of the century, but his successors kept the tradition alive. Today, there is a regular concert series that features St. Bartholomew's Choir as well as visiting choirs and orchestras, and organ recitals on the impressive Aeolian-Skinner (one of New York's largest pipe organs; viewing and demonstration by appointment). There is also a "Music in the Chapel" series, Wednesdays at 6:30, featuring solo instrumental, vocal, and chamber music recitals.

ST. JEAN BAPTISTE CHURCH (see Amor Artis in "Vocal Chords")

ST. MICHAEL'S CHURCH
225 W. 99th St., at Amsterdam Ave.   222-2700
Subway: 1, 2, 3 or 9 to 96th St.

Recently refurbished, St. Michael's is both visually stunning and acoustically pleasing. Maybe that's why so many groups like to perform here. One of the finest early-music ensembles in the country, the a cappella women's quartet Anonymous 4, is in residence here, and its annual Christmas concert is a highlight of the season. The church also houses the von Beckerath organ, built in 1967, one of the best church instruments you'll hear in New York City. It's so fine, in fact, that a series, "Bach on the Upper West Side," was created just to show it off and raise money to help with its maintenance.

ST. PAUL'S CHAPEL (see Noonday Concerts in "The Best Things in Life Are Free")

ST. PETER'S CHURCH AT THE CITICORP CENTER

619 Lexington Ave., at 54th St.   935-2200
Subway: E or F to 53d St.; 6 to 51st St.

For jazz lovers, St. Peter's is paradise in midtown. Reverend John
Garcia Gensel, who recently retired, was not called pastor to the jazz
community for nothing. Under his leadership the church's jazz
programs grew by leaps and bounds. It has a weekly Sunday Jazz
Vespers followed by a concert, and its Midtown Jazz at Midday series
(Wednesdays at 12:30) presents guest artists who give concerts in
the informal setting of the Church's living room. (Do bring your
lunch.) For those whose tastes run in different directions, Early
Music at St. Peter's offers programs by choice groups like Artek (see
p. 55) and Parthenia: A Consort of Viols. (Information for this series:
460-5713.)

ST. THOMAS CHURCH FIFTH AVENUE

1 W. 53d St.   757-7013   **Subway:** E or F to 53d St.; B, D, F or Q to 47th-
50th St./Rockefeller Center

St. Thomas is a magnificent gothic church where music is much
exalted. Free Sunday afternoon organ recitals on the church's
Aeolian-Skinner and the weekly choral Eucharists and Evensongs are
just the tip of the iceberg. There is a full-fledged concert series (with
full-fledged prices), often with the Orchestra of St. Luke's (see p. 66)
or Concert Royal (see p. 57). But Christmas is when St. Thomas
truly enters its glory, with programs by the church's renowned choir
of 12 men and 18 boys, and an annual "Messiah" performance that
rises above most others (see p. 114). St. Thomas has the only fully
accredited church-related choir school for boys in the country.
Entrance is by audition and testing, and it is a very competitive
process.

STEPHEN WISE FREE SYNAGOGUE
30 W. 68th St., near Columbus Ave.   877-4050
Subway: 1 or 9 to 66th St.; B or C to 72d St.

One of the city's big vocal events takes place at the Stephen Wise
Free Synagogue every fall. It is the annual Judith Raskin Memorial
Concert, named for the remarkable American lyric soprano who died
in 1984. (She got her start singing in the synagogue's choir for $11 a
week!) This free concert, co-sponsored by the Metropolitan Opera
where Raskin later sang, showcases the winner of the Met's National
Auditions. In the spring, the synagogue puts on "Sing a Song of
Love," an annual fund raiser with groups like the Harlem Spiritual
Ensemble joining Wise's choir for an ecumenical cabaret.

TEMPLE EMANU-EL
1 E. 65th St., at Fifth Ave.   744-1400 **Subway:** N or R to Fifth Ave.
Temple Emanu-El is the largest Jewish house of worship in the
world and one of the most prestigious. Every year, on the first
Sunday in May, it holds an "Ecumenical Concert" with choirs from
local churches joining the Temple's own. At other times during the
year, Temple Emanu-El holds occasional performances, mostly of
liturgical music, and since it has the resources to hire a pick-up
orchestra, it can program some major works. For its 150th
anniversary year in 1995, for example, the choir presented Bloch's
"Sacred Service" and Bernstein's "Chichester Psalms."

TRINITY CHURCH
74 Trinity Place, at Wall St.   602-0768
Subway: 4 or 5 to Wall St.; 1, 9, N or R to Rector St.

Dating back to 1696, this historic church is a wellspring of music in
Lower Manhattan. Its Aeolian-Skinner organ is the fifth largest in
the city, and a recital series offers a chance to hear this marvelous
instrument. Trinity has an excellent choir, which presents four

concerts a year, including a complete performance of "Messiah" at Christmastime, and an Eastertime concert of a Bach Passion or similarly appropriate work. Suggested donations are $30 in the nave and $15 for side seats (limited view).

(See also: Winter Star in "It's Christmastime in the City")

WASHINGTON SQUARE CHURCH
135 W. Fourth St., near MacDougal St.   777-2528
Subway: A, C, D, E or F to W. 4th St.; N or R to 8th St.

Like most everything in Greenwich Village, music at Washington Square Church is just a little off the beaten track. This is not where you go for a Bach Cantata or period-instrument concert. What you do go to hear are avant-garde groups like First Avenue (see p. 171) as well as a multitude of world music concerts. The church has hosted West African Griots, Lebanese singers, Hawaiian slack key guitarists, and many others from virtually every corner of the globe. There is also a Sunday morning Jazz Liturgy, and the People's Voice Café, a popular folk music gathering, is held here on weekends.

IT'S CHRISTMASTIME IN THE CITY

The Christmas–Chanukkah season is one of the most magical times in New York, and musically the city is at it's busiest. It seems that every concert hall, from the largest to the smallest, and every church and synagogue, is vibrating with music.

There are dozens of performances of Handel's "Messiah" (including some you can participate in) and other liturgical offerings. There are Christmas and Chanukkah pageants, jazz interpretations of the Nativity, winter solstice and Kwanzaa celebrations. There is truly too much happening to describe it all here. When the time comes, keep your eye on the print media; most local papers and magazines do extensive listings of holiday events a week or two before Christmas.

HANDEL'S "MESSIAH"

If there's one piece of music that says "Christmas" it's Handel's popular oratorio, "Messiah," which in December is as ubiquitous as Christmas trees and department store Santas. (One year I counted 17 performances in one week.) Here are some that stand out, but again, check local listings for dates and times:

•Concert Royal and the St. Thomas Choir at St. Thomas Church (see p. 110): If you like a "Messiah" with a cast of thousands then this one is not for you. If you like a superbly sung, smaller-scale "Messiah," closer to the way Handel probably intended it, then be sure to hear this one.

•Concordia Orchestra (see p. 57) at **Alice Tully Hall**: Marin Alsop and her group perform an interesting crossover "Messiah." It's a jazz-pop-rock version called "Too Hot to Handel."

•The Handel and Haydn Society of Boston at **Avery Fisher Hall**: This organization gave the first American performance of "Messiah" in 1818 and has sung it every Christmas season since 1854. The music is second nature to this group, and its annual performances in Boston and New York reflect it.

•Musica Sacra (see p. 97): For years this excellent chorus has presented one of the most popular "Messiahs" in town. Unfortunately, because of financial problems, they had to cancel their annual **Carnegie Hall** performances in 1994, but the tradition lived on at Madison Avenue Presbyterian Church. Let's hope they'll return to Carnegie.

•Virgin Consort at the Church of St. Mary the Virgin (see p. 105): Like most music at St. Mary's, this is an excellent rendition, performed with a period-instrument ensemble.

A few other groups that make valiant efforts every year—with varying degrees of success—are the Choir and Orchestra of St. Ignatius Loyola (see p. 104); the National Chorale (see p. 98) at **Avery Fisher Hall**; the Oratorio Society of New York (see p. 215) at **Carnegie Hall**; and the Trinity Church Choir (see p. 111).

If you're not content being a mere listener, several organizations sponsor "Messiah" sing-alongs, where the audience is the chorus. Here are a few:

•Musica Viva at All-Souls Unitarian Church (see p. 97): New York's only "Messiah" sing-along with a fully professional orchestra. Information: 535-5530.

•National Choral Council (see p. 98) at **Avery Fisher Hall**: The Council's annual "Messiah Sing-Ins" are among the most popular in town. It's a chorus of thousands, with organ accompaniment and two dozen conductors, each conducting a different segment. Polished, it's not. Fun, it is. (The National Choral Council also sponsors a Holiday Sing at Grand Central Terminal.) Information: 333-5333.

•Riverside Church Choir (see p. 108). Information: 222-5900.

•West Village Chorale (see p. 218). Information: 924-0562.

If "Messiah" is not your cup of eggnog, you might enjoy one or more of the following:

"AMAHL AND THE NIGHT VISITORS"

Gian Carlo Menotti composed this popular children's opera in 1951 for NBC-TV, and ever since it has been a Christmastime favorite around the world. Here in the Big Apple, there are two groups that mount annual productions of this delightful work: The Little Orchestra Society (see p. 60) at **Avery Fisher Hall**, and Il Piccolo Teatro dell'Opera (see p. 84) at a different venue each season.

AMOR ARTIS CHORUS AND ORCHESTRA'S ANNUAL BACH CONCERT

(see St. Jean Baptiste Church in "Get Me to the Church")

ANONYMOUS 4 (see St. Michael's Church in "Get Me to the Church")

"BENDING TOWARD THE LIGHT: A JAZZ NATIVITY"

This is a fully staged, elaborately costumed dramatization of the Christmas story, featuring some of the world's biggest jazz stars (Lionel Hampton, Tito Puente, Dave Brubeck) in the cast. In this version, "Silent Night" is played in darkness on tenor sax and "We Three Kings" announces the arrival of the Jazz Kings. There's an all-star jazz orchestra and a 25-voice choir. At **Avery Fisher Hall**.

"BRANDENBURG" CONCERTOS

Why these popular Bach masterpieces have taken a place next to "Messiah" as representative Christmas music is a mystery to me, but in the past few years, performances of the six concertos have cropped up around town during the holiday season. Three groups keeping the tradition going are: Bargemusic (see p. 74), which presents three of the "Brandenburgs" during Christmas week and finishes the set a week later; the Chamber Music Society of Lincoln Center (see p. 12) and Chamber Music at the Y (see p. 21), both of which do all six in one sitting.

"THE CHANUKKAH STORY"

The Western Wind, a vocal sextet, and the actress Tovah Feldshuh present an engaging narration of the origins of the Chanukkah tradition, with musical selections from the 14th-century Sephardim of Spain to modern times. At the **Kaye Playhouse**.

CHANTICLEER

A highly polished male a cappella group, Chanticleer presents a wonderful selection of sacred and secular Medieval and Renaissance holiday music in the **Metropolitan Museum of Art**'s Medieval Sculpture Hall, in front of the dazzling Christmas tree.

"A CHRISTMAS CAROL"

This family-oriented musical adaptation of the Dickens classic, from the composer Alan Menken ("Aladdin," "Beauty and the Beast"), has wonderful costumes and dazzling special effects. It's sure to be a hit with the kids. At the **Paramount**. Information: 465-6741.

CONCERT FOR PEACE

Every New Year's Eve the Brooklyn Philharmonic crosses the East River and heads uptown to the **Cathedral of St. John the Divine** for a wonderful evening of free music. Joining them are guests like folksinger Odetta, flutist Carol Wincenc, and soloists from the Metropolitan Opera.

DICAPO OPERA THEATRE (see "A Night at the Opera")

ENSEMBLE FOR EARLY MUSIC (see Early Music Foundation, p. 58)

The Ensemble's holiday offering is "Daniel and the Lions," a delightful medieval Christmas pageant at the **Cathedral of St. John the Divine**. Based on a 12th-century French Benedictine manuscript, this show is the group's signature production, and it's quite a spectacle.

FIRST NIGHT NEW YORK

A potpourri of all sorts of family-oriented, alcohol-free activities for New Year's Eve and Day at sites around the city, First Night includes concerts, dancing, ice skating, and the like. One ticket ($15, $5 for children under 12) gets you into as many events as you can endure. Happy hangover-free New Year! Information: 922-9393.

I GIULLARI DI PIAZZA (see p. 84)

One of I Giullari's most memorable shows is "La Cantata dei Pastori," an exuberant production based on a 17th-century

Neapolitan shepherd's play. With puppets and jugglers, period-instrument players, whimsical masks and costumes, and an excellent cast, this is a delightful holiday treat. At the Synod House of the **Cathedral of St. John the Divine**.

KWANZAA

A wintertime festival of things African, Kwanzaa has been adopted by many African-Americans as the December holiday of choice. The literal translation is "first fruits of the harvest" and although the harvest in this part of the world has long passed, no matter. Kwanzaa is a colorful celebration of a rich culture. Related events usually include a fair share of music and dance, and pop up at various places each year. Some likely spots include the American Museum of Natural History (see p. 153) and S.O.B.'s (see p. 162).

LITTLE ORCHESTRA SOCIETY (see p. 60)

Annual Candlelight Concert at the Greek Orthodox Archdiocesan Cathedral of the Holy Trinity, 319 E. 74th St.

A 20-year-old tradition, the Little Orchestra's Christmas concert is one of the highlights of its season. The program always includes a major choral work, sung by the Metropolitan Singers/Greek Choral Society (see p. 211). Information: 704-2100.

MIDNIGHT MASS AT ST. PATRICK'S CATHEDRAL

Fifth Ave. at 50th St.
Subway: B, D, F or Q to 47th–50th St./Rockefeller Center

O.K., Midnight Mass is not exactly a musical event. Nonetheless, it does draw a big crowd of spectators who come to witness the high pageantry. It is preceded by a free concert at 11 P.M., but tickets, which are required for both the service and the concert, go fast. To get some, send a self-addressed, stamped envelope to 460 Madison Ave., New York, N.Y. 10022. Information: 753-2261. If you are too late, don't despair: there are many other churches that offer beautiful Midnight Masses.

NEW YORK CITY BALLET'S "THE NUTCRACKER"

Yes, I know it's dance, but since Christmas in New York wouldn't be complete without "The Nutcracker" I decided to include it. The music is by Tchaikovsky, after all, and one of the great ballet scores of all times. The company has presented this beloved work in the Big Apple every season since 1954, and it is one of the true joys of the holidays. At the New York State Theater, Lincoln Center. Information: 870-5570.

NEW YORK CITY GAY MEN'S CHORUS (see "Amateur Night")

NEW YORK POPS (see p. 64)

The Pops' annual holiday concert at **Carnegie Hall** is fast becoming a New York Christmas tradition. It's an exuberant evening of traditional and contemporary carols, songs and spirituals, with a soloist or two and a choir. Tickets are $13 to $60.

NEW YORK STRING ORCHESTRA SEMINAR AT CARNEGIE HALL

Founded by the late Alexander Schneider and now led by Jaime Laredo, the orchestra performs two concerts, one on Christmas Eve, the other a day or two before New Year's. Its members are young musicians (ages 15–22) who come together for ten days of chamber music and orchestral coaching, culminating in the two performances. Alumni include Yo-Yo Ma, Shlomo Mintz, and Cho-Liang Lin, which should give you some idea of the quality of the players. Information: 229-5689.

92D STREET Y CHANUKKAH CELEBRATION

The Y has a holiday party every year, an event for children and adults alike, which might include Israeli folk dancing, klezmer music, or even jazz. A recent one was "Eight Tales For Eight Nights," a potpourri of songs and stories, with a narrator, a cantor, and an Orchestra.

PAUL WINTER CONSORT'S "SOLSTICE LIVE"

Paul Winter's homage to the longest night of the year is one of the most exciting events of the season, with music, lights, dancers, and a sense of jubilation. At the **Cathedral of St. John the Divine**.

RADIO CITY MUSIC HALL (see p. 22) CHRISTMAS SPECTACULAR

This is it, folks, the one and only extravaganza, with live animals on stage and the Rockettes kicking up a storm. It's the annual Christmas Spectacular, one of the most popular holiday shows in town—so popular, in fact, that tickets, which go on sale in August, sell like hotcakes. Information: 307-1000.

SOUTH STREET SEAPORT CHORUS TREE

Fulton and South Sts.   732-7678
Subway: A or C to Broadway–Nassau St.; J, M, Z, 2, 3, 4 or 5 to Fulton St.

From Thanksgiving through New Year's the Seaport's famous singing Christmas tree comes to life for the holiday season. Forty choristers from the St. Cecilia Chorus (see p. 216), in Christmas tree formation, give free performances of holiday tunes.

TALLIS SCHOLARS

One of the finest early-music choral groups in the world, the British-based Tallis Scholars show up in New York each holiday season for an outstanding concert of Renaissance Christmas music. Their performances are unsurpassable. They're not always at the same location each year, so check local listings.

VIENNA CHOIR BOYS

Now here's a group with a history. The Vienna Choir Boys was founded in 1498 by Emperor Maximilian I. Mozart wrote music for it. Schubert sang in it. Bruckner was its organist. Of course you don't really need to know any of this to enjoy Vienna's annual Christmas program at **Carnegie Hall**. It is one of—if not the—best boy's choirs in the world.

THE VINEYARD

The Vineyard Theatre produces an original opera geared toward children and family audiences every Christmas season. These delightful one-act works are created by composer James Kurtz and librettist Barbara Zinn Krieger (the Vineyard's director), and have included "Aldo and the Magic Lamp" and "Appelemando's Dreams." At the Vineyard's 26th Street theater, 309 E. 26th St., near Second Ave. Information: 353-3874.

THE WAVERLY CONSORT

The Waverly Consort's presentation of "The Christmas Story" at the Cloisters (see p. 75) is a fully staged, beautifully costumed enactment of the nativity, based on medieval manuscripts and played on reproductions of period instruments. It's a spectacular Christmas show at a very special location.

WINTER STAR

At Trinity Church (see p. 111)   602-0768

"The Winter Star" is the name of a charming Christmas Eve presentation at Trinity Church for and by children, meaning that the kids are taught parts to play in this short Nativity Play, briefly rehearsed, and then it's onto the stage for Junior's first break in the theater. The show is followed by a Christmas Eve service.

IN THE GOOD OLD SUMMERTIME

Despite the sometimes brutal weather, there are some distinct advantages to summer in the city, and one is the steady supply of free music. From May through September just about every park, plaza, square, and public atrium is transformed into a concert hall, with free or inexpensive music at almost any time of the day or night. There are orchestras, string quartets, jazz trios, rock bands, klezmer groups, big bands, and more. And if you have access to transportation, music festivals on the grounds of spectacular mansions or in quaint villages are within easy reach nearby.

Some summertime offerings, in fact, are quintessential Big Apple events of which even the most jaded New Yorkers never seem to tire. Free parks concerts by the Metropolitan Opera and the New York Philharmonic draw hundreds of thousands of listeners year after year. The Mostly Mozart Festival attracts a loyal audience that comes for the high-quality orchestral and chamber music, while Summergarden offers a taste of 20th-century masterpieces.

For those whose tastes run in different directions, there's the JVC Jazz Festival, Central Park SummerStage, Hot Prospects, and many other first-rate pop, rock, and jazz series.

The only drawback is the fickle weather—this being New York in the summer, inevitably something is bound to get rained out. But don't worry, most events have prescheduled rain dates.

So don't pack that beach bag yet! You don't know what you might be missing right here at home.

BAM OUTSIDE: MUSIC AT METROTECH
MetroTech Commons, Myrtle Promenade, between Flatbush Ave. and Jay St., Brooklyn 718-797-5959 **Subway:** A, C or F to Jay St./Borough Hall; M, N or R to Lawrence St./MetroTech

Free outdoor concerts, sponsored in part by the **Brooklyn Academy of Music**, smack in the heart of downtown Brooklyn, are performed by a wide variety of performers. Past seasons have featured the Persuasions, Senegalese percussionist Mor Thiam and his Drums of Fire, and Jean-Paul Bourelly, the funk-blues guitarist.

BATTERY PARK CITY
416-5354
Between Vesey and Chambers Sts. **Subway:** 1, 2, 3 or 9 to Chambers St.; N or R to Cortlandt St.

All summer long the Battery Park City Authority sponsors an impressive array of free concerts by jazz, pop, rock, cabaret, classical, and other performers, usually at 6:30 P.M. in Hudson River Park (Warren St. at the river), or on the esplanade, which runs along the river the length of BPC. Three series, "Sounds at Sunset," "Cabaret Series" and "Sounds on the Hudson," offer enjoyable music and wonderful views of the Statue of Liberty and sunset over New York harbor. Some of the classical concerts take place indoors at Stuyvesant High School (Chambers and West Sts.).

BRONX ARTS ENSEMBLE (see "The Bronx and Staten Island, Too")

BROOKLYN MUSEUM (see "The Bronx and Staten Island, Too")

BRYANT PARK YOUNG PERFORMERS SERIES
Sixth Ave. at 42d St.   983-4143 **Subway:**7 to 5th Ave.; B, D, F or Q to 42d St.

Thanks to extensive rehabilitation, Bryant Park is now one of the nicest small parks in Manhattan, with a gorgeous perennial garden and several outdoor cafés. All summer long, classical and jazz musicians from around the city take to the bandshell here. The music is free, and if you can tune out the din of midtown, you'll find these concerts a pleasant lunchtime diversion.

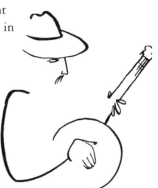

CELEBRATE BROOKLYN
Performances at Prospect Park Bandshell, entrance at Prospect Park West at 9th St., Brooklyn   718-965-8999 or 718-855-7882
Subway: F to 7th Ave./Park Slope; 2 or 3 to Grand Army Plaza

One of the longest running, free outdoor arts festivals in town, Celebrate Brooklyn is also one of the most comprehensive. It presents jazz, classical, rock, world music, fusion. . .you name it. There's plenty of room (1,600 seats in the bandshell and another few thousand on the surrounding lawns) and plenty of great entertainment.

CENTERSTAGE AT THE WORLD TRADE CENTER
Church St., between Liberty and Vesey Sts. 435-4170
Subway: 1, 9, N or R to Cortlandt St.; A, C or E to Chambers St.;
2 or 3 to Park Pl.

Free noontime concerts on the plaza of the World Trade Center, every day of the week in July and August, as follows: "Opera Mondays" (with singers from the New York City Opera); "Swingin' Tuesdays"; "Jazz Wednesdays"; "Oldies Thursdays," and "Country Fridays." Pack a lunch and enjoy.

CENTRAL PARK SUMMERSTAGE
Rumsey Playfield, mid-park at 72d St. 360-CPSS (2777)
Subway: B or C to 72d St.

You couldn't ask for a more all-encompassing series than SummerStage. Programs include hard and soft rock, pop and folk, calypso and zydeco, African and Caribbean, and even opera, now that the New York Grand Opera (see p. 129) is under the SummerStage aegis. All performances, except for an occasional benefit, are free.

CLASSICAL JAZZ (see Jazz at Lincoln Center in "All That Jazz")

COOPER-HEWITT NATIONAL DESIGN MUSEUM
2 E. 91st St., at Fifth Ave. 860-6321
Subway: 4, 5 or 6 to 86th St.

The museum (one of New York's real gems) hosts four free Tuesday evening concerts in conjunction with a lecture series. Each summer the focus is on a specific ethnic culture, Latino, Native-American, and so on.

FESTIVAL OF AMERICAN MUSIC THEATRE (see National Chorale in "Vocal Chords")

GOLDMAN MEMORIAL BAND
1501 Broadway Suite 2401, New York, N.Y. 10036   944-1501

For almost 80 years the Goldman Memorial Band has provided New Yorkers with free summer entertainment in the European concert band tradition. Founded in 1911, it's one of the oldest professional music groups in the city. The band often plays music written expressly for it, and some notable composers have done just that, including Respighi, Howard Hanson, and Morton Gould. Its series is divided between Lincoln Center's Damrosch Park and Seaside Park in Brooklyn.

HOT PROSPECTS
Prospect Park Concert Grove, Lincoln Rd. entrance, Brooklyn 718-965-8999/8961 **Subway:** D to Prospect Park

Cool off with these free Sunday afternoon performances by groups like the Afro-Cuban drummers Los Afortunados, the Andean music ensemble Inkhay, and Amanecer, a flamenco music and dance troupe.

IL PICCOLO TEATRO DELL'OPERA (see "A Night at the Opera")

JAZZ IN JULY (see 92d Street Y in "I'll Take Manhattan")

JULIUS GROSSMAN ORCHESTRA
Municipal Concerts, Inc.
P.O. Box 26, Oakland Gardens, Flushing, N.Y. 11364   718-776-5914

Since the 1950's, Julius Grossman has been bringing free music to areas where concerts are otherwise rare events. His well-rehearsed group plays in parks, community centers, churches, and other such venues, to appreciative audiences. Although the orchestra is a year-round operation, the bulk of its activities is in the summer (the rest of the year 11 of its string members perform chamber programs). Grossman is a sort of musical psychic who can spot big talents before they are widely known. Among his discoveries were Pinchas Zukerman, Erie Mills, and Young-Uck Kim, who appeared as soloists with the orchestra early in their careers.

JVC JAZZ FESTIVAL
787-2020

First it was the Newport Jazz Festival, then it was the Kool Jazz Festival. Now it's sponsored by JVC (the electronics company), which has kept this incredible festival going strong. For a week or so at the end of June, almost all the major Manhattan venues, and a few elsewhere, are turned over to the best jazz acts you'll ever see gathered in one city at one time. There is almost too much going on at JVC: unless you know how to be in more than one place at the same time, you're bound to miss some remarkable show.

LINCOLN CENTER FESTIVAL
721-6500 (CenterCharge)

As this book was being written, plans were underway for a major international summer festival at Lincoln Center, scheduled to open in July 1996. Headed by John Rockwell, a former New York Times music critic, the new festival's scope is ambitious, with a wide variety of grade-A classical and contemporary music and dance, stage works, and non-Western arts. (Serious Fun!, Lincoln Center's popular summer series of avant-garde and performance art, will be superceded by this yet to be named festival.) Keep your eyes and ears on this one . . . it should be an exciting addition to the New York summer arts scene.

LINCOLN CENTER OUT-OF-DOORS
875-5400

Here is street theater at its best. For almost the entire month of August, all the outdoor spaces around Lincoln Center (the Fountain

Plaza, the North Plaza, and Damrosch Park) come alive with free performances by just about any type of group you can imagine. The cliché "something for everyone" definitely applies. And the shows take place at all hours of the day and evening, so virtually anyone can work one or two into his or her busy schedule.

MARTIN LUTHER KING JR. CONCERT SERIES
Wingate Field, Winthrop St. near Kingston Ave., Brooklyn   718-469-1912
Subway: 2 or 5 to Winthrop St.

A Brooklyn summer tradition, this weekly free series, which runs from mid-July through August, features artists with wide musical appeal. The roster has included Little Richard, the O'Jays, the Mighty Sparrow, and the Stylistics. There is always a Gospel night, and a Caribbean night, too.

METROPOLITAN OPERA IN THE PARKS
362-6000

Can't afford to hear Pavarotti at the Met? Then catch him—or other stars from the world's most esteemed opera company—in Central, Van Cortlandt, and other city parks, for free. Concert versions of the Met's most popular productions feature many of the same singers who appear in the house the rest of the year. And with a new sound system manufactured a few years ago, the quality of the amplification is not bad at all. (The New York Philharmonic uses it for its Parks Concerts, too.)

MIDSUMMER NIGHT SWING
Fountain Plaza at Lincoln Center   875-5446

Here's your big chance to learn to mambo, tango, or two-step. For 20 nights from June to August, the fountain plaza at Lincoln Center is transformed into a huge dance club, where New Yorkers dance to the sounds of the best bands around. You have to pay $7.50 to get in on the dance lessons, but if you just want to hear the music, you can hang out anywhere on the plaza and boogie to your heart's content.

MOSTLY MOZART FESTIVAL
at **Avery Fisher Hall**   875-5030

The mother of all urban summer music festivals, Mostly Mozart has become as integral to summer in New York as the Mets and the Yankees, the Fourth of July fireworks and the Mister Softee truck. When this series began in 1966 no one would have predicted its almost instant success. Under music director Gerard Schwarz, it's achieved international stature, drawing the best soloists and chamber groups. So if you love Mozart—or Bach, Haydn, Schubert, Beethoven, or Brahms, for that matter—don't miss out. Tickets are moderately priced and often include bonus recitals before the concerts.

NAUMBURG ORCHESTRA
1165 Park Ave., New York, N.Y. 10128   876-6677

Elkan Naumburg, a rags-to-riches Bavarian immigrant, began a series of free orchestral concerts in Central Park in 1905. Since then, the orchestra bearing his name has delighted New Yorkers with free concerts each summer. Until 1981, they were held at the Naumburg Bandshell on the mall, then the series moved to Damrosch Park at Lincoln Center. These are not fly-by-night gigs, but excellent concerts led by top-notch conductors, sometimes with winners of the prestigious Naumburg Foundation Competitions as soloists.

NEW YORK GRAND OPERA
245-8837
at Rumsey Playfield, Central Park (see Central Park Summerstage, p. 125)

This is an ambitious company that mounts fully staged operas, free of charge, five times a summer. For the past several years NYGO has been steeped in Verdi, in a valiant attempt at producing all his operas. While you may not be familiar with all the singers, performances are generally quite respectable.

NEW YORK PHILHARMONIC PARKS CONCERTS
875-5709

The Philharmonic's Parks Concerts have drawn more than 11 million listeners since they began in 1965, and it's easy to understand why. What can beat lying under the stars with your spouse, lover, friends, or even your dog, sipping a glass of chardonnay, enjoying a delectable picnic, listening to a concert by one of the world's great orchestras, and all for free? Many of these concerts end with a super fireworks display. This is a New York ritual not to be missed.

RIVER MUSIC
c/o Circum Arts
31 W. 21st St., New York, N.Y. 10010   496-4549

A relatively new series, River Music presents high-quality classical, jazz, and ethnic music concerts on Roosevelt Island, a planned urban community with a small town atmosphere. Most concerts take place at the Chapel of the Good Shepherd (543 Main St.), a 107-year-old church turned community center, or on the adjacent plaza. One of the fun things about River Music is getting there—you can take the Roosevelt Island tram from Second Ave. and 59th St. in Manhattan, a ride that offers spectacular views of the city.

ROCKEFELLER CENTER LUNCHTIME CONCERTS   632-3975 OR 698-8676
Subway: B, D, F or Q to 47th–50th St./Rockefeller Center

Swing bands, country groups, folk singers, and jazz ensembles are just some of the types of musicians you'll hear in Rockefeller Center's free summer series. The concerts are at 12:30 P.M. in two locations, the garden at 1251 6th Ave. (near 49th St.), and the McGraw-Hill Park, off 49th St. between 6th and 7th Aves.

ROOFTOP CONCERTS AT TWILIGHT
YWCA of New York, 610 Lexington Ave., at 53d St.   755-4500
Subway: E or F to Lex. Ave. or 6 to 51st St.

For a modest $8, you can hear some of the brightest stars on the
New York music scene at the YWCA's rooftop music series. From
mid-June to mid-July, jazz and world-music performers provide an
hour or so of hip music. In case of rain, the concerts are in the Y's
Hitchcock–Rockefeller Auditorium.

SEUFFERT BAND
Forest Park Music Grove
Forest Park Drive, off Woodhaven Blvd., Queens   718-428-1973
Subway: J or Z to Woodhaven Blvd., then the Q11 bus to the Park Dr.

Like the Goldman Memorial Band (see p. 126), at its free concert
series the Seuffert plays music written specifically for concert band
(meaning no strings) as well as transcriptions of orchestral music,
some of which are seldom played on other band programs.

ST. MARK'S PARK (see Third Street Music School Settlement in
"Mama, I Want to Sing")

SUMMERGARDEN
Museum of Modern Art Sculpture Garden
14 W. 54th St., between Fifth and Sixth Aves.   708-9491   **Subway:** E or F
to 5th Ave.; B, D, F or Q to 47th–50th St./Rockefeller Center

For nine consecutive weekends beginning in July, young artists from
the Juilliard School perform a series of free concerts exploring a
particular aspect of 20th-century music. The programs are well
planned and well played, and sitting in the museum's sculpture
garden, surrounded by exquisite art and listening to Debussy or
Messiaen, is about as civilized as civilized can get. The competing
traffic noise is the only drawback here.

SUMMERPIER
Pier 16 at the South Street Seaport
Fulton and South Sts.   732-7678 **Subway:** A or C to Broadway–Nassau
St.; J, M, Z, 2, 3, 4 or 5 to Fulton St.

The Seaport is the setting for a mixed bag of concerts throughout the
summer featuring local and touring rock and pop groups, classical
choral and instrumental ensembles, all of high calibre, all of them free.

WASHINGTON SQUARE MUSIC FESTIVAL
Washington Square Park, Washington Square S. and LaGuardia Pl.
431-1088 **Subway:** A, B, C, D, E, F or Q to W. 4th St.;
N or R to 8th St.; 6 to Astor Pl.

The Washington Square Music Festival is one of the oldest running
free outdoor summer concert series in New York. For the month of
July the festival's resident orchestra or visiting chamber groups play
classical music—and classic jazz. It's a good venue for emerging
musicians (two who made appearances early in their careers are
Marilyn Horne and Wynton Marsalis . . . need we say more?)

WORLD FINANCIAL CENTER SUMMER ARTS PROGRAM
Plaza outside the Winter Garden (see p. 25)   945-0505 **Subway:** 1 or 9 to
Rector St. or Cortlandt St.; C or E to World Trade Center; 2 or 3 to Park Pl.

Summertime at the World Financial Center is jam-packed with all
sorts of free music and dance events. You'll hear anything from a
string quartet to a program of cowboy music.

WQXR CONCERT SERIES
At Damrosch Park, Lincoln Center   633-7600
New York's classical music radio station presents several free hour-
long concerts in Damrosch Park from mid-June to mid-July, broadcast
live on the station. They host vocal and instrumental groups like the
Gregg Smith Singers (see p. 96) and the Western Wind.

A WEEKEND IN THE COUNTRY. . .

Here is a smattering of some perennial favorite summer festivals, no more than an hour and a half by car from midtown Manhattan.

CARAMOOR FESTIVAL

Katonah, N.Y.   914-232-1252

On spectacular grounds, mainly classical from June through August, with some pop and jazz concerts.

CHARLES IVES CENTER FOR THE ARTS

Danbury, Conn.   203-837-9226

Home of the Ives Symphony Orchestra. A potpourri of pop, rock, jazz, and classical presentations.

JONES BEACH THEATER

Wantagh, L.I. 516-221-1000

Major pop and rock stars on the summer circuit stop here for a gig.

LONG ISLAND SUMMER FESTIVAL

Planting Fields Arboretum, Oyster Bay, L.I.   516-922-0061

The annual Mozart and Beethoven Festivals take place on the grounds of some of the prettiest gardens in the tri-state area.

NORFOLK CHAMBER MUSIC FESTIVAL

Norfolk, Conn.   203-542-5537

At Yale's summer home for fine visiting chamber ensembles you'll hear groups like the Cleveland String Quartet or the New York Woodwind Quintet, and lots of wonderful guest artists.

OPERA FESTIVAL OF NEW JERSEY

Lawrenceville   609-936-1500

Three quality productions, from mid-June to mid-July, sung in English.

ALL THAT JAZZ...AND ROCK AND POP

From Harlem to TriBeCa and beyond, jazz is thriving in the Big Apple. In Greenwich Village alone there are probably more clubs clustered together than in any other single neighborhood in the country.

Even the major classical organizations have caught the fever. There's the Carnegie Hall Jazz Band, Jazz at Lincoln Center, and Jazz in July at the 92d Street Y. Churches are also swinging: St. Peter's in midtown, Church of the Heavenly Rest on the Upper East Side, and St. Ann's in Brooklyn Heights are drawing audiences eager to explore this most American of art forms.

So how do you keep on top of what's going on? A good place to start is Jazzline (479-7888), a 24-hour recorded announcement of many jazz events taking place around town. It's sponsored by the Jazz Foundation of America, which also offers a free referral service for booking musicians (213-3866).

Many newspapers and magazines have extensive weekly listings of the jazz and rock clubs. Two of the most comprehensive appear in the Village Voice and the New York Press, but the Sunday New York Times, the New Yorker, and New York magazine also have ample listings.

The places listed here represent only a small fraction of what's out there in the New York jazz, pop, and rock worlds. Also included are some of the better cabarets and blues clubs. (You'll find that many venues don't stick to just one type of music but offer an eclectic mix.) Where cover charges and minimums remain constant, they've been indicated. Where charges are not specified, it's because they vary from show to show.

A word about the clubs: many require reservations, so to be on the safe side, call ahead. Also ask about a dress code. Some of the fancier cabarets require ties and jackets for men. You may also want to check smoking regulations, since the laws that apply to restaurants do not necessarily cover the clubs. If you're bothered by smoke, ask to be seated as far away from it as possible.

Finally, with the exception of a few clubs, like the Village Vanguard and the Blue Note, many, particularly rock clubs, open and close in New York as fast as the doors on a subway train. If you're not 100% sure that a place still exists, it's best to check ahead before you trek downtown, or you might end up singing the blues.

JAZZ AND CABARET

THE ALGONQUIN HOTEL OAK ROOM (see "A Fine Romance")

BIRDLAND
2745 Broadway, at 105th St. 749-2228 **Subway:** 1 or 9 to 103d St.
No cover; $7 music charge at tables, none at bar.

This attractive restaurant and club, with its colorful bands of neon, is named after the club where the incomparable Charlie "Yardbird" Parker used to play. It's a favorite hangout for neighborhood residents who come for the moderately priced food as well as the fine music. Not all tables offer a great view of the performers, however, so it pays to get one downstairs rather than on the mezzanine.

THE BLUE NOTE
131 W. Third St., near Sixth Ave. 475-8592
Subway: A, B, C, D, E, F or Q to W. 4th St.
Cover and minimums vary with each show. (Tends to be expensive.)

The Blue Note is one of New York's top jazz clubs, which is both the good news and the bad. Good because you can count on hearing the biggest names in the field all year round; bad because it tends to be crowded, overpriced, and, some say, serves mediocre food. Still, it's an exciting place, and if you can manage to stay up past 2 A.M., you can drop by and hear the performers jam after the regularly scheduled shows. Or come on a Sunday for jazz brunch, or a Monday night, when lesser-known talents are on stage. The Blue Note is also one of the only clubs with its own giftshop.

BRADLEY'S
70 University Pl., near 10th St. 228-6440
Subway: N or R to 8th St.; 6 to Astor Pl.
$12–$15 cover; $8 minimum

Bradley's is a cozy, dark room that attracts the finest musicians, both as performers and as listeners. It began as a piano and bass room, but now duos, trios, and even larger groups appear regularly. One of Bradley's best features is its acoustics, which are as good as it gets.

CABARET CONVENTION

Sponsored by the Mabel Mercer Foundation
230 E. 49th St. 4–D, New York, N.Y. 10017   980-3026

When the annual cabaret convention rolls into town, hang on to
your seat! If you are a cabaret lover, then for one week in October
you'll be in musical heaven, as just about every big name on the
cabaret circuit shows up at **Town Hall**, where the festivities take
place, to deliver a song or two. And it's only $15 a ticket.

CAFÉ CARLYLE AND BEMELMANS BAR

At the Hotel Carlyle
35 E. 76th St., at Madison Ave.   744-1600   **Subway:** 6 to 77th St.
$40 cover; no minimum

The Carlyle is practically synonymous with Bobby Short, who year
after year appears for two long runs, in the spring and the fall. The
rest of the time, people like Barbara Cook and Eartha Kitt grace the
stage. It's a very stylish club (with a stylish crowd and prices to
match). Across the floor is Bemelmans Bar, named for the painter
who, it is said, paid his hotel bill with the room's now-famous
murals. Quality piano playing is Bemelmans' specialty.

CARNEGIE HALL FOLK AND CABARET SERIES

Two of Carnegie Hall's increasingly popular series are "Cabaret
Comes to Carnegie," featuring vocalists like Karen Mason and
Phillip Officer, and the "Carnegie Hall Folk Festival," which focuses
on American themes like baseball, the circus, and cowboys. (Both
take place in **Weill Recital Hall**.)

CARNEGIE HALL JAZZ BAND

Carnegie Hall jumped on the jazz bandwagon in 1992 and got Jon
Faddis to steer the fledgling big band to success. He did this by
offering exciting concerts with major artists, shows with themes like

"Benny Goodman Revisited" and "'S Wonderful, 'Marvelous: A Celebration of American Song and Songwriters." Though the programs tend to look at jazz through historically tinted glasses, they are, nevertheless, satisfying.

COTTON CLUB
666 W. 125th St., west of Broadway 663-7980
Subway: 1 or 9 to 125th St.
Cover varies; usually $20–$25, including dinner.

In Harlem's heyday, the Cotton Club (then farther uptown) was *the* jazz spot in New York. It was Duke Ellington's hangout for years, and legendary artists like Cab Calloway and Ethel Waters were regulars. Now, some of these people are still there, in a manner of speaking—their portraits hang on the walls. There's still good jazz at the Cotton Club, as well as blues and Gospel. And the southern cooking isn't bad, either!

DANNY'S SKYLIGHT ROOM CABARET AND PIANO BAR
346 W. 46th St., between Eighth and Ninth Aves. 265-8133
Subway: 1, 2, 3, 7, 9, A, C, E, N, R or Shuttle to Times Square/42d St.
$6–$15 cover; $10 minimum (pre-show dining in restaurant applied)

Because of its proximity to the theater district, this small, affordable piano bar and cabaret is a hangout for Broadway types and, if you're lucky, you might spot one or two bona fide stars. But even if you don't, you'll get your money's worth in the Skylight Room, where the shows take place. (There is no cover or minimum at the separate piano bar.) On Thursdays, Danny's has a cabaret–jam session for only $3 cover and no minimum.

EIGHTY EIGHTS
228 W. 10th St., between Bleecker and Hudson Sts. 924-0088
Subway: 1 or 9 to Christopher St.
$10–$15 cover; 2 drink minimum

There are 88 keys on a piano, and each one is put to excellent use at this popular Village piano bar and cabaret. You can sing along with the piano player in the bar, or, upstairs in the stylish cabaret, hear an eclectic variety of jazz, comedy, and musical revues.

FAT TUESDAYS
190 Third Ave., at 17th St. 533-7900
Subway: 4, 5, 6, N or R to 14th St.; L to 3d Ave.
$20 cover; $7.50–$10 minimum

Once a German beer hall, Fat Tuesdays is now a small (read cramped) club where you're practically on top of the musicians. Downstairs you'll find good mainstream jazz at reasonable prices, while upstairs there's a bar and restaurant, with live music only at Sunday brunch.

HEAVENLY JAZZ (see Church of the Heavenly Rest in "Get Me to the Church")

HIGHLIGHTS IN JAZZ (see Pace Downtown Theater in "I'll Take Manhattan")

IRIDIUM
44 W. 63d St., at Columbus Ave. 582-2121 or 956-4676
Subway: 1 or 9 to 66th St.; A, B, C or D to 59th St./Columbus Circle
$10–$15 cover; $10 minimum at tables

Iridium is the West Side's newest and only seven-day-a-week jazz club. You can't miss the entrance: it looks like something out of a Dali painting, with contorted shapes sculpted in gilded metal.

While the upstairs restaurant offers good food and a close-up view of the plaza at Lincoln Center, the downstairs jazz room features live music by younger, up-and-coming musicians. Good solo piano playing keeps things warm before the scheduled shows begin.

JVC JAZZ FESTIVAL (see "In the Good Old Summertime")

JAZZ AT HENRY STREET (see Henry Street Settlement in "Mama, I Want to Sing")

JAZZ AT LINCOLN CENTER
875-5299

In 1991 Lincoln Center saw a good opportunity knocking at its door and got trumpeter Wynton Marsalis to let it in. Marsalis, Jazz at Lincoln Center's artistic director, has successfully led the series into the big time with swinging year-round concerts featuring the Lincoln Center Jazz Orchestra and dynamite guests, plus lectures, films, and new commissions.

Jazz For Young People, the children's component, is a splendid series modeled after the New York Philharmonic's Young People's Concerts (see p. 189), where kids can get answers to questions like "What is improvisation?" and "Who was Louis Armstrong?"

JAZZ AT NOON
Upstairs at Sardi's
234 W. 44th St., between Broadway and Eighth Ave. 221-8440
Subway: 1, 2, 3, 7, 9, A, C, E, N, R or Shuttle to Times Square/42d St.
$6 cover; $15 minimum

Founded by Les Lieber (who is still the director, and blows a mean pennywhistle, not to mention saxophone), Jazz at Noon was formed in the 1960's to give corporate executives, lawyers, doctors, stock brokers, and other jazz devotees a chance to meet for lunch and a jam session. They've been doing that, Fridays at noon, for 30 years now, at various locations, making it one of the oldest continually running jazz series in town. Past luminaries who have joined them include Benny Goodman, Dizzy Gillespie, and Illinois Jacquet. This is a great series, but, feminists beware: it's very male-oriented.

JAZZ COMPOSERS COLLECTIVE
43 E. 10th St., New York, N.Y. 10003   995-1552
The Collective is a musician-run, nonprofit organization dedicated to bringing original live jazz to audiences, with the emphasis on original. It presents concerts all around the city (often at Greenwich House, see p. 00), featuring works and improvisations by composers on the cutting edge. The collective also publishes a newsletter.

JAZZ IN JULY AND JAZZ PIANO AT THE Y (see 92d St. Y–Tisch Center for the Arts in "I'll Take Manhattan")

JAZZ INSTITUTE OF HARLEM (see Aaron Davis Hall in "I'll Take Manhattan")

JAZZ LIVE (see Flushing Town Hall in "The Bronx and Staten Island, Too")

JAZZMOBILE
154 W. 127th St., New York, N.Y. 10027   866-4900
Billy Taylor started this jazz concert hall-on-wheels, which trucks great music into neighborhoods around town. Every summer there's usually a big blow-out or two at Grant's Tomb (Riverside Dr. at 122nd St.). It's a wonderful program, making good jazz available to the multitudes sans the fancy club prices.

KNICKERBOCKER BAR AND GRILL
33 University Place, at Ninth St. 228-8490 **Subway:** N or R to 8th St.; 6 to Astor Pl.

This historic establishment has been on the scene almost forever (in the club world, a century is a long time!). Harry Connick, Jr. got his jump-start here before hitting the big-time, and the club still attracts top performers (Cyrus Chestnut, Ron Carter), with the focus on piano–bass duos. One of the restaurant's most prominent features is the original Hirschfeld drawings on the walls.

KNITTING FACTORY
74 Leonard St., near Church St.   219-3055 or 219-3006
Subway: 1 or 9 to Franklin St.; A, C or E to Canal St.

I guess I should say the *new* Knitting Factory, since this mainstay of the downtown scene recently moved here from its former location on Houston St. This popular club doesn't fit neatly into any particular category, since jazz, rock, performance art, film, and even poetry readings are equally at home here. Despite its new, more genteel look, the Knitting Factory retains its adventurous spirit. There is a front bar featuring espresso, cappuccino, and teas, a bar with 18 microbrewed beers on tap, a recording studio with its own label, the 80-seat Alterknit Theater, and the main performance space and balcony. The framed bits of the old Factory's sweater collection is a fitting reminder of the club's humble origins.

LYRICS AND LYRICISTS (see **92d Street Y–Tisch Center for the Arts** in "I'll Take Manhattan")

MICHAEL'S PUB
211 E. 55th St., between Second and Third Aves.   758-2272
Subway: E, F, N or R to Lex. Ave.; 4, 5 or 6 to 59th St.
Tues.–Thur., $15 cover, Fri.–Sat., $20; 2 drink minimum (Mon., no cover, $35 minimum)

Yes, Woody Allen still shows up here on Monday nights with his clarinet to play with the New Orleans Funeral and Ragtime Orchestra. Other nights you may catch Mel Torme or some other great artist at this East Side institution, where you'll hear the finest traditional jazz in a posh setting.

MIDTOWN JAZZ AT MIDDAY AND JAZZ VESPERS (see St. Peter's Church in "Get Me to the Church")

NEW SCHOOL FOR SOCIAL RESEARCH
66 W. 12th St., near Sixth Ave.   229-5690   **Subway:** 1, 2, 3, 9, F or L to 14th St.

The New School's Jazz and Contemporary Music Program has a few jazz series open to the public, the most notable being Jazz at Six, a lecture–performance course that can be attended either for credit or on a per evening basis.

NOT JUST JAZZ SERIES (see Town Hall in "I'll Take Manhattan")

RAINBOW AND STARS (see "A Fine Romance")

RUSSIAN TEA ROOM (see "A Fine Romance")

SMALLS
183 W. 10th St., at Seventh Ave.   929-7565   **Subway:** 1 or 9 to Christopher St. $10 cover

Smalls is just that: small and intimate. The acts here are mostly younger, lesser-known musicians, but that doesn't mean lesser quality. And with jam sessions going from two to eight in the morning, it's one of the only all-night clubs in Manhattan. To top it off, food and drinks are free!

S.O.B.'S (see "Around the World")

SWEET BASIL
88 Seventh Ave. S., near Bleecker St. 242-1785
Subway: 1 or 9 to Christopher St. $15 cover; $10 minimum

Long a Village fixture, Sweet Basil is one of the most reliable jazz rooms in town. No matter who is there, and the variety of performers is large, you get a good show and a clientele appreciative of the music. Try it for Sunday brunch when there is no music charge (but a $6 minimum), and you might catch the indefatigable Doc Cheatham, who still shows up with his trumpet.

TAVERN ON THE GREEN CHESTNUT ROOM (see "A Fine Romance")

VILLAGE VANGUARD
178 Seventh Ave. S., at 11th St. 255-4037
Subway: 1, 2, 3 or 9 to 14th St. $12–$15 cover; $10 minimum

The Vanguard is known by some as the Carnegie Hall of jazz. It was established in 1935 by impresario Max Gordon, who ran it with love and devotion until his death in 1989. Virtually every prominent jazz performer has played in this hallowed basement. Their names— Mingus, Davis, Monk—read like a Who's Who of jazz, and tribute is paid to many of them with their photographs on the walls. The Vanguard is a small triangular room, with a capacity of about 125 and excellent acoustics, where great talents still appear week after week. Despite its illustrious history, the club remains as it always has been: simple, unassuming, and wonderful.

VISIONES
125 MacDougal St., at W. Third St. 673-5576 **Subway:** A, B, C, D, E, F or Q to W. 4th St. $0–$15 cover; $10 minimum at tables

Visiones is a well-run, hospitable Spanish restaurant that serves good food and a wide variety of jazz, from the most traditional to progressive and fusion. It's also a great find for late-nighters, with weekend shows lasting well into the wee hours.

WEST END GATE
2911 Broadway, at 114th St. 662-8830 **Subway:** 1 or 9 to 116th St. $5–$10 cover for jazz shows; no minimum

Jack Kerouac, Allen Ginsberg, and other beat generation legends used to gather here, but now this renovated West Side restaurant attracts a Columbia University crowd, who come for the inexpensive food and the assortment of events: everything from stand-up comics and backgammon tournaments to jazz improvisations.

ROCK, POP, AND BLUES CLUBS

ACADEMY THEATRE
234 W. 43d St., near Seventh Ave. 249-8870 **Subway:** 1, 2, 3, 7, 9, A, C, E, N, R or Shuttle to Times Square/42d St.

Not exactly a theater (drinks are served during the performances) but not exactly a club (it's open only for specific shows), the Academy—an old movie theater—has become one of the city's major rock venues. "Young" barely begins to describe the crowd, which can get a bit rowdy. If you go, you might want some cotton for your ears, since the decibel level is high. There is a balcony with reserved seating, where you can avoid the mob scene below.

A.K.A.
77 W. Houston St., at W. Broadway 673-7325 **Subway:** N or R to Prince St.; A, B, C, D, E, F or Q to W. 4th St. $5–$10 cover

A recent arrival on the scene, A.K.A. is one of those places (there are a growing number of them) that specializes in rock-funk-jazz hybrids. Unlike many rock clubs, which are in dingy basements, A.K.A. is on the second floor, and actually has a decent view. It's not well marked, so if you're not familiar with the neighborhood it can be hard to find.

APOLLO THEATER (see "I'll Take Manhattan")

BEACON THEATRE
2124 Broadway, at 74th St. 496-7070 **Subway:** 1, 2, 3 or 9 to 72d St.

The Beacon is the Upper West Side's smaller, funkier counterpart to Radio City Music Hall. With 2,708 seats, it is one of the major rock venues in town. A handsomely renovated old theater with good acoustics, it attracts mainstream rock and pop groups, as well as punk, funk, and fusion bands.

THE BITTER END
147 Bleecker St., near LaGuardia Pl. 673-7030 **Subway:** A, B, C, D, E, F or Q to W. 4th St. $5 cover; 2 drink minimum at tables

I don't know why it's bitter, but the Bitter End, along with a few other clubs of that ilk in the neighborhood (the Rock 'n Roll Café and Kenny's Castaways), presents an assortment of bands each night. Some you've heard of, some you haven't: take your chances.

THE BOTTOM LINE

15 W. Fourth St., at Mercer St. 228-7880 **Subway:** A, B, C, D, E, F or Q
to W. 4th St.; N or R to 8th St.; 6 to Astor Pl.
Tickets: $12.50–$17.50; no minimum

A bit of rock, a little jazz, some funk, that's what you'll find at the
Bottom Line, a friendly club where some of the hottest stars have
appeared (though usually while they were just warm). After 20 years,
the Bottom Line has become old reliable on the club/theater circuit.
It specializes in singer-songwriters but delves into all sorts of
mainstream rock, jazz, and folk.

BROWNIES

169 Ave. A, near 10th St. 420-8392
Subway: L to 1st Ave. Around $6 cover

Your basic East Village club, Brownies recently upgraded its sound
system, and it's now one of the better ones around. Bookings include
some of the above-average local alternative rock bands.

CBGB/OMFUG AND CBGB'S 313 GALLERY

315 and 313 Bowery, at Bleecker St. 982-4052; Gallery: 677-0455
Subway: B, D, F or Q to Broadway/Lafayette St.; 6 to Bleecker St.
$3–$10 cover; no minimum

CB's is the revered birthplace of punk rock. It's a cramped room with a
good (but loud) sound system. Eclectic is the keyword here, where just
about every type of alternative rock group shows up. In case you're
wondering, it stands for Country, Blue Grass, Blues and Other Music
For Uplifting Gourmandizers. The mix of punk rockers and tourists
makes for quite a scene. CB's Gallery (an honest-to-goodness art
gallery) is a slightly more sedate version of the main space next door,
usually presenting acoustic guitarists or avant-garde improvisers.

CHICAGO B.L.U.E.S.

73 Eighth Ave., at 14th St. 924-9755
Subway: A, C or E to 14th St.; L to 8th Ave.
$5–$10 cover; 2 drink minimum at tables; none at bar

New York's only authentic Chicago-style blues club reopened in
August 1994 after a short-lived incarnation as Zanzibar, and it
already has a steady clientele. It's a comfortable club that imports not
only the best midwest blues singers to the Big Apple, but also the
bands they've been working with, making for a better-quality show.

THE COOLER

416 W. 14th St., near Ninth Ave. 229-0785 Subway: A, C or E to 14th
St.; L to 8th Ave. $5–$10 cover (free on Mon.); no minimum

At the Cooler, drains in the concrete floor and meat-hanging apparatus
are the not-so-subtle reminders of the club's former incarnation as a
meat locker. Musically, the club is a sort of mini Knitting Factory (see
p. 142). The acoustics leave something to be desired, but the
sensational jazz and indie rock make it worth a little ringing in the
ears. You can also watch the acts from the bar, via video.

FEZ

380 Lafayette St., at Great Jones St. 533-2680 or 533-7000
Subway: B, D, F or Q to Broadway/Lafayette St.; 6 to Bleecker St.
$7–$15 cover; 1 drink minimum

Here's a refreshing change from many of the rock clubs, which can
be so loud and crowded you can barely think. Located under the chic
Time Café, Fez is an intimate space that presents a variety of
interesting acts—rock, jazz, and experimental. Top-flight acoustic
groups are a specialty here, and the Mingus Big Band still draws a
big crowd every Thursday night.

IRVING PLAZA
17 Irving Pl., at 15th St.   777-6800 **Subway:** L, N, R, 4, 5 or 6 to 14th St./Union Sq. Tickets can range from $5 to $35 depending on show.

This former Polish veterans meeting hall has a big dance floor and a narrow balcony, and presents rock acts one rung down from those featured at the Academy. Jazz and theater are also at home here. If the downstairs action gets too much, head on upstairs—where there is a quieter lounge—and watch the show on closed-circuit television.

THE KITCHEN (see "Yeah, But Is It Music?")

LIMELIGHT
660 Sixth Ave., at 20th St.   807-7850 **Subway:** F to 23d St.
Cover: $15 weeknights; $20 weekends

Once a church, Limelight was turned into a dance club in the 1980's. But the stained-glass window overlooking the dance floor is about all that remains here to remind us of things sacred, unless you worship heavy metal bands with names like "Pungent Stench" or "Psychosis."

MADISON SQUARE GARDEN AND THE PARAMOUNT (see "I'll Take Manhattan")

MAXWELL'S
1039 Washington St., Hoboken, N.J.   201-798-0406
Transportation: PATH Train to Hoboken, then taxi to 11th and Washington Sts. (The club is about half a mile from the PATH station.)
Tickets, $6–$10

Maxwell's is one of the few clubs that New Yorkers will actually cross the Hudson to visit. While many rock clubs don't last more than a few seasons, Maxwell's has endured. It's a small, plain room, but it's become a vital link on the alternative rock circuit. Anyway, Hoboken is right across the river, not at all hard to reach.

MERCURY LOUNGE
217 E. Houston St., at Essex St.   260-4700   **Subway:** F to 2d Ave. or
Delancey St.; J, M or Z to Essex St. $5–$12 cover; no minimum

One of the newer—and already better—clubs in town, the Mercury
Lounge is a modest room with brick walls that one rock pundit said
"pulls off an unlikely combination of elegant understatement and
East Village cool." It has an excellent sound system and brings in
local and touring bands of many varieties, from folk to funk.

PALLADIUM
126 E. 14th St., between Third and Fourth Aves.   473-7171
Subway: L to 3d Ave.; N, R, 4, 5 or 6 to 14th St. $20 cover; no minimum

Though the disco craze of the 70's has died down, the Palladium is
still going strong, remaining the city's premier dance palace.
Formerly a concert hall where rock reigned, it's now a snazzy, high
tech space with a moving bank of video monitors, laser lights, and a
dance floor that can transform itself to various sizes. Friday is live
rock night.

ROSELAND BALLROOM
239 W. 52d St., between Broadway and Eighth Ave.   247-0200
Subway: 1, 9, C or E to 50th St. $12–$30 cover; no minimum

The city's most famous dance hall now books hard rock, Latin,
reggae, and other types of bands. But if waltzing or fox-trotting is
more your style, you can still do it here, on Thursdays (for $7) and
Sundays (for $11).

TRAMPS
51 W. 21st St., between Fifth and Sixth Aves.   727-7788
Subway: F, N or R to 23d St.   Cover varies; 2-drink minimum

One of the leading blues clubs in the city, Tramps also books reggae,
zydeco, Cajun, and even Irish rock. At its old location on 15th

Street, the club was a small, undistinguished place; now it's bigger, has a good dance floor, and a sister café next door where lesser-known acts appear.

WEBSTER HALL
125 E. 11th St., near Third Ave.   353-1600
Subway: L to 3d Ave.; N, R, 4, 5 or 6 to 14th St. $12–$20 cover; no minimum

Its ads tout it as "shocking by its size, breathtaking by its beauty, inspiring by its power." (You'd think they were talking about the pyramids of Giza or the Great Wall of China.) But where else can you find a 4-story club with a rock and reggae room, a disco, a huge dance floor, and a coffeehouse, all under one roof?

WETLANDS PRESERVE
161 Hudson St., at Laight St.   966-4225
Subway: 1 or 9 to Canal St.   Cover usually around $8; no minimum

Maybe the only rock club in town with such an up-front political consciousness, Wetlands actually has two full-time activists on staff who coordinate the Tuesday night "ecosalons," gatherings with guest speakers, videos, and what-not about all sorts of environmental and other politically correct concerns. But you don't have to care about whales or rainforests to enjoy the music, which goes on all week long and spans blues to hardcore rock.

AROUND THE WORLD

New York City is often called a melting pot, but that's a misrepresentation, if you ask me. It seems more a savory stew, with individual and distinctive flavors.

Just walk around town and you'll see: an enclave of Indians or Koreans here, an Italian or Hispanic neighborhood there. Chinatown is an old, bustling Asian community, while Brooklyn's Atlantic Avenue is a thriving Arabic-speaking district. Astoria is home to many Greeks, Yorkville is home to Germans and Hungarians. Brighton Beach (nicknamed Little Odessa-by-the-Sea) is heavily settled by Russian immigrants, the East Village is largely Ukrainian, and Harlem is distinctively African-American. This is what makes New York New York.

Our cultural diversity is reflected in the many types of ethnic music that can be heard all around the city. There are Chinese opera companies and steel drum bands, salsa groups and Greek nightclubs. In the Big Apple you can travel around the globe without ever leaving town.

The ethnic mosaic of New York is a whole book in itself. But a musical guide would be amiss were it not to include at least some ethnic and folk music establishments, so here is just a sampling. For folk music fans, a handy service is Folk Fone, a 24-hour information line listing events around the city: 674-2508.

With some exceptions, I've omitted restaurants and clubs with live music. There are so many that it's difficult to single them out, and besides, I'm not familiar enough with them to make recommendations.

Some organizations listed here, like the Austrian or Italian Cultural Institutes, have names that sum up their focuses; generally, these places offer classes, lectures, and/or sponsor performances; in these instances, no further explanation is given . . . unless they have an exceptional concert series worth pointing out.

AMERICAN MUSEUM OF NATURAL HISTORY
Central Park West at 79th St.   769-5000 **Subway:** B or C to 81st St.

In conjunction with its fascinating exhibits about peoples and places around the world, several times a year the museum sponsors ethnic festivals that explore many facets of the cultures found in New York's communities. These well-run programs of music, dance, theater, and food have included African, Bulgarian, and Chilean Festivals (and that's just A, B, and C).

AMERICAS SOCIETY (see Music of the Americas)

ASIA SOCIETY
725 Park Ave., at 70th St.   517-ASIA (2742) **Subway:** 6 to 68th St.

Traditional and contemporary Asian music are given thoughtful performances in the Society's cherrywood-paneled Lila Acheson Wallace Auditorium, by both Asian and Western musicians. The concerts are frequently accompanied by lectures or discussions, and offer insights into the many varied Asian cultures.

ASSOCIATION FOR PUERTO RICAN-HISPANIC CULTURE
c/o Peter Bloch
83 Park Terrace West, New York, N.Y. 10034   942-2338

AUSTRIAN CULTURAL INSTITUTE
950 Third Ave., 20th Fl., New York, N.Y. 10022   759-5165

BHARATIYA VIDYA BHAVAN, U.S.A.
Institute of Indian Culture
305 7th Ave., 17th Fl., New York, N.Y. 10001   989-8383

BLARNEY STAR
43 Murray St., near Church St. 732-2873
Subway: 2, 3, 4, 5, J, M or Z to Fulton St.; 4, 5 or 6 to Brooklyn
Bridge/City Hall; N or R to City Hall
$10 admission, no minimum.

If you're willing to travel to the lower tip of Manhattan, this pub
has great live Irish music on Friday nights. (Dining is available, too.)

CAJUN CONNECTION (see "A Fine Romance")

CARIBBEAN CULTURAL CENTER
408 W. 58th St., New York, N.Y. 10019   307-7420

CHINA INSTITUTE IN AMERICA
125 E. 65th St., New York, N.Y. 10021   744-8181

ETHNIC FOLK ARTS CENTER
131 Varick St., Rm. 907, New York, N.Y. 10013   691-9510

EFAC sponsors a wide assortment of activities, but its richest
program by far is the Folk Parks Music and Dance Festivals. These
free, day-long multicultural extravaganzas, held in parks around the
city, feature concerts, dance workshops, and ethnic foods of many

countries and nationalities, offering audiences a chance to experience, in a single event, the music and dance traditions of New York's diverse cultures.

FRENCH INSTITUTE/ALLIANCE FRANÇAISE (see Florence Gould Hall in "I'll Take Manhattan")

GAMELAN SON OF LION (see "Yeah, But Is It Music?")

GOETHE HOUSE NEW YORK
1014 Fifth Ave., at 82d St.   439-8700   **Subway:** 4, 5 or 6 to 86th St.

Goethe House is a German cultural center, which presents music by composers having a direct connection to the contemporary German music scene. One of the more interesting concerts mounted here recently featured the music of Friedrich Nietzsche (yes, *that* Nietzsche).

HELLENIC CULTURAL CENTER
27-09 Crescent St., at Newtown Ave., Astoria   718-626-5210
Subway: N to 30th Ave. (Grand Ave.)

Astoria, in Queens, is the heart of New York City's Greek community, and the Hellenic Cultural Center's activities reflect the neighborhood's rich heritage.

HISTORIC RICHMOND TOWN
(formerly the Richmond Town Restoration)
441 Clark Ave., Staten Island   718-351-1617
Transportation: Staten Island Ferry to terminal, then the S74 bus

Historic Richmond Town is the only restored village within New York City's borders. Among its 30 buildings, some dating back to the 1600's, is an authentic 1820's tavern (meaning no heat or electricity) where folk music is presented on Saturday nights at 7:30

and 9—by the heat of a wood stove in the winter—while people in period costumes serve wine, beer, and hot cider. The tavern seats about 45; reservations suggested. Admission: $7.

HOSTOS CENTER FOR THE ARTS (see "The Bronx and Staten Island, Too")

INTERNATIONAL HOUSE OF NEW YORK
500 Riverside Dr., at 122d St.   316-8400   **Subway:** 1 or 9 to 125th St.

International House is actually a residence for students, visiting professors, and scholars from around the world, who come to study at nearby Columbia University, the Manhattan School of Music, and other institutions. But it also presents cultural programs, often reflecting the global makeup of its residents. Not all programs are open to the public. Call the Programs Dept. and ask to be on the mailing list.

IRISH ARTS CENTER
553 W. 51 St., between 10th and 11th Aves.   757-3318
Subway: C or E to 50th St.

The American home for Irish music, the center offers classes in bagpipes, Irish song, fiddle, tinwhistle, and even the bodhran (goatskinned drum). They were the first to bring the popular singing group the Chieftains to this country, and continue to sponsor concerts by Irish musicians. The Center holds a huge outdoor Irish music festival each June (lately it's been at the College of Mount St. Vincent in the Bronx).

ITALIAN CULTURAL INSTITUTE
686 Park Ave., at 69th St., New York, N.Y. 10021   879-4242

JAPAN SOCIETY

333 E. 47th St., between First and Second Aves.   832-1155
Subway: 4, 5, 6, 7 or Shuttle to Grand Central

A leading showcase for traditional and contemporary Japanese performing arts, the Japan Society has a full complement of concerts, from shakuhachi flute music to a Jazz from Japan series.

JEWISH MUSEUM

1109 Fifth Ave., at 92d St.   423-3200 **Subway:** 6 to 96th St.

Concerts with Jewish themes, often in conjunction with current exhibits. You might catch a klezmer band, Yiddish folk singers, or even a jazz ensemble. The museum recently renovated its 224-seat concert hall, turning it into a well-equipped, comfortable auditorium.

(See also Bridgehampton Chamber Music in "I Hear a Symphony")

THE KLEZMATICS

c/o Springer
12 Newell Ave., New Brunswick, N.J. 08901   908-828-7458

Klezmer music is enjoying a big resurgence, and the Klezmatics is one of the groups that has helped bring that about. Self described as a "radical Jewish roots band," imagine a cross between traditional Eastern European Jewish celebration music and jazz, rock, and avant-garde improvisation and you'll have some idea of what this six-member group is all about. Born on the Lower East Side in 1986, the Klezmatics' concerts—at **Symphony Space**, La MaMa (see p. 00) and many other New York venues—are full of fervor and joy.

KOREAN CULTURAL SERVICE

460 Park Ave., near 57th St., New York, N.Y. 10022   759-9550

KOSCIUSZKO FOUNDATION (see "I Hear a Symphony")

LOTUS FINE ARTS CENTER
109 W. 27th St., between Sixth and Seventh Aves.   627-1076
Subway: 1 or 9 to 28th St.

A school and performance venue for multicultural studies, Lotus's emphasis is on South India, but you'll also find classes and performances representing Native American, African-American, and other cultures. About once a month the center sponsors a weekend festival highlighting one particular ethnic group, with music, dance, and food. It also hosts a new-music series called "Warmer by the Stove: Improvised Music, Intermedia, and Free Hot Chocolate." You're bound to like at least one out of the three!

MAHRAJAN AL-FAN, A DAY OF ARAB WORLD CULTURE (see Brooklyn Museum in "The Bronx and Staten Island, Too")

MAISONS FRANÇAISES
•at Columbia University, Buell Hall
Broadway at 116th St.   854-4482
•at New York University
16 Washington Mews, near Fifth Ave.   998-8750

Both Columbia's and N.Y.U.'s French societies sponsor numerous performances, lectures, and other events pertaining to music, dance, art, and theater, enough to satisfy any Francophile's appetite.

METROPOLITAN GREEK CHORALE (see "Amateur Night")

EL MUSEO DEL BARRIO
1230 Fifth Ave., at 104th St.   831-7952 **Subway:** 6 to 103d St.
For Hispanic painting, sculpture, and photography, this Upper East Side museum can't be beaten. In addition to its art exhibits, El Museo del Barrio sponsors music, dance, theater, and other live Latin-oriented presentations.

MUSEUM FOR AFRICAN ART

593 Broadway, at Houston St. 966-1313 **Subway: B, D, F or Q to**
Broadway/Lafayette St.; 6 to Bleecker St.; N or R to Prince St.

A prominent center for African art and culture, this SoHo museum
often offers live cultural events in conjunction with exhibits. These
might include storytelling or dance performances, with drumming
or other musical accompaniment.

MUSIC FROM CHINA

170 Park Row, #12D, New York, N.Y. 10038 962-5698

An eight-member ensemble consisting of traditional Chinese
instruments like the pipa (lute), di (flute), and zheng (zither), Music
From China performs ancient music, regional folk, and new music,
much of which it commissions. You'll find the group in many
locations, including the New York Public Library for the Performing
Arts (see p. 49), the Amercian Museum of Natural History (see p.
153) and **Weill Recital Hall**.

MUSIC FROM JAPAN

7 E. 20th St., near Fifth Ave., Suite 6F 674-4587 **Subway: N or R to 23d St.**
Most performances are at the Asia Society (see p. 153).

In addition to being the foremost presenter of traditional and
contemporary Japanese music in the United States, Music From Japan
has a new Resource Center for Japanese Music, a custom-designed
database offering access to scores, books, magazines, CDs, and recordings of Japanese composers. (Admission free, by appointment only.)

MUSIC OF THE AMERICAS

at the Americas Society
680 Park Ave., at 68th St. 249-8950 **Subway: 6 to 68th St.**

Latin American classical music has yet to achieve the same kind of
international status enjoyed by the art and literature of the region.

Music of the Americas hopes to change that. Sponsored by Chamber Music International, this series presents composers and performers from Argentina, Brazil, Cuba, Mexico, and other Latin American countries. Single tickets: $20; 4-concert series, $60.

NATIONAL MUSEUM OF THE AMERICAN INDIAN

One Bowling Green, at State St.   825-6700
Subway: 4 or 5 to Bowling Green; 1, 9, N or R to South Ferry

After residing on Audubon Terrace in upper Manhattan for more than 60 years, this splendid museum recently set up shop at a new home in lower Manhattan. Along with its exhibits, it occasionally presents performances of American Indian music.

NEAR EASTERN MUSIC ENSEMBLE

571 82d St., Suite 6, Brooklyn, N.Y. 11209   718-745-5159

Ever hear of the oud? Know what a nay is? Attend a concert by the Near Eastern Music Ensemble and you'll find out. Simon Shaheen, a master of the oud (an Arabic lute), founded this group to increase awareness and appreciation of Arabic music. His seven-member ensemble performs a vast repertoire, from classical and folkloric music to contemporary works by living composers. Their concerts, at major halls, colleges, and museums in New York, America, and Europe, have established them as the foremost exponent of Near Eastern music in the United States. (And, by the way, a nay is a wooden flute.)

NEW YORK PINEWOODS FOLK MUSIC CLUB

817 Broadway, 6th Fl., New York, N.Y. 10003   674-2418

Pinewoods sponsors an amazing variety of national and international folk concerts by top performers at churches, schools, and halls all around New York City. The club also runs Folk Fone, an indispensable service for folk music lovers (see chapter introduction), and publishes a monthly newsletter for members with a calendar of events so numerous it's exhausting just to look at it.

NORTH/SOUTH CONSONANCE (see "Yeah, But Is It Music?")

PADDY REILLY'S
519 Second Ave., at 29th St.   686-1210 **Subway:** 6 to 28th St.
Irish music every night at 9:30, with a traditional seisiun (jam session) on Thursdays. $5 cover; no minimum.

PEOPLE'S VOICE CAFÉ (see Washington Square Church in "Get Me to the Church")

REPERTORIO ESPAÑOL
Gramercy Arts Theatre
138 E. 27th St., between Lexington and Third Aves.   889-2850
Subway: 6 to 28th St.
A highly accomplished Spanish theater company, Repertorio Español presents delightful productions of zarzuelas (Spanish operettas). In 1995 it instated a Hispanic chamber music series, which got off to a rousing start with the Cuban-born clarinetist Paquito D'Rivera.

RUSSIAN CHAMBER CHORUS OF NEW YORK (see "Amateur Night")

SCHOMBURG CENTER FOR RESEARCH IN BLACK CULTURE
515 Lenox Ave., at 135th St.   491-2200 **Subway:** 2 or 3 to 135th St.
Not a performance venue per se, this well-equipped research center (affiliated with the New York Public Library) hosts concerts, films, and other events pertaining to African-American culture. It also houses a comprehensive recordings collection of African and African-American folk music and jazz.

S.O.B.'S
204 Varick St., at W. Houston St.   243-4940 **Subway:** 1 or 9 to Houston St.

S.O.B.'s is a good-looking club that started out presenting only Brazilian music but now covers the whole range of African and Caribbean music as well. You'll hear visiting African rock bands and the best Latin American jazz, Salsa, and rap. The name stands for Sounds of Brazil, and the decor—straw huts, faux palm trees, and the like—helps create a tropical ambiance. This is a real dancing club, and the tiny dance floor is always crammed with samba-ing bodies. ($15 to $20 cover charge; $15 minimum at tables.)

SONIDOS DE LAS AMERICAS FESTIVAL (see American Composers
Orchestra in "I Hear a Symphony")

SPANISH INSTITUTE–CENTER FOR AMERICAN-SPANISH AFFAIRS
684 Park Ave., New York, N.Y. 10021   628-0420

SWISS INSTITUTE
495 Broadway, 3d Fl., New York, N.Y. 10012   925-2035

TAIPEI THEATER (see "I'll Take Manhattan")

THALIA SPANISH THEATRE
41-17 Greenpoint Ave., 2 blocks south of Queens Blvd.
Sunnyside, Queens   718-729-3880 **Subway:** 7 to 40th St./Lowery St.

Primarily a venue for Spanish plays, the Thalia also produces concerts of Spanish music and has an excellent series of zarzuelas.

THIASOS CAFÉ
59 W. 21st St., at Sixth Ave. 727-7775 **Subway:** F to 23d St.

An "authentic" Greek restaurant with "special" prices (their words, not mine), Thiasos also presents "authentic" Greek bands.

UKRAINIAN INSTITUTE
2 E. 79th St., at Fifth Ave.   772-2884 or 288-8660 **Subway:** 6 to 77th St.

The Ukrainian Institute's chamber music program, Music at the Institute, is an outstanding series featuring either Ukrainian performers or composers (or sometimes both). Concerts are on weekends, generally about once a month.

UPTOWN COFFEEHOUSE AT THE SOCIETY FOR ETHICAL CULTURE
4450 Fieldston Rd., Riverdale, Bronx   718-549-5478
Subway: 1 to 231st St., then the Bx10 or Bx20 to 239th St.

Hosted by the Riverdale–Yonkers Society for Ethical Culture, the Coffeehouse presents traditional and contemporary folk music in a congenial, pleasant atmosphere. Admission: $7 for adults; $3 for children under 12.

WORLD MUSIC INSTITUTE
49 W. 27th St., Suite 810, New York, N.Y. 10001   545-7536

World Music Institute sponsors a mind-boggling array of performers

from virtually every corner of the globe, from A (for Andean, African, and Asian) to Z (for Zimbabwean and Zydeco) and everything in between. The programs are fascinating cultural travelogues that entertain as well as educate. They take place at many venues around the city, so call for one of their detailed schedules. (See also Interpretations in "Yeah, But Is It Music?")

YEAH, BUT IS IT MUSIC?

Contemporary music, once the Achilles heel of concert programmers, has gone mainstream. It used to be like pulling teeth to get the average audience to listen to anything that smacked of modernism. Now, it's rare for a program at, say, the New York Philharmonic not to include a 20th-century work. Experimental music, once confined mainly to small downtown lofts and galleries, has moved uptown: Bang on a Can, the festival that once defined "downtown music," now happily resides at Lincoln Center.

For composers writing today almost anything goes. The lines separating so-called "low-brow" from "high-brow" are blurry. Pop and rock, jazz improvisation, computers and electronics all share a part in shaping the "serious" music of today.

New York City is home base to dozens of new-music groups, which perform everything from the early 20th-century classics by composers like Debussy, Stravinsky, and Ives to works by the most far-out composers of our day. Various terms are used to describe them: avant-garde, minimalist, ambient, new-age, downtown. Don't worry about the categories—just be willing to open your ears to new sounds.

An excellent source of information about new-music concerts is the Calendar for New Music, a monthly publication put out by the SoundArt Foundation. It lists virtually every performance in the New York area with contemporary music on the program. A yearly subscription is $13 (or $23 for two years); students, $9. Write to the SoundArt Foundation, Inc., P.O. Box 850, Philmont, N.Y. 12565 (518-672-4775).

Another good sourcebook is "Einstein's Guide to the Musical Universe," put out by Roulette (see p. 179) and its record label, Einstein Records. It's a comprehensive list of national avant-garde and new-music performance venues, presenters, newspapers, radio stations, schools, and more. Cost: $35. Write or call Roulette. (Incidentally, the title of this chapter was coined by Roulette-Einstein as a logo available to concert presenters to bring about recognition for experimental music; I'm grateful for their permission to use it here.)

Here are some organizations that specialize in contemporary music. Included are several "performance art" spaces, marked with "PA" next to their names. Though performance art is much broader than music alone and encompasses all the arts, music often plays a vital role in performance works. Unless otherwise specified, all ticket prices in this chapter fall in the "inexpensive" range (free to $15). But that's not a guarantee, so call ahead.

ALTERNATIVE MUSEUM
594 Broadway, at Houston St.   966-4444
Subway: B, D, F or Q to Broadway/Lafayette St.

This staple of the SoHo art world presented its first concert series in 1978, when it created the World Music Program, a forerunner of the

World Music Institute (see p. 163). Now concerts at the Alternative focus on contemporary American music from a wide variety of traditions, including jazz, avant-garde, improvisation, and multi-media by artists like Rashied Ali, Hamiet Bluiett, and Matt Darriau.

AMERICAN FESTIVAL OF MICROTONAL MUSIC

318 E. 70th St., Suite 5FW, New York, N.Y. 10021   517-3550

Most of us were taught that there are 12 fixed half tones in an octave. In fact, within these 12 intervals is a universe of tones closer together—microtones—and many composers (Partch, Cage, Ligeti, among others) have experimented with tunings that venture far beyond the traditional. The American Festival of Microtonal Music, founded in 1981 by bassoonist and composer Johnny Reinhard, showcases this sometimes exotic-sounding music. Reinhard has an annual New York series at various venues, and all he asks is that his audiences "drive out preconceived ideas about how music should sound and open up to how the music does sound."

BANG ON A CAN FESTIVAL

222 E. Fifth St., New York, N.Y. 10003 777-8442

Even though the quintessential "downtown" festival has moved uptown to Lincoln Center, it hasn't lost its adventurous spirit. Bang on a Can was started in 1987 by three composers who had one aim in mind—to make hearing new music more fun. They offered concerts in a relaxed atmosphere where audiences and composers could mingle freely. The group's presentation of cutting-edge works from across the new-music spectrum caught on big-time, becoming one of the most popular events in town. The Bang on a Can All Stars, a core ensemble of the festival's regular musicians, continues to break new ground in experimental chamber music, while the festival's new Spit (no, it's not a misprint) Orchestra hopes to do the same for works demanding a larger performing force.

COMPOSERS CONCORDANCE
P.O. Box 20548 (PABT), New York, N.Y. 10129   564-4899
Performs at the Kosciuszko Foundation (see p. 60)

Composers Concordance plays an important role in developing new audiences for concert music being written today. It presents affordable programs by contemporary American composers, focusing on works by minorities and women. In a ten-year period it has given more than 200 premieres.

COMPOSERS' FORUM
73 Spring St., New York, N.Y. 10012   334-0216

This 60-year-old organization (founded as part of the WPA Federal Project) says it is "committed to presenting and supporting composers whose diversity of style and approach reflects present reality." Whatever . . . Concerts under its aegis take place at many venues around town, and it sponsors a free New Music/New Composers series showcasing public readings of previously unperformed works by emerging composers. This allows the audience to witness firsthand the encounter between composers and performers as new works are brought to life.

CONSORTIUM SERIES
55 Perry St., New York, N.Y. 10014   229-1766

The Consortium is a concert series sponsored by several foundations, founded to review the major developments of 20th-century music. Each program (there are three a year) includes a work by a pre-World War II master, the post-1945 generation of Americans, and a promising young American composer. In New York, the series is at the **Miller Theatre**; it's also at Harvard University in Cambridge, Massachusetts.

CONTEXT
28 Avenue A, between Second and Third Sts.   505-2702
Subway: F to Second Ave.

Context is a two-story work–performance space with 11 studios for recordings and rehearsals and a black box theater seating about 100. The focus here is on music and dance (the theater's maple floors are particularly suited to the latter). Performances are a mix of jazz, opera, solo recitals, and performance art, and there's a monthly dance program.

CONTINUUM
333 West End Ave., New York, N.Y. 10023   662-2967
3-concert series at **Alice Tully Hall** and the **Miller Theatre**

One of New York's pioneer new-music groups, this 30-year-old instrumental–vocal ensemble has introduced audiences to many creative geniuses of the 20th century. For instance, its performances have helped firm up the reputations of Henry Cowell, Sofia Gubaidulina, Alfred Schnittke, and others as masters of our time. Each season Continuum presents a series of retrospective concerts offering a new slant on a major 20th-century composer or significant related theme.

CROSSTOWN ENSEMBLE
237 E. 18th St., New York, N.Y. 10003   780-9281

This fledgling group got off to a promising start in 1995 with a concert at the New York Academy of Art mixing established European masters with avant-garde cult figures and up-and-coming American composers, reflecting the ensemble's aim to present programs with broad reaches. A 20-member instrumental ensemble, Crosstown is a welcome addition to the New York new-music scene.

DA CAPO CHAMBER PLAYERS

215 W. 90th St., 1F, New York, N.Y. 10025   873-1065

An award-winning quintet consisting of violin, cello, flute, clarinet, and piano, Da Capo offers a comfortable mix of the traditional and the modern, programming Brahms and Mozart side by side with both the masters and the lesser-known composers of the 20th century. The group was formed in 1970, and has since commissioned more than 70 works by composers, including a number of Pulitzer Prize winners, whose names read like a veritable Who's Who of modern music.

DANCE THEATER WORKSHOP (BESSIE SCHÖNBERG THEATER)

219 W. 19th St., near Seventh Ave.   924-0077 **Subway:** 1 or 9 to 18th St.

Every now and then Dance Theater Workshop kicks off its toe shoes, puts up its feet, and turns up the music. One of its best series is Big City Musics, a hybrid jazz-avant-fusion affair, with performers like Lenny Pickett, Myra Melford, and Gary Lucas. Another, New Song, takes a provocative look at contemporary trends in songs and song-making.

DOWNTOWN MUSIC PRODUCTIONS

310 E. 12th St., 2H, New York, N.Y. 10003   477-1594

One music critic said Downtown Music Productions specializes in "concerts with an attitude." From Halloween shows for kids to music by Holocaust composers, Downtown presents a wide variety of unusual programs of mostly 20th-century music. It has produced original operas for adults (Marshall Coid's "The Bundle Man") and for children (Nicholas Scarim's "The Magic Feather"). At its annual AIDS benefit, you'll hear works by composers who are living with, or have died of, the disease.

ECLECTIX CHAMBER ORCHESTRA

105 Duane St., Suite 14C, New York, N.Y. 10007   566-2217

Eclectix is a new-music group dedicated to melodic music, or, more precisely, music in the tradition of Debussy, Gershwin, and Ellington. Which means that for the uninitiated new-music listener, Eclectix's programs are a little easier on the ears than those of some of the other groups listed here. Performances take place at CAMI Hall (see p. 11) and other venues.

ENSEMBLE 21

523 W. 112th St., #21, New York, N.Y. 10025   663-5191

Like most groups of this sort, the cooperative of young artists called Ensemble 21 was established in hopes of making new music more accessible to a wider audience. Its creative programming and skilled performances have helped do just that. The Ensemble plays several concerts each season, commissions new works, and sponsors a solo recital by a young performer committed to 20th-century repertoire.

ESSENTIAL MUSIC

c/o Meader Associates
270 Lafayette St., Suite 502, New York, N.Y. 10012   966-0693

This percussion-based ensemble is steeped in the American experimental tradition of John Cage, Henry Cowell, and others. Known for its intensity and daring, Essential Music has a stated mission to "explore this rich legacy [of Cage and Cowell] and its present and future heirs." In its relatively short lifetime—it was founded in 1987—the ensemble has played an extraordinarily large and unusual repertoire of new and/or neglected music.

EXPERIMENTAL INTERMEDIA
224 Centre St., at Grand St.   431-5127 **Subway: J, M, N, R, Z or 6 to** Canal St.

Back in 1973, composer and film maker Phill Niblock opened up his loft on Centre Street for a series of concerts, and it became the musical branch of the Experimental Intermedia Foundation. It has since turned into one of the city's major alternative spaces for experimental music, as well as film and video. Scores of innovative composers have paraded through here over the years, for concerts that sometimes go on for hours and hours (bring your no-doze). If we're lucky, there will be many more to come.

FIRST AVENUE
c/o Matt Sullivan
226 E. Second St., New York, N.Y. 10009   529-4737
3 concerts at Washington Square Church (see p. 112)

No, not the street, First Avenue is a electro–acoustic trio in residence at Princeton University. What's electro–acoustic? It's a combination of acoustic instruments and electronic or synthesized sounds. William Kannar (bass), C. Bryan Rulon (synthesizers) and Matt Sullivan (oboe) have been on the scene since 1981, improvising, educating, and provoking audiences with their maverick approach.

FRIENDS AND ENEMIES OF NEW MUSIC
300 W. 108th St., New York, N.Y. 10025   749-1324
4-concert season at Greenwich House Music School (see p. 195)
and **Merkin Concert Hall**

This cleverly named group is actually a coalition of three composers, Tom Cipullo, John Link, and Ben Yarmolinsky. Their concerts are a forum both for their own music and for works by a host of other composers, from the most recognizable, like Copland, Carter, and

Bernstein, to young composers writing today. Performers in these events are some of the most competent new-music specialists now on the scene. Friends and Enemies also sponsors a composition contest; winning works are performed at the concerts.

GAMELAN SON OF LION

305 Call Hollow Rd., Stony Point, N.Y. 10980   914-354-2349

The gongs and angklungs used by this group are most closely associated with the music of Indonesia. But Gamelan Son of Lion is most definitely not an Indonesian music group. It is a new-music ensemble founded in 1976 by the composer and ethnomusicologist Barbara Benary, who made the instruments used by the group—about 20 gongs and metallophones (similar to xylophones), supplemented by an assortment of flutes, drums, clarinet, and—yes!—hubcaps. Works on Gamelan's programs reflect a myriad influences—classical, jazz, klezmer, atonal, minimalist, and more.

GUGGENHEIM MUSEUM SOHO

575 Broadway, at Prince St.   423-3877 **Subway:** N or R to Prince St.; 6 to Spring St.

The SoHo branch of the Guggenheim hosts two intriguing series, "Second Helpings" and "Works & Process."

•Second Helpings: Co-sponsored by the St. Luke's Chamber Ensemble (see p. 66), Second Helpings gives repeat performances of recent chamber works by younger, emerging composers and revives lesser-known works by those already established. It's a great idea, since often one hearing is not enough for new music to sink in. The informal concerts take place in the museum's galleries instead of a concert hall, thus promoting interaction among audience, performers, and composers.

•Works & Process: Here's a rare opportunity to see bits and snatches of operas, dances, and other works in the making, and hear ideas about interpretation and creation from the creators themselves. Performances are sometimes at the museum, sometimes off-site.

INTERNATIONAL OFFESTIVAL

311 W. 43d St., New York, N.Y. 10036   307-6000

This inventive festival is held each April through June and focuses mainly on experimental theater and performance art. The OFFestival also imports interesting music groups from around the world. Some who have appeared in the past include Batucada (Brazilian street drummers), Atma! (Indian musicians and dancers), RhythMania (a Japanese rock group), and the Charlie Palmieri Quartet (salsa).

INTERPRETATIONS SERIES

Sponsored by the World Music Institute (see p. 00), this series, going on ten years old, is one of the city's most spirited surveys of new music. It explores the relationships between the artists who create and those who interpret, and features top contemporary music and multimedia artists (baritone Thomas Buckner is one of its mainstays). Most performances take place at **Merkin Concert Hall**.

THE KITCHEN (PA)

512 W. 19th St., near Tenth Ave.   255-5793 **Subway:** 1 or 9 to 18th St.

Anyone and anything can—and usually does—turn up at the Kitchen, one of New York's most influential performance art spaces. Since its establishment in 1971, this hub of the avant-garde has set the standards for the genre. Housed in a 19th-century ice house, the Kitchen presents music, dance, theater, and video, singly or in any combination, by well-known artists and newcomers on the scene. These are not mere performances, they are happenings. The recently established Electronic Café International is a sort of musical rest stop on the worldwide information highway. Here you can grab a cup of coffee, sit back, and watch performers in several cities linked interactively on a "virtual stage." Its founders think of it as "the café for the global village." Whatever.

LA MAMA E.T.C. (PA)
74A E. Fourth St., between Second and Third Aves.   475-7710
Subway: B, D, F or Q to Broadway/Lafayette St.; 6 to Bleecker St.;
F to 2nd Ave.

One of the oldest, boldest experimental venues in the country, La MaMa has three stages (the First Floor Theater, the Club, and the Annex), where something unusual is usually happening at each one. Shows run the gamut from tedious to exciting, but they're almost always interesting. Though theatrical events are more common here, La MaMa presents some of the most innovative musicians on the new-music circuit. At La MaMa La Galleria (6 E. 1st St.), there is a terrific "Composer Series" offering musicians an informal and supportive atmosphere to present new works while at the same time helping to develop audiences for experimental music.

LEAGUE OF COMPOSERS/ISCM
30 W. 26th St., Suite 1001, New York, N.Y. 10010   627-1851

A marriage of the League of Composers and the American section of the International Society for Contemporary Music (no wonder they use the abbreviation), this is the country's oldest contemporary-music organization. (The League was founded in 1923 and the merger took place in the 1950's.) It sponsors a concert series at various New York City venues and a national composers contest, and it commissions new works.

MUSIC FOR HOMEMADE INSTRUMENTS
262 Bowery, near Houston St.   226-1558 **Subway:** F to Second Ave.

The name says it all! The composers in this collective write works for instruments made from trash and found objects—anything from styrofoam boxes (used as resonators) to cardboard tubes, refrigerator pans, chemical drums, wires, nuts and bolts, and other hardware. In keeping with the group's recycling aesthetic, at its home-base concerts on the Bowery, returnable beverage containers are accepted for admission in lieu of cash!

MUSIC OF OUR TIME (see Chamber Music Society of Lincoln Center in "I'll Take Manhattan")

MUSIC UNDER CONSTRUCTION AT THE CONSTRUCTION COMPANY
10 E. 18th St., between Fifth Ave. and Broadway   924-7882
Subway: L, N, R, 4, 5 or 6 to 14th St./Union Sq.

A loft with room for about 80, the Construction Company was originally a theater and dance space, but in the last few years music has been lovingly embraced. The music series (five performances a year) is administered by composers who write new works specifically for these events. One usually a involves a choreographer.

MUSICIANS' ACCORD: A NEW MUSIC PROJECT
245 E. 24th St., 3E, New York, N.Y. 10010   229-5599

Musicians' Accord presents concerts of 20th-century chamber music of all styles, including the "classic" repertoire, like Debussy and Stravinsky, as well as brand-new works, many of them commissioned premieres (there have been close to 100 in the past 15 years). The group is in residence at City College (see **Aaron Davis Hall** in "I'll Take Manhattan"), and perform there several times a year, with additional concerts at other venues.

NEWBAND
Box 443 Nyack, N.Y. 10960   914-358-2759

Since its birth in 1977, Newband has championed some of the most offbeat music of our time. It specializes in alternative tunings (see

American Festival of Microtonal Music, p. 166) and unusual instruments—in fact, the entire collection of composer–inventor Harry Partch's homemade instruments is on permanent loan to Newband's founder Dean Drummond. When Newband is on stage, you'll see instruments you've probably never dreamed of: the Chromelodeon (a 43-tone-per-octave reed organ), Cloud Chamber Bowls, and Drummond's own invention, the Zoomoozophone, a 31-tone-per-octave percussion instrument.

NEW JUILLIARD ENSEMBLE (see Juilliard School in "The Best Things in Life Are Free")

NEW MUSIC CONSORT (see Manhattan School of Music in "The Best Things in Life Are Free")

NEW SOUNDS LIVE (see **Merkin Concert Hall** in "I'll Take Manhattan")

NEW YORK CONSORTIUM FOR NEW MUSIC
215 W. 90th St., Suite 1F, New York, N.Y. 10025
873-1065

The N.Y. Consortium is a joint venture of five groups—Continuum, Da Capo Chamber Players, New Music Consort, New York New Music Ensemble, and Newband (see individual entries in this chapter)—a sort of united front for promoting new music. Its best venture is the annual Sonic Boom Festival, held in the fall, where each member group plays one concert, and all participate in a joint effort. For the past few seasons, the **Miller Theatre** has hosted Sonic Boom.

NEW YORK NEW MUSIC ENSEMBLE
48 Horatio St., New York, N.Y. 10014   633-6260
3-concert season at **Merkin Concert Hall**

A six-member group made up of flute, clarinet, violin, cello, piano, and percussion, the New York New Music Ensemble believes that thoughtfully programmed and ardently performed concerts can reach both the new-music aficionado and the uninitiated listener. The ensemble presents interesting programs and theater works in concert, and also offers informal home-listening sessions with a featured composer, by special arrangement.

NEW YORK UNIVERSITY NEW MUSIC ENSEMBLE
N.Y.U. School of Education
35 W. 4th St., New York, N.Y. 10012   998-5441

The N.Y.U. New Music Ensemble performs mostly improvisatory music, particularly ethnic and jazz-influenced works, as well as experimental and interactive computer music. N.Y.U. composers are, of course, given top billing.

NEXT STAGE COMPANY
145 W. 46th St., New York, N.Y. 10036   354-6121

A consortium of music, dance, drama, film, and the visual arts, Next Stage states its goal as creating a home in which artists of many disciplines can develop their skills in a collaborative environment. The theater is a renovated gym at the Church of St. Mary the Virgin (see p. 105), which now makes a functional black box theater. In addition to multimedia shows, Next Stage's resident Music Ensemble presents concerts by a host of young composers associated with the consortium.

NEXT WAVE FESTIVAL (see **Brooklyn Academy of Music** in "The Bronx and Staten Island, Too")

NORTH/SOUTH CONSONANCE

P.O. Box 698, Cathedral Station, New York, N.Y. 10025   592-3532
4 to 8 concerts a season, mostly at **Christ** and **St. Stephen's Church**
(see p. 104)

Composer and pianist Max Lifchitz, this group's founder and
director, was born in Mexico City, so it's not surprising that
North/South's gaze is mainly on the South (meaning Latin America),
although Russian and European works also appear on the programs
from time to time. The group plays chamber music of many
configurations, mostly by living composers.

PARNASSUS

258 Riverside Drive, 7-C, New York, N.Y. 10025   864-4197

Parnassus is one of the country's largest and most respected new-
music groups. Established in 1974, under its founder Anthony Korf
the 16-member ensemble has given more than 150 premieres by
mostly, though not exclusively, American composers. Through its
own commissioning program Parnassus has increased the
contemporary chamber repertory by more than 50 works. Although
programs are not always what you'd call easy listening, the
ensemble's 3-concert season in New York is well attended.

PERFORMANCE SPACE 122 (P.S. 122) (PA)

150 First Ave., at 9th St.   477-5288
Subway: L to First Ave.; 6 to Astor Pl.; N or R to 8th St.

Aspiring musicians, choreographers, and performance artists flock to
this converted East Village public school, hoping to get their big
breaks. Some of them—Eric Bogosian and Bill Irwin, for example—
did start out here, and return from time to time to show their
gratitude. Meredith Monk and Zeena Parkins also set up shop here,
as does a host of lesser-known but equally engaging artists. P.S. 122
puts on an "Avant-Garde-Arama," where over the course of a few

days you get a bit of this, a bit of that, and some of whatever is left over. Performances run from the ridiculous to the sublime, but whatever they are, you can count on them being different.

PRISM CHAMBER ORCHESTRA
c/o Elm Management
411 W. 21st St., New York, N.Y. 10011   741-0011

Prism was founded by the late conductor Robert Black, who was one of New York's major new-music advocates. After his untimely death at age 43 in 1993, the orchestra's voice was temporarily quieted, but now Prism is back on the scene under a newly reorganized board determined to carry on Black's original mission to present "innovative works of bold artistic vision." Varying in size as needed per concert, from small groups to full chamber orchestra, the ensemble has an eclectic repertoire, which includes rarely performed works by established composers as well as commissioned music by emerging composers.

QUINTET OF THE AMERICAS
134 Bowery, New York, N.Y., 10013   431-8786

Founded in Bogotá, Colombia, in 1976, the Quintet of the Americas is a traditionally configured woodwind ensemble (flute, clarinet, oboe, bassoon, and horn) that plays contemporary music from the Western hemisphere, leaning heavily toward Latin American countries. Although they are in residence at Northwestern University outside Chicago, they still call New York home, and have a regular Big Apple series, at various venues over the years.

ROULETTE
228 W. Broadway, at White St.   219-8242   **Subway:** A, C or E to Canal St.

This 75-seat loft space in still-burgeoning TriBeCa is one of those venues that could just as easily have landed in the chapter on jazz and rock music, since a lot of both goes on at Roulette. But the experimental nature of its performances won them a spot here. Between 60 and 90 concerts are presented yearly, ranging from improvisation and music for homemade instruments to classically oriented soloists, composers, and chamber groups. Le Salon de Roulette, an informal cocktail–concert series with food, drink, and music ($15 for nonmembers), provides the chance to mingle with other supporters of the avant-garde.

S.E.M. ENSEMBLE
25 Columbia Place, Brooklyn, N.Y. 11201   718-488-7659

S.E.M. plays Cagean and post-Cagean works, and the programs are far from light, so if you like to leave a concert humming the tunes, you might be better off somewhere else. But if you're willing to stretch your listening limits, you'll probably discover some exciting new music. By the way, in homage to Cage (for whom chance played a major role in his compositional techniques), the name S.E.M. means nothing in particular, and was chosen randomly. This extraordinary group has a Manhattan series at the Paula Cooper Gallery (155 Wooster St.) and a Brooklyn Heights series at the Willow Place Auditorium (26 Willow St., between Joralemon and State Sts.).

SONIC BOOM FESTIVAL (see New York Consortium for New Music)

SPECULUM MUSICAE
423 W. 118th St., New York, N.Y. 10027   864-0638
3-concert series at **Merkin Concert Hall** and the **Miller Theatre**

For a quarter of a century, Speculum Musicae has been giving its audiences consummate performances of 20th-century music. The ensemble, made up of 12 of the most accomplished musicians on the New York new-music scene, is one of the most versatile around, with a repertoire spanning the classics of Schoenberg and Webern to newly commissioned works by today's composers. The group has given 42 world, 17 American, and 22 New York premieres, often using interactive computer systems and other electronic technology.

THAT! NEW MUSIC GROUP

235 W. 22d St., Suite 1D , New York, N.Y. 10010   645-0718

What's That? Why, it's a new new-music group, which describes itself as a music theater company, that's what! Theater, because the music, which is the main focus, is performed in a theatrical manner, with lighting, costumes, props, staging. Meaning that during a performance you might see the pianist shredding paper, or the violinist blowing up balloons, or hear spoken text above the music. The aim? To use visual elements as a tool, helping increase familiarity with new music. Hmm, we shall see . . .

WARMER BY THE STOVE (see Lotus Fine Arts Center in "Around the World")

WASHINGTON SQUARE CONTEMPORARY MUSIC SOCIETY

New York University Music Dept.
24 Waverly Place, Rm. 268, New York, N.Y. 10003   691-9184

The Society itself is not a performing group, but an organization that sponsors concerts by expert New York new-music specialists and guest ensembles. Most performances are either at N.Y.U. or at **Merkin Concert Hall**.

CHILDREN'S CORNER

Once upon a time music was an indispensable element in public education, considered as basic as reading, 'riting and 'rithmetic. Sadly, that is no longer the case. As funding for music and arts education wanes, MTV and boom boxes are replacing more formal programs as many children's only sources of music.

Parents, don't despair! In New York, a city with lots of kids and lots of musicians, there are still many organizations that care whether children grow up knowing that a Prelude is not just a car and a Symphony is something other than a candy bar.

A few examples: The New York Philharmonic continues to charm—and educate—new generations of listeners with its Young People's Concerts. Carnegie Hall has entered its second decade of "Link Up!," a program designed to teach elementary school kids basic music concepts and increase their exposure to orchestral music. With its Chamber Music Beginnings, the Chamber Music Society of Lincoln Center is making sure that youngsters don't grow up ignorant of chamber music. The Metropolitan Opera Guild and others are doing the same for opera. Jazz for Young People is Jazz at Lincoln Center's way of teaching children about a music form intricately linked with American history and culture. Truly, New Yorkers can be proud of the commitment our local performing arts groups have made to our city's younger citizens.

Here is a small sampling of children's programs that for the most part take place outside the schools and are geared to ensure that music remains an important ingredient in every child's development.

AMATO OPERA "OPERAS IN BRIEF" (see "A Night at the Opera")

AMERICAN SYMPHONY ORCHESTRA (see p. 55)   581-1365
A new program, "The Red, White and Bluejeans Music Machine," was developed by the orchestra in collaboration with P.D.Q. Bach (alias Peter Schickele). For kids ages seven through thirteen, this **Alice Tully Hall** series uses a variety of imaginative and informative materials, including booklets, cassettes, video—and of course live performances, to explore a vast range of musical ideas ("Who Needs a Conductor, Anyway?" was the theme of the inaugural program). Tickets are $20.

BOYS CHOIR OF HARLEM
P.O. Box 669, Triborough Station, New York, N.Y. 10035   289-1815
In 1968 this group started as a small church choir. Today it's one of the most prestigious boys choirs in the world. Although members come from all over New York City, a large number are from Harlem. The choir gives special emphasis to the works of African-American composers, spirituals, and popular music, and it performs citywide, nationally, and even internationally. The group has its own

accredited school (coed, as all public schools must be), the Choir Academy of Harlem, at Madison Ave. and 127th St.

BRONX ARTS ENSEMBLE (see "The Bronx and Staten Island, Too")

CHAMBER MUSIC BEGINNINGS
Chamber Music Society of Lincoln Center (see p. 12)   875-5788

Chamber music is often overlooked when introducing young children to the world of music. The Chamber Music Society hopes to correct that oversight with its Chamber Music Beginnings program. It familiarizes elementary and middle school students to the genre through performances with commentary by artists and guests of the Society. For high school students, programs include: "Open Rehearsals—Musicians Up Close," "The Performance Awareness Seminar," and the "Composer Apprentice Scholarship." The annual "Young Musicians Concert" at **Alice Tully Hall** is a public performance by selected high school ensembles that receive coaching from Society members.

CHILDREN'S FREE OPERA AND DANCE
Sponsored by the St. Luke's Chamber Ensemble (see p. 66)   840-7470

The St. Luke's Chamber Ensemble has an exceptionally strong commitment to educational programs for children. Since 1976, it has presented Children's Free Opera and Dance, four weeks of free performances (two in the fall, two in the spring) for children from all five boroughs at places like **Alice Tully Hall**, **Town Hall**, and the **Brooklyn Academy of Music**. Attendance is through the schools, which are admitted on a first-come first-serve basis.

CHILDREN'S ORCHESTRA SOCIETY, INC.
65-03 180th St., Fresh Meadows, N.Y. 11365   718-358-4866

For about ten years now the husband-and-wife team of Michael Dadap and Yeou-Cheng Ma have led the Children's Orchestra Society, a 120-member group of young instrumentalists founded by Ms. Ma's father a quarter of a century ago. Its members, ages seven to seventeen, meet weekly for classes and coaching in one of the Society's three orchestras (a training orchestra for kids under ten; a middle or chamber orchestra, and the advanced group, the Symphonic Ensemble). Some members have gone on to careers in music (like Ms. Ma's well-known younger brother Yo-Yo), but according to Ms. Ma, the aim is not so much to create musicians as to give the kids a taste of what it takes to make it in life: teamwork, perseverance, and commitment. Acceptance is by audition and family interview; performances take place throughout the year.

FAMILY MUSIK
At the **92d Street Y**   415-5440

The composer–conductor Robert Kapilow created this series to give kids a chance to participate in music-making, through storytelling and other interactive means. Its 1994 debut featured two "pocket operas," one an adaptation of Dr. Seuss's "Green Eggs and Ham," the other playwright Terrence McNally's first children's work, "You and Hugh." These fun-filled performances are done with members of the New Jersey Chamber Music Society. Ticket prices: $25 for one child and one adult; additional seats, $10. Subscriptions available.

GROWING UP WITH OPERA
Sponsored by the Metropolitan Opera Guild (see p. 87 769-7028)

"Growing Up With Opera" is a wonderful program whose aim is to cure "operaphobia" by giving kids (and their parents) a positive first experience in the genre. Performances are abridged, sung in Englis'

and presented in theaters small enough so that everyone is close to the action. Single tickets are $15 to $25; season membership, which includes three performances, an invitation to the Meet the Cast Party, and a home activity book, is $50.

HAYDN SEEK CONCERTS
253 W. 91st St., 5B, New York, N.Y. 10024   877-4475

One of the city's newest children's series comprises chamber music concerts designed with preschool kids in mind. Ticket holders are given cassettes for home listening so that children can become familiar with the music in advance. A short, informal talk precedes the 45-minute program, during which each instrument is introduced, and a word or two about concert manners is offered. Tickets (including the cassette) are $15; children under five are admitted free.

INTERSCHOOL ORCHESTRAS OF NEW YORK
1556 Third Ave., Suite 601, New York, N.Y. 10128   410-0370

InterSchool Orchestras of New York is one of the most respected youth orchestras on the east coast. It gives talented public and private elementary through high school students the opportunity to rehearse with prominent coaches and perform in venues as varied as the Jewish Home for the Aged and **Alice Tully Hall**. The program is made up of three orchestras (plus two for beginners), the most advanced being the ISO Orchestra, a full-scholarship group. Each rehearses one afternoon a week. Except for the beginners' orchestras, entrance is by audition only.

INTRODUCTION TO OPERA (see Empire State Opera in "A Night at the Opera")

JAZZ FOR YOUNG PEOPLE (see Jazz at Lincoln Center in "All That Jazz")

KIDSCLASSICS AT THE COLDEN CENTER
718-793-8080

Hosted by Goliard Concerts (see p. 59), this 5-concert series for six-to ten-year-olds introduces a new family of instruments each month (voices, woodwinds, strings, and brass) and then combines them all in the final concert (appropriately called "Tutti"). They feature classical, light classical, and jazz, and use an illustrated workbook with puzzles, a glossary, and a list of materials you can bring from home to play along. Children also meet Rude Ralph, who teaches them about concert etiquette the fun way. Ticket prices: Five for $20, or $5 each concert. For older children there is also a KidsClassics II series of three concerts with more advanced themes ($8 per concert; $21 for three).

LITTLE ORCHESTRA SOCIETY (see p. 60)
704-2100

"Lollipops Concerts" for children ages three to five, at **Florence Gould Hall**; "Happy Concerts for Young People" for children five to twelve, at **Avery Fisher Hall**

Long before many of the organizations in this section were born, the Little Orchestra Society was quietly busy introducing youngsters to classical music through its two programs, the "Lollipops Concerts" and the "Happy Concerts," which, at the time of this writing, are almost 50 years old. The repertory for these concerts is interesting and easy to digest, and often includes premieres. Hats off to Dino Anagnost, the orchestra's music director, who meets the difficult challenge of keeping the children engaged in the proceedings while maintaining a high-quality performance level. Ticket prices: Happy Concerts: Single tickets, $15 to $32; four-concert series, $50 to $105. Lollipops: Single tickets, $32; 3-concert series, $90.

METROPOLITAN MUSEUM OF ART
Children's Choice: Saturday Afternoon Treats 570-3949

Seven programs, for kids ages seven to twelve, each lasting about an hour. They range from "An Introduction to Gilbert and Sullivan" to "What Is Jazz," which one year was cleverly answered by Billy Taylor and his jazz trio. Single tickets are $15 ($70 for the entire series). All adults must be accompanied by a child!

NATIONAL CHORAL COUNCIL (see "Vocal Chords")

NEW YORK ALL-CITY HIGH SCHOOL MUSIC PROGRAM
N.Y.C. Board of Education Division of High Schools
110 Livingston St., Room 816, Brooklyn, N.Y. 11201   718-935-3441

This 60-year-old program gives gifted public high school kids the chance to participate in an orchestra, chorus, marching band, concert band, or jazz band. Auditions (children must have certain skills to get in) are held in the fall. Rehearsals are held once a week, and each group performs throughout the year. The orchestra is the jewel in All City's crown, and gives two or three concerts a year, including one at **Alice Tully Hall**, often with prestigious guest conductors (Leonard Bernstein was one back in the 40's).

NEW YORK PHILHARMONIC YOUNG PEOPLE'S CONCERTS 875-5656
At **Avery Fisher Hall** 875-5656

Anyone who grew up watching Leonard Bernstein's Young People's Concerts on TV probably has a soft spot for these imaginative programs. They have become models for similar ones all around the country, offering exposure to the orchestra in ways that are educational, thought-provoking, and fun. The conductor and players speak directly to the children, making these first musical encounters a personal experience, and written materials are used to enhance what is being seen on the stage.

All Young People's Concerts are preceded by a "Children's Promenade," a colorful hour of demonstrations, music-making activities, and the chance for kids to meet members of the orchestra. Ticket prices: Single tickets, $6 to $20; 4-concert series, $20 to $80.

NEW YORK PUBLIC LIBRARY (see "The Best Things in Life Are Free")

NEW YORK YOUTH SYMPHONY
Carnegie Hall, Room 504
881 Seventh Ave., New York, N.Y. 10019   581-5933

Although the musicians in the Youth Symphony are amateurs as young as 12 (and no older than 22), this award-winning ensemble sounds as good as many a professional orchestra. Entry is by audition only (in September), and standards are high. Past members have gone on to hold seats in major orchestras, and some even to big solo or conducting careers. (Recognize the names Itzhak Perlman and Ransom Wilson?) The orchestra plays six free concerts a season, three at **Carnegie Hall** and three at the **Colden Center**, and presents fine young soloists in their orchestral debuts. Tickets for the concerts must be obtained by mail. Call for information.

In addition to the performances, members are coached by members of the New York Philharmonic, and may participate in the

Symphony's Chamber Music Program. An Apprentice Conducting Program offers opportunities for a select few to study under the guidance of the music director. There is no tuition or membership fee for any of these programs; the application fee is $45.

PHILHARMONIA VIRTUOSI "CUSHION CONCERTS" (see "I Hear a Symphony")

QUEENS OPERA ASSOCIATION (see "A Night at the Opera")

RIVERSIDE CHURCH CHILDREN'S CONCERT SERIES (see p. 108)
222-5900

Only a few years old, this series has already attracted much attention. Aimed at kids ages four and up, performers introduce children to different types of music and instruments. Engaging presentations of works like "Carnival of the Animals" and other favorites charm audiences of all ages.

RUG CONCERTS (see Diller-Quaile School in "Mama, I Want to Sing")

ST. THOMAS CHURCH BOYS CHOIR (see "Get Me to the Church")

WINTER STAR (see "It's Christmastime in the City")

MAMA, I WANT TO SING

Finding a good music teacher needn't be a difficult task. Like choosing a good doctor, lawyer, or plumber, word of mouth is one of the best ways. If you know someone taking lessons, or whose children are, talk with them about their experiences. When you call the prospective teachers, don't be afraid to ask lots of questions: where they studied, how much teaching experience they've had, whether they are more comfortable with children or adults. Don't be swayed by lots of concert experience—the best performers are not necessarily the best teachers. Find out if you can talk to other students; arrange to sit in on a lesson.

Don't forget to ask in advance how much a teacher charges, since rates vary, and how much time your money is buying—don't assume it's an hour. And don't assume that more expensive means better instruction.

Another way to find a teacher is to contact the Music Teachers National Association. It publishes a free annual directory of affiliated teachers in every state, and affiliation implies a fairly high level of competency. Write to the association at the Carew Tower, 441 Vine St. (Suite 505), Cincinnati, Ohio 45202 (telephone: 513-421-1420).

The National Federation of Music Clubs, one of the largest music associations in the world, is another organization that might help steer you in the right direction. Although it does not have a teacher referral per se, one of its major focuses is music education. Contact the national office: 1336 North Delaware St., Indianapolis, Ind. 46202 (telephone: 317-638-4003).

In New York City, Local 802 of the American Federation of Musicians does maintain a free referral service for local teachers who are union members. Call and request the Teachers Registry. Information: 245-4802.

Many stores that sell musical instruments keep lists of teachers on hand, and a few will make free referrals. Also, the placement offices at the Juilliard School, Manhattan School of Music, and Mannes College of Music can put you in touch with students who give private lessons.

Finally, as an alternative to private lessons at home, neighborhood music schools offer reasonably priced private or group instruction by accomplished teachers for both children and adults. Following is a sampling of some of them. Since all offer lessons in voice, piano, and most orchestral instruments, as well as related theory, ear-training, and history courses, that information is not specified in each entry. Instead, a few outstanding highlights for each are detailed. Many have orchestras, choral, and chamber ensembles, as well as excellent free concerts, and some offer Suzuki instruction (for an explanation, see School for Strings). For a catalogue with complete course descriptions, a schedule of events, and travel information, call the school.

AMERICAN INSTITUTE OF GUITAR (see Guitar Stage in "The Best Things in Life Are Free")

BLOOMINGDALE HOUSE OF MUSIC
323 W. 108th St., New York, N.Y. 10025   663-6021

This 30-year-old school is named for the neighborhood in which it's located (though no one calls it that anymore). For toddlers, Bloomingdale has a Music and Movement class, which emphasizes improvisation, movement, and even playing simple instruments. Classes in composition and computers in music are offered, and there is an Orff teacher training-program, based on composer Carl Orff's pedagogical theories. Ensembles include a jazz and an African-American percussion ensemble. The Gotham Ensemble, Bloomingdale's new-music chamber group-in-residence, appears regularly in the school's fine concert series.

BRONX HOUSE MUSIC SCHOOL
990 Pelham Parkway South, Bronx, N.Y. 10461   718-792-9720

Students at this 82-year-old school range in age from two to ninety-two, and teachers here are attentive to the needs of all ages. In addition to the standard instruments, the school has ten state-of-the-art electronic keyboards, and a powerful computer cum software for music notation and recording. There are ample studios and rehearsal rooms, and a 300-seat hall used for concerts.

BROOKLYN CONSERVATORY OF MUSIC (2 BRANCHES)
•Brooklyn branch:
58 Seventh Ave., Brooklyn, N.Y. 11217   718-622-3300
•Queens branch:
140-26 Franklin Ave., Flushing, N.Y. 11355   718-461-8910

The Brooklyn Conservatory, which will celebrate its 100th birthday in 1997, offers quality instruction at modest prices. It has a jazz studies program, a teen music-theater course, and individual choruses for children and adults. For those wishing to make music a career, there is a professional division leading to undergraduate or graduate diplomas, and an opera ensemble for professional singers. The Brooklyn branch has a 100-concert-a-year series with a strong jazz bent.

BROOKLYN MUSIC SCHOOL

126 Saint Felix St., Brooklyn, N.Y. 11217   718-638-5660

With the **Brooklyn Academy of Music** as its neighbor, a 300-seat theater, and 20 grand pianos, the Brooklyn Music School is well equipped for fine instruction and performance opportunities. Founded as a settlement school in 1912, it presents many public concerts, and holds a monthly Singer's Forum where voice students meet in a master class set-up.

DALCROZE SCHOOL OF MUSIC

877-2127

This is the only Dalcroze teachers training school in the Americas authorized by Dr. Emile Jaques-Dalcroze, whose creative approach to music education it champions. Until recently the 80-year-old school was located on E. 73d St., but it now splits its week between the Upper East and the Upper West Sides. Classes are held Mondays and Saturdays at the Rudolf Steiner School (15 E. 78th St.); Tuesdays through Thursdays at the Lucy Moses School (see p. 198) which has taken over the young people's program. The adult and certification programs are still under the aegis of the independently operated Dalcroze School.

DILLER-QUAILE MUSIC SCHOOL
24 E. 95th St., New York, N.Y. 10128   369-1484

If you've ever taken piano lessons, you're probably familiar with the name Diller-Quaile, whose piano books are used by teachers around the world. Founded in the 1920's, the school has a long history of teacher training and offers nationally accredited pedagogy courses for faculty members and the community at large. Adult programs include opera classes, master classes by distinguished guest artists, a recorder ensemble, and a community chorus. A Friday afternoon and Saturday morning series of family-oriented "Rug Concerts" give youngsters a chance to see, hear, and touch everything from whistles and horns to harps and castanets.

DOROTHY DELSON KUHN MUSIC INSTITUTE
OF THE JEWISH COMMUNITY CENTER
Two locations on Staten Island: •North Shore J.C.C., 475 Victory Blvd. 718-981-1500 •South Shore J.C.C., 1297 Arthur Kill Ave. 718-356-8113

Among the ensembles available to students here are a piano improvisation group, a teen jazz ensemble, and a Jewish music ensemble. Students are given the chance to play joint recitals with faculty members. There is also a Suzuki violin program.

GREENWICH HOUSE MUSIC SCHOOL
46 Barrow St., near Seventh Ave., New York, N.Y. 10014   242-4770

This small school has occupied the same two brownstones on a tree-lined Village street since 1914 and remains dedicated to quality teaching at low prices. Among its excellent programs are Dalcroze Eurhythmics classes for the very young (beginning at age two), which explore the basic elements of music through movement, storytelling, games, and simple percussion instruments.

The 90-seat Renee Weiler Concert Hall, one of the most active small halls in the city, is located here. Innovative series like "Inner

Ear," "Village Variations," and "Mostly New Music" take place at Weiler Hall, and most concerts are under $10. Across Seventh Ave., at 27 Barrow, is the parent organization, Greenwich House, a community and senior center where excellent concerts are presented in the 200-seat Hayden Auditorium.

HARLEM SCHOOL OF THE ARTS
645 St. Nicholas Ave., near 141st St., New York, N.Y. 10030 926-4100

Founded by the acclaimed soprano Dorothy Maynor, HSA has been serving the local community since 1964. Its 1,500 students receive high-quality music, theater, and dance training in a supportive environment. The school offers a jazz and African-American music progam, along with career guidance for singers making the transition from college-level training to professional careers. A Performance Etiquette series, created for audience development, is one of the school's unique programs.

HENRY STREET SETTLEMENT/ABRONS ARTS FOR LIVING CENTER
466 Grand St., New York, N.Y. 10002   598-0400

In terms of cultural activities and community involvement, the Henry Street Settlement is to the Lower East Side what the 92d Street Y is to the Upper East Side. Established in 1893, it's one of the oldest arts schools in the city, with three indoor theaters, including the 350-seat Harry De Jur Playhouse (a historic national landmark), an outdoor ampitheater, art galleries, classrooms, practice facilities, and rehearsal spaces.

Henry Street holds workshops in opera, Latin music, and jazz, and students can perform in the Symphony Orchestra, the chorus, the Opera Workshop productions, or the jazz and chamber ensembles. The Settlement is also an active concert venue, with fully staged operas, orchestral concerts, a 20-year-old jazz series, and a summertime cabaret series.

JEWISH ASSOCIATION FOR SERVICES FOR THE AGED (JASA)
40 W. 68th St., New York, N.Y. 10023   501-1027

JASA has a continuing education program in the arts and
humanities for New Yorkers 55 and older. For a $25 registration fee,
participants may take two of the dozen or so courses in music and
the arts that are offered, including "A History of North America in
Song" or "The Poet Lyricists of Tin Pan Alley" as well as piano or
violin lessons. Students can also attend concerts, dance and theater
events, and an unlimited number of lectures, for only $2.

THE JUILLIARD SCHOOL
60 Lincoln Center Plaza (Broadway at 65th St.), New York, N.Y. 10023
799-5000

•Pre-College Division: Since 1916, Juilliard has offered classes in
musical performance to pre-college age students in what is now
called the Pre-College division (formerly the Preparatory Division).
This is an internationally preeminent training ground for
exceptionally talented young musicians,
and entrance is by rigorous audition and
testing. More than 50 faculty members,
themselves active performers,
work with the school's 325
students, ages seven to
eighteen, on Saturdays.
The division has three
orchestras and choruses,
which present public
performances at the
Juilliard Theater, and
more than 25 chamber
groups.
•Evening Division: This is

where adults can take classes and group lessons. Some unusual courses include "Performance Anxiety," which explores the psychology behind pre-concert jitters; "Signing for the Theater," which gives proficient interpreters the chance to sign as actors; and a course in Alexander Technique, a mind–body system that promotes the awareness, and changing of, habitual body language. Some classes are available for credit.

(See also "The Best Things in Life Are Free")

LIGHTHOUSE MUSIC SCHOOL
111 E. 59th St., New York, N.Y. 10022   821-9660

One of the few music schools in the country serving the blind and visually impaired, Lighthouse not only teaches students, but also trains sighted musicians to work with the blind. Instruction in Braille music reading is a strong component of the curriculum, and the school has a large library of Braille and large print scores. Ensembles include a jazz workshop, mixed chorus, and the only opera workshop that we know of for blind and partially sighted singers.

LUCY MOSES SCHOOL FOR MUSIC AND DANCE
(FORMERLY THE HEBREW ARTS SCHOOL)
129 W. 67th St., New York, N.Y. 10023   362-8060

The Lucy Moses School is located smack in the center of Manhattan's musical heartland, with Lincoln Center a short walk down Broadway and the Juilliard School just two blocks away. As part of the Abraham Goodman House, the school focuses on Jewish culture and observes the Jewish calendar (meaning, among other things, no classes on Saturdays). But it is a nonsectarian institution open to all. One of its best features is **Merkin Concert Hall**. Another is the Birnbaum Library, which has a remarkable collection of Jewish music and original manuscripts. Yet another is its new jazz department. The resident Rottenberg Chorale and Chamber Singers is one of New York's preeminent coed ensembles performing a wide range of Jewish music. (Entrance by audition only.)

(See also: Dalcroze School, p. 104 ; Special Music School of America, p. 201)

MANHATTAN SCHOOL OF MUSIC PREPARATORY DIVISION

120 Claremont Ave. (Broadway at 122d St.), New York, N.Y. 10027 749-2802

Every Saturday more than 400 preschool, elementary, and secondary school students fill the studios and classrooms at the Manhattan School for intensive training in every area of musical performance. A typical study program includes a private lesson, theory and ear training classes, performance in a large ensemble (orchestra, chorus, or chamber group) and elective courses in such subjects as composition, conducting, and electronic music. Enrollment is by audition, held in September, January, and May.

(See also "The Best Things in Life Are Free")

MANNES COLLEGE OF MUSIC

150 W. 85th St., New York, N.Y. 10024 580-0210

•Preparatory School: Five hundred students, ages four to eighteen, are enrolled in Mannes's prep division, where they receive comprehensive training by the distinguished faculty. Classes are held weekday afternoons and on Saturdays. Unlike its sister schools Juilliard and the Manhattan School, no audition is required for enrollment. Auditions are for placement only, except for the honors program for extraordinarily gifted students.

•Extension Division: At Mannes's Extension Division you'll find beginners taking lessons just for enjoyment, as well as professional musicians seeking to refine their skills, or perhaps even learn a few new ones. In addition to private lessons, students have a wide array of courses to choose from: Jazz Improvisation, Schenkerian Analysis, Scoring Music on the Computer, and dozens of others.

(See also: "The Best Things in Life Are Free")

MIND-BUILDERS CREATIVE ARTS CENTER

3415 Olinville Ave., near Gun Hill Rd., Bronx, N.Y. 10467
718-652-6256

One of the only arts education institutions in this area of the city, Mind-Builders is committed to fostering an appreciation of African-American and Latino cultures. Founded in 1978, this minority-owned organization offers a variety of programs in music, dance, and theater, including a Positive Youth Troupe, a musical theater group of 30 teenagers who perform original plays dealing with inner-city adolescent issues like drug use, teenage pregnancy, and family relationships.

92D STREET Y SCHOOL OF MUSIC

1395 Lexington Ave., New York, N.Y. 10128   415-5580

The Y has one of the most complete music education programs in the city, both for adults and for children, and 9,000 students participate in them annually. There are classes in music appreciation and world music, plus lectures and performance workshops. For intrepid adults who want to be on stage, there are several amateur performing opportunities, including the Broadway at the Y Chorus, a chamber music program with coaching sessions culminating in concerts, the Classic Guitar Ensemble, and the Y Symphonic Workshop, primarily a reading orchestra that gives two public performances a year (audition required). For more serious children, a Young Artists Program offers not only private lessons, but also classes, ensembles, and the chance for lots of performance experience.

(See also **92d Street Y** in "I'll Take Manhattan")

SCHOOL FOR STRINGS
419 W. 54th St., New York, N.Y. 10019 315-0915

You've probably seen them on television or in magazines: three- and four-year-olds sawing away en masse on violins and cellos. These are Suzuki students, using a method developed by the Japanese educator Sinichi Suzuki. His theory is that, given a positive environment, very young children can learn to play an instrument by listening, repetition, and reinforcement. The School for Strings is just such an environment for violin, cello, or piano students. Its success rate is impressive, but parental involvement is crucial to this system, so, Mom and Dad, if you don't have the time, you'd best look elsewhere.

SPECIAL MUSIC SCHOOL OF AMERICA
This unique school was the brainchild of Russian pianist Vladimir Feltsman, who saw the need in this country for a public school where exceptionally talented youngsters could receive a superior academic and musical education under one roof. The school, scheduled to open in the fall of 1996, will begin with a kindergarden and first grade, then eventually extend through high school. Classes will be limited to 15 students, and entrance will be by evaluation. Operated by the N.Y.C. Board of Education, the school will be located at the Abraham Goodman House-Lucy Moses School of Music (see p. 198). Interested parents should contact Community School District 3, Office of Alternative Schools, 300 W. 96th St., New York, N.Y. 10025 (678-2885).

THIRD STREET MUSIC SCHOOL SETTLEMENT
235 E. 11th St., New York, N.Y. 10003 777-3240
The school is not on Third Street at all. In 1974 it moved north eight blocks to a renovated hospital building, gaining more space but keeping its original name. It was founded in 1894 (when a piano lesson cost a dime), making it one of the oldest community music

schools in the country. A century later, it is a thriving center for the study of the arts, with a 300-seat auditorium, 24 studios with pianos, and a library with more than 10,000 scores, books, and recordings. Advanced students have the opportunity to perform in the Baroque and jazz ensembles, or in the 30-voice mixed Chamber Chorus of New York (open to adults only, by audition).

From October through May, the Settlement presents a marvelous free concert series on Friday evenings at 7:30, as well as student recitals on Saturday afternoons; in the summer, it sponsors an outdoor lunchtime series at St. Mark's Park, Second Ave. at 10th St., featuring new music groups, world music, and jazz.

TURTLE BAY MUSIC SCHOOL
244 E. 52d St., New York, N.Y. 10022 753-8811

It started in 1925 with six students. Since then, thousands of New Yorkers have availed themselves of Turtle Bay's excellent instruction. The children's division has an Orff program for preschoolers, while for adults there are Monday Night Sings open to the community, Opera at Turtle Bay for singers with professional aspirations, and Acting For Singers, a workshop focusing on stage movement and dialogue delivery. There's also a harmonica ensemble and a day-long chamber music festival. The Meridian String Quartet is in residence, and performs in the school's enjoyable concert series.

AMATEUR NIGHT

If you're a music lover who wants to perform just for the sheer pleasure of it, New York offers many wonderful opportunities for you to dust off that old violin or warm up those rusty vocal chords. Join the thousands of doctors, lawyers, bus drivers, bankers, housewives, teachers—you name it—who are active in the city's amateur choruses, orchestras, and chamber groups.

Amateur here means unpaid, and does not refer to a group's quality. Levels can vary from inexperienced and unpolished to highly skilled, professional-sounding ensembles. Most groups require auditions, which can be either formal or relaxed. Some may simply invite you to play or sing at a rehearsal, while others require sight reading, a performance, and/or an interview. Call to find out requirements.

Volunteer ensembles offer more than just the chance to make

music. There are fund-raising activities, committees, ticket sales, and even parties. The social networks that form can be very rewarding, but you must be willing to devote time and energy to the group.

A financial commitment may be involved as well, since many groups have dues, plus separate sheet-music fees. Singers generally pay more than instrumentalists, since choruses, which must hire orchestras for their performances, exact steeper dues. Some have sliding scales, or reduced rates for students and seniors, so if money is an issue, ask.

For singers who want to try out their vocal chords before committing to joining a chorus, some groups have annual summer sings—weekly read-throughs of choral masterpieces open to the general public for a small fee (see Summer Sings in this chapter).

In addition to the groups listed here, most neighborhood music schools offer opportunitites to play or sing in ensembles, but you must be a registered student (see "Mama, I Want to Sing"). The rehearsal information included here is the regular weekly schedule. Most groups add extra rehearsals right before performances.

AMATEUR NIGHT AT THE APOLLO (see Apollo Theatre in "I'll Take Manhattan")

AMATEUR CHAMBER MUSIC PLAYERS
1123 Broadway, Rm. 304, New York, N.Y. 10010   645-7424
This organization enables amateur musicians from around the world to find others of similar abilities with whom to play chamber music. For a suggested annual contribution of $15, you receive a directory of members, self-graded as to level of proficiency. The rest is up to you. ACMP also publishes a newsletter with general information, members' comments, anecdotes, and suggestions.

BIG APPLE CHORUS, MANHATTAN CHAPTER
986-1910 (Phone only)

Take a deep breath and say: Society for the Preservation and
Encouragement of Barbershop Quartet Singing in America. That's
the organization you'll become part of if you join the Big Apple
Chorus, whose members enjoy this special brand of four-part male a
cappella singing. The Manhattan chapter was chartered in 1945, and
its original roster included Governor Al Smith, Arthur Godfrey, and
Irving Berlin. In preparation for national contests and an annual
Carnegie Hall concert in June, members rehearse on Wednesdays
from 7:30 P.M. to 10:30 P.M. at the Norman Thomas High School
(Park Ave. at 33d St.). Membership: $108 first year; $100 thereafter.
There are also several other chapters in the metropolitan area. To
find out more, call 800-876-SING (7464). A similar organization for
women is the Sweet Adeline Society: 800-992-SING (7464).

BLUE HILL TROUPE
P.O. Box 6800 Yorkville Station
New York, N.Y. 10128   988-9102

Blue Hill Troupe started in 1924 when a group of New Yorkers,
summering in Blue Hill, Maine, put on a production of "H.M.S.
Pinafore" using a boat for a stage and car headlights for
illumination. These dedicated Savoyards kept their troupe going in
the city, and have presented a Gilbert and Sullivan operetta every
year since. They now mount two productions a year, one in the
spring at the John Jay College Theater (Amsterdam Ave. and 59th
St.) and a smaller scale performance in November. And here's a nice
touch: proceeds from all performances are donated to a different
charity each season.

Getting into Blue Hill is something along the lines of being
approved by a co-op board. First you must be sponsored by a
member and pass the membership committee. Then, you audition

(late September/early October) and attend a party where you are sized up. Once you're in, however, you're in for a good time. Rehearsals: Tuesdays, 7:30 P.M.–9:30 P.M. Membership: $50 annually.

BMCC DOWNTOWN SYMPHONY
Borough of Manhattan Community College
199 Chambers St., Rm. S121, New York, N.Y. 10007   346-8170

Though the Downtown Symphony is connected to BMCC, the majority of its members are music lovers from the community, as well as students and college staff. Its series of four or five free concerts a year is held at the Tribeca Performing Arts Center (see p. 24). Auditions: September. Rehearsals: Tuesdays, 5:30 P.M.–7:30 P.M. No membership fees.

BOYS CHOIR OF HARLEM (see "Children's Corner")

BRONX SYMPHONY ORCHESTRA (see Lehman Center in "The Bronx and Staten Island, Too")

BROOKLYN HEIGHTS ORCHESTRA
P.O. Box 020334, Brooklyn, N.Y. 11202   718-625-6531 or 718-951-5792

Members of this well-established orchestra come from all over town, and include lawyers, doctors, and other professionals as well as freelance musicians who play professionally in other groups. It plays five concerts a year at the Church of St. Ann and the Holy Trinity (see p. 104), with a repertory encompassing the standard concert fare: symphonies by Mozart, Beethoven, and Mahler, concertos and overtures, and an occasional new work. Auditions: call for appointment. Rehearsals: Mondays, 7:30 P.M.–10 P.M. No membership fees.

BROOKLYN PHILHARMONIA CHORUS
c/o First Presbyterian Church
124 Henry St., Brooklyn, N.Y. 11021   718-596-6119

Not as well known as some other local volunteer choral groups, this
one has been around longer than many. (It turns 40 in the 1995-96
season.) It presents two or three concerts a year at various venues in
the borough, and sometimes in Manhattan. With 65 members, its
repertory ranges from big works like "Carmina Burana" to light
opera and smaller-scale pieces. Auditions: September and January.
Rehearsals: Tuesdays, 7 P.M.–10 P.M. Membership: $65 annually;
buy your own scores.

CANTICUM NOVUM SINGERS
2 Cove Road, South Salem, N.Y. 10590 914-763-3453

Harold Rosenbaum, who directs the professional New York Virtuoso
Singers (see p. 100), also leads this elite, volunteer chamber choir,
which has appeared in concerts around the city. It has its own series
(three to five concerts a year) and often appears with the American
Symphony (see p. 55) and other orchestras. Auditions: As needed;
call for information. Rehearsals: Mondays, 7:15 P.M.–10 P.M. No
membership fess, but you must buy four tickets to sell, in advance.

I CANTORI DI NEW YORK
P.O. Box 4165, New York, N.Y. 10185   439-4758

One of New York's most respected chamber choirs, I Cantori di New
York has a 3-concert season in Manhattan, plus additional
performances around the metropolitan area. Its concerts encompass a
broad range of music, from early works like Gluck's "Telemacco" (I
Cantori gave its modern stage premiere) to contemporary composers
like Bartok and Dallapiccola. Auditions: Early September.
Rehearsals: Thursdays, 7 P.M.–10 P.M. Membership: $75 annually,
plus music costs.

CENTRAL CITY CHORUS
593 Park Ave., New York, N.Y. 10021   838-0808

A highly accomplished 60-voice chorus, Central City concentrates on repertoire rarely performed by most other amateur groups around town. It has presented concert versions of Purcell operas and lesser known works by Hindemith, Britten, and Messiaen. But if you like singing the standards, Central City does them, too. The chorus performs three concerts a season at Central Presbyterian Church (Park Ave. at 64th St). Auditions: Late August/early September. Rehearsals: Thursdays, 7:30 P.M.–10 P.M. Membership: $85 annually, plus music fees.

COLLEGIATE CHORALE
Carnegie Hall Studios, Rm. 154
154 W. 57th St., New York, N.Y. 10019   664-1390

This chorus was founded at Marble Collegiate Church in 1941 by Robert Shaw, a name practically synonymous with choral music. It has appeared under many of the world's greatest conductors (Toscanini, Bernstein, et al.) and has been featured in several of the annual prestigious Richard Tucker Foundation Galas. The Chorale has 150 active singing members who perform three concerts a year, two in a major hall and one in a church. Auditions: Yearly, end of summer, beginning of fall, plus reauditions as necessary. Rehearsals: Mondays, 7 P.M.–9:45 P.M. Membership: $135 annually, plus music fees.

COLUMBIA UNIVERSITY ORCHESTRA
703 Dodge Hall, New York, N.Y. 10027   854-5409

Columbia's is the oldest continually operating university orchestra in the United States, established in 1896 by the American composer Edward MacDowell. Its free concerts, held at the **Miller Theatre** three to five times a year, feature big programs with well-known soloists like Claude Frank and Roberta Peters, and they sometimes include premieres by major composers. Members are students and faculty from the college as well as music lovers from the local community. Auditions: September and January. Rehearsals: Mondays, 6 P.M.–8:30 P.M. No membership fees.

CORNERSTONE CHORALE

178 Bennett Ave., at 189th St., New York, N.Y. 10040   781-7247

Catering to the Washington Heights–Inwood community, the Cornerstone Chorale is a solid group of about 40 singers, who perform music from Mozart to Gershwin. They do about four concerts a season at the Cornerstone Center (at the above address), a local church that opens its doors to various community groups. Auditions: No formal process. Rehearsals: Thursdays, 7:30 P.M.–9:30 P.M. Membership: $25 per concert.

DESSOFF CHOIRS

P.O. Box 3370, New York, N.Y. 10163   935-2551

One of New York's oldest choral groups, the Dessoff Choirs was founded in 1924. Its mission was to bring to the stage unusual or previously unperformed works, including music by pre-Bach masters like Palestrina, Lassus, and Monteverdi (this was before the early-music craze swept the country). Now directed by Amy Kaiser, the Choirs has a 3-concert season and regularly gives the premieres of important works, some of them commissioned. (And, yes, it's choirs, plural. That's because within the larger organization there are various subgroups, like a chamber choir, a men's choir, and a women's choir.) Auditions: End of the summer, with mandatory reauditions every few years. Rehearsals: Wednesdays, 7 P.M.–9:30 P.M. Membership: $130 annually, plus a $30 music fee.

DOCTORS ORCHESTRAL SOCIETY

P.O. Box 20360, DHCC, New York, N.Y. 10017   802-5368

Formed in the 1930's by a group of physicians, the Doctors Orchestral Society is one of New York's oldest community orchestras. A large core of its members still are doctors, though it attracts players from other professions and freelance musicians. Its 4-concert season is held at the former Stuyvesant High School—now called the High School for Health Professions (an appropriate coincidence) at 345 E. 15th St. Over the years the orchestra has had some fine soloists—Yo-Yo Ma was one, before he became famous. Auditions: Call for information. Rehearsals: Thursdays, 7:30 P.M.–10 P.M. Membership: $25 to $50 annually.

FOREST HILLS SYMPHONY ORCHESTRA

160-08 25th Drive, Flushing, N.Y. 11358   718-746-9122

This group draws an appreciative audience at its 3-concert series held at the Forest Hills Jewish Center (106-06 Queens Blvd.). Auditions: No formal process; prospective players can sit in on rehearsals. Rehearsals: Wednesdays, 7:30 P.M.–10 P.M. No membership fees.

GREENWICH VILLAGE ORCHESTRA

P.O. Box 1110, Madison Square Station, New York, N.Y. 10159   969-0197

Don't let the name fool you: members of this respected community orchestra come from New Jersey, upstate New York, and out on Long Island, as well as the Village and other city neighborhoods. Its conductor, Robert Grehan, leads the orchestra in seven concerts a year at the Washington Irving High School (Irving Place at 16th St.), and often some fine soloists join him for concertos. Grehan's standards are high, and the result is thoughtfully programmed and well-played concerts. Auditions: No formal process. Rehearsals: Tuesdays, 7 P.M.–10 P.M. No membership fees.

LAVENDER LIGHT GOSPEL CHOIR

70A Greenwich Ave., Suite 315, New York, N.Y. 10011
714-7072

A gay Gospel choir? Well, why not! This one was
formed in 1985 to create an environment where
black gays and lesbians could celebrate both those
aspects of their identities. Since then, the choir
has performed all over town, in two solo concerts a
year at the Tribeca Performing Arts Center (see p.
24) and at other special presentations. (Its full
name is Lavender Light: the Black and People of
All Colors Lesbian and Gay Gospel Choir. But you
can just call it Lavender Light.) Auditions:
January–February, and mid-August. Rehearsals:
Mondays, 6:30 P.M.–9:30 P.M. Membership: $3 weekly.

METROPOLITAN GREEK CHORALE

975 E. 17th St., Brooklyn, N.Y. 11320   718-253-3779

You don't have to be Greek to be in the Chorale, though most of its
40 members do come from the greater New York area Greek
communities. Since its debut concert in 1968, this volunteer chorus
has performed dozens of works, many of them premieres, by Greek
and Greek-American composers, making the Chorale an important
vehicle for Hellenic music. Auditions: Call for appointment.
Rehearsals (and some performances): Sunday afternoons at the Greek
Orthodox Church of the Annunciation (West End Ave. at 91st St.).
No membership fees.

METROPOLITAN SINGERS/THE GREEK CHORAL SOCIETY

220 W. 42d St., 18th Fl., New York, N.Y. 10036   704-2100

This 100-voice chorus broke away from the Metropolitan Greek
Chorale in the 1970's and has had a strong life of its own ever since.

Closely associated with, though independent from, the Little Orchestra Society (see p. 60), Metropolitan Singers/The Greek Choral Society appears with the orchestra in its annual performances of "Amahl and the Night Visitors" (see p. 115) and the Candlelight Christmas Concerts (see p. 118). Though programs occasionally feature Greek music, that is no longer the main focus, and most members are not of Greek origin. The chorus does, however, perform at the Greek Orthodox Archdiocesan Cathedral of the Holy Trinity (319 E. 74th St.). Auditions: September and January. Rehearsals: Sundays, 3 P.M.–6 P.M. Membership: $85 annually.

NEW AMSTERDAM SINGERS

P.O. Box 373, Cathedral Station, New York, N.Y. 10025   769-4798

The 70-voice New Amsterdam Singers is known for its thoughtful programming and impeccable performances. Its 3-concert season might encompass an evening of Renaissance works, or a program devoted solely to recently composed music. Clara Longstreth, the director, is a master at weaving themes through the fabric of her programs, such as "The Seasons of Life," musical settings of poetry about youth and age, or "Serious Folk," composers inspired by traditional melodies. NAS or its 18-voice chamber chorus often participate in other events, like the popular Wall-to-Wall series at **Symphony Space**. Auditions: Late August–early September. Rehearsals: Tuesdays, 7 P.M.–9:45 P.M. Membership: $135 annually (includes music).

NEW AMSTERDAM SYMPHONY ORCHESTRA

138 W. 18th St., New York, N.Y. 10011   741-0011

The primary goal of this well-established orchestra is the showcasing of emerging conductors, soloists, composers, and orchestral players. Its programs are fairly conservative, sticking mostly to the warhorses, but performances (including those of the guest conductors and soloists) are of a higher calibre than most nonprofessional groups. Although New Amsterdam is open to new members, particularly string players, there is no formal audition process as such; generally members are recruited by word of mouth. Rehearsals: Wednesdays, 7:30 P.M.–10 P.M. No membership fees.

NEW YORK CHORAL SOCIETY

Carnegie Hall Studios, Rm. 154
154 W. 57th St., New York, N.Y. 10019   247-3878

With 180 voices, the New York Choral Society is one of the larger and livelier choruses in the city. Almost 40 years old, it gives masterful performances of the standard large choral works, as well as lesser-known and completely new music. Through its commissioning program, the chorus has presented premieres of several important works. In addition to its own 3-concert season, the Society frequently appears as guest artist with orchestras and at galas. Auditions: Late August, early September, and as needed. Rehearsals: Tuesdays, 7 P.M.–10 P.M. Membership: $140 annually, includes music.

(See also Summer Sings, p. 217)

NEW YORK CITY GAY MEN'S CHORUS

55 Christopher St., New York, N.Y. 10014   924-7770

It's not the oldest gay chorus in the country (San Francisco holds that distinction), but the 190-voice N.Y.C. Gay Men's Chorus is probably the most famous, and one of the best. Its repertory encompasses everything from opera to pop and show tunes, with emphasis on new works by gay composers. The chorus performs a 3-concert season at **Carnegie Hall**, and each one draws a big, enthusiastic crowd. The highlight is the annual Gay Pride Week concert in June. The annual Christmas concerts are festive affairs, with special guest stars, like Marilyn Horne or Ann Hampton Callaway adding a merry touch.

When the chorus was formed in 1979, AIDS was not in the lexicon, but now the disease—which has affected the lives of many chorus members—has become a focus, and a big part of the group's agenda is community outreach.

Auditions: September, January, and March. Rehearsals: Mondays, 7:30 P.M.–10:30 P.M. Membership: $100 annually (payable monthly by arrangement); one-time music fee of $20.

NEW YORK CITY LABOR CHORUS
c/o Fund for Labor Education
2109 Broadway, Suite 206, New York, N.Y. 10023   677-3900

If you're looking for the union label, you'll definitely find it here. The multi-ethnic, multi-generational N.Y.C. Labor Chorus is made up of 60 singers, mostly union members from the New York Metro Area Postal Union, United Federation of Teachers Local 1199, and many others. The only chorus of its kind in the country, it was founded in 1991 and has performed in a variety of settings, including parades and demonstrations, and presented concerts at **Avery Fisher Hall**. The chorus specializes in songs of labor struggles and social protest, but also sings jazz, gospel, folk, and classical music. Auditions: No formal process. Rehearsals: Mondays, 6 P.M.–8 P.M. Membership: $5 a year.

NEW YORK MANDOLIN ORCHESTRA
c/o the McBurney YMCA
215 W. 23d St., New York, N.Y. 10011
Attn: Lucky Checkley, manager (No phone calls, please.)

A Beethoven symphony performed by 45 mandolins? Well, stranger things have been heard! Besides, this 50-year-old orchestra incorporates a flute, a clarinet, and a concertina, too! In addition to transcriptions of symphonic works, the orchestra performs music actually written for mandolin ensemble—it's even had a hand in commissioning some. So if you play the mandolin (or the violin, which is tuned the same way) you may want to check this one out. Auditions: No formal process; come to a rehearsal, Tuesdays, 7 P.M.–9 P.M., at the Y. Membership: $100 annually.

ORATORIO SOCIETY OF NEW YORK
Carnegie Hall Studios, Rm. 504
881 Seventh Ave., New York, N.Y. 10019   247-4199

Legend has it that Andrew Carnegie, president of the Oratorio Society for more than 30 years, built his hall just so the chorus would have a permanent place to perform. (It has sung there every year since **Carnegie Hall's** opening season more than a century ago.) Leopold Damrosch (of Damrosch Park renown, and founder of the New York Philharmonic, for which the hall was also built), established the chorus in 1873. Since then, it's performed under the batons of Tchaikovsky, Mahler, Bernstein, and Copland, among others, and some of opera's most illustrious stars have been soloists at its performances. The 200-voice chorus has a 3-concert season, the highlight being the annual performance of "Messiah," which it has presented at Christmastime since 1891 (see p. 120). Auditions: late August, early September. Rehearsals: Thursdays, 7 P.M.–9:30 P.M. Membership: $125 annually (scholarships available).

RIVERDALE CHORAL SOCIETY
P.O. Box 436, Riverdale, N.Y. 10471   718-543-3866

This group, now in its fourth decade, presents two major concerts a year, plus several smaller performances at nursing homes and community centers. It does excerpts from the big blockbusters ("Judas Maccabeus," etc.) and smaller works. Auditions: September and January. Rehearsals: Tuesdays, 7:30 P.M.–10 P.M. Membership: $65 semiannually, plus music charges.

ROTTENBERG CHORALE AND CHAMBER SINGERS (see Lucy Moses School in "Mama, I Want to Sing")

RUSSIAN CHAMBER CHORUS OF NEW YORK
731 W. 183rd St. Suite 11, New York, N.Y. 10033   928-1402

Slavic music lovers will find a haven in this decade-old chorus dedicated to secular and sacred Russian music. The group sings mostly in Russian, but you don't have to know the language, as all texts are transliterated. The chorus gives between six and ten performances a year, mostly at New York area churches. Auditions: Call for appointment. Rehearsals: Wednesdays, 7 P.M.–10 P.M. Membership: $70 annually, includes music.

ST. CECILIA CHORUS
P.O. Box 421, FDR Station, New York, N.Y. 10150   718-428-0007

The patron saint of music has smiled graciously upon this chorus for whom it is named. The 140-voice group (originally all women but now coed) has been a vital part of the New York music scene since 1906, giving more than 60 world and American premieres. The chorus sings three concerts a year, two at **Carnegie Hall** and one in a church. Its annual Christmas program is refreshingly not always "Messiah," though it does perform the old war-horse every now and then. Forty St. Cecilia choristers also transform themselves into a tree—the annual South St. Seaport Chorus Tree, that is (see p. 00). Auditions: September and January. Rehearsals: Mondays, 7:30 P.M.–10 P.M. Membership: $100 annually, plus music fees.

STONEWALL CHORALE
P.O. Box 920, Old Chelsea Station, New York, N.Y. 10011   262-9544

Before there was the New York City Gay Men's Chorus there was the Stonewall Chorale, the city's oldest gay and lesbian music organization. The chorus performs three concerts a season at the

Fashion Institute of Technology (227 W. 27th St.), and holds auditions for each. Performances are polished and enthusiastic, and cover a wide range of repertory, often including works by gay composers. Auditions: Call for information. Rehearsals: Tuesday, 7:30 P.M.–10 P.M. Membership: $200 annually, or $5 per rehearsal (scholarships available).

SUMMER SINGS

Several choral groups open their ranks to the public in the summer for informal rehearsal–performances, so if you've always wanted to belt out the "Ode to Joy" from Beethoven's Ninth, or the "Dies Irae" from the Verdi Requiem, here's your chance. It's a way for choruses to attract new members while providing singers an opportunity to work with the Big Apple's finest choral directors. Admission is modest ($10 at most), and scores are provided. Some even serve refreshments, adding a social element. Three popular Summer Sings are held by the New York Choral Society (see p. 213), twice a week at CAMI Hall (see p. 11); the St. George's Choral Society, weekly at St. George's Episcopal Church, 209 E. 16th St. Information: 460-0940; and the West Village Chorale (see p. 218), weekly at the Church of St. Luke in the Fields (487 Hudson St., in Greenwich Village).

SWEET ADELINE SOCIETY (see Big Apple Chorus, p. 205)

VILLAGE LIGHT OPERA GROUP
P.O. Box 143, Village Station, New York, N.Y. 10014
978-3668 or 243-6281

VLOG members are among the most enterprising around. They present two shows a year at the Fashion Institute of Technology (227 W. 27th St.), usually one Gilbert and Sullivan and one American musical ("Brigadoon," "Carousel") or light opera ("The Merry

Widow," "New Moon"). Members handle every aspect of the performances, from sets and costumes and marketing and ticket sales to the actual singing and dancing. Only the leads are sometimes outsiders (the 60-year-old theater group predates Actors Equity, so union members are allowed to perform). The shows are delightful, the singing excellent, and what's sometimes lacking in polish is made up for in enthusiasm.

If you're interested in joining, you may try it out for one show; then you are invited into membership. Auditions: Advertised in Backstage magazine; call for information. Chorus rehearsals: Mondays, 7:30 P.M.–10 P.M. Membership: $25 annually.

WEST VILLAGE CHORALE
At the Church of St. Luke in the Fields
487 Hudson St., New York, N.Y. 10014   570-7301

The 40-member West Village Chorale performs a wide range of traditional and contemporary music in two annual concerts at its home base, the Church of St. Luke in the Fields. It also sponsors three winter sings and a series of popular weekly summer sings (see p. 217). Since its inception in 1971, the group has fostered close ties with the local community—its annual Christmas Carol Walk through the streets of the West Village is a popular holiday activity, as is its "Messiah" sing-along. Auditions: September for the winter concert; January for the spring. Rehearsals: Tuesdays, 7 P.M.–9 P.M. Membership: $60 per semester, plus music fees.

Y SYMPHONIC WORKSHOP (see 92d St. Y Music School in "Mama, I Want to Sing")

THE SHOP AROUND THE CORNER

New York is as famous for its shopping as for its cultural attractions. So if you're in the market for musical items, you've come to the right place.

You'll find record shops that specialize in every type of music, from classic opera to punk rock. There are superstores (like Tower and HMV) that have large, eclectic inventories, and dozens of smaller ones that cater to more arcane tastes. Looking for an out-of-print jazz album? Check out the Jazz Record Center. A 1960's rock LP? Try Bleecker Bob's, or the House of Oldies. Craving a Callas "Carmen?" Gryphon to the rescue.

Professional and amateur performers and students will find shops to buy sheet music, scores, and books. If you need a music-related gift, there's Rita Ford's for the perfect music box, or the Lincoln Center Shops for striking posters or pretty jewelry. Whether you have one dollar to spend or thousands, you can go on a music-shopping spree in New York and return home satisfied.

Here are some of the stores that sell records and CD's, sheet music, books, specialty items, and musical knickknacks. Everything, in fact, but instruments. Many of the record shops deal in used merchandise, so if you're looking to sell old albums or CD's, check with them about their policy. Some pay cash, others do trades or give store credit.

RECORD SHOPS

A CLASSICAL RECORD
547 W. 27th St., 6th Fl., between 10th and 11th Aves.   675-8010
Mon.–Sat., 10 A.M.–5 P.M.

In stock are 75,000 rare LP's, mostly classical, but also vintage jazz and show music. A catalogue, which rates the conditions of the albums, is available for $10. Entire collections bought.

ACADEMY BOOK STORE
10 W. 18th St., near Fifth Ave.   242-4848
Mon.–Sat., 9:30 A.M.-9 P.M.; Sun., 11 A.M.–7 P.M.

Books are the mainstay here, but Academy also has hundreds of used classical and jazz LP's and CD's for sale. They also buy used albums.

BATE RECORDS
140 Delancey St., between Norfolk and Suffolk Sts.   677-3180
Open daily, 10 A.M.–7 P.M.

Bate is a cornucopia of Latin music, including disco, reggae, and rap, with an excellent selection of new and old salsa.

BLEECKER BOB'S
118 W. Third St., near MacDougal St.   475-9677
Sun.–Thur., noon–1 A.M.; Fri.–Sat., noon–3 A.M.

No, it's not a mistake: Bleecker Bob's is not on Bleecker Street. Rock music lovers know this Village fixture well, since it carries a mind-boggling array of alternative and hard-to-find rock, exotica, funk, jazz, and imports, mostly LP's. And in the back you'll find an awesome assortment of tee-shirts.

COCONUTS MUSIC AND MOVIES
1980 Broadway, at 67th St.   362-0344 Open daily, 9 A.M.–midnight
Coconuts is a complete home-entertainment mart, selling records, tapes, CD's, and videos—all under one roof—at reasonable prices. There is a separate room for classical music, and a good selection of just about everything else. Cococuts is a chain, with several other stores around the city. Hours vary at each.

COLONY
1619 Broadway, at 49th St. 265-2050
Open daily, 10 A.M.–1 A.M. (midnight on Sun.)

Located in the heart of the theater district, Colony is a veritable New York institution. It has an impressive collection of new and out-of-print albums of all varieties, sheet music, and even posters and some gift items. The salespeople know the merchandise and will help you find what you're looking for.

DOWNSTAIRS RECORDS
35 W. 43d Street, between Fifth and Sixth Aves.   354-4684
Mon.–Fri., 10 A.M.–6:30 P.M.; Sat., 11 A.M.–6 P.M.

This is a real collector's store. It's chock full of oldies, mostly stuff from the 50's through the 70's, with lots of 45's. Just don't look for it downstairs—it's on the second floor!

FINYL VINYL
89 Second Ave., between Fifth and Sixth Sts.   533-8007
Mon.–Sat., noon-8 P.M.; Sun., 1 P.M.–6 P.M.

If the sound quality of CD's leaves you cold, Finyl Vinyl is the place
for you. It sells vinyl only, specializing in pop and rock from the
50's, 60's, and 70's. Let's hear it for the good old days.

FOOTLIGHT RECORDS
113 E. 12th St., between Third and Fourth Aves.   533-1572
Mon.–Fri., 11 A.M.–7 P.M.; Sat., 10 A.M.–6 P.M.; Sun., noon–5 P.M.

Footlight carries the original Broadway cast albums and movie
soundtracks that you can't seem to find anywhere else. The store is a
treasure trove for out-of-print and hard-to-find LP's. There is also a
decent number of jazz, spoken word, and other varieties—just no
classical.

GOLDEN DISC
239 Bleecker St., at Sixth Ave.   255-7899
Mon.–Tues., 11:30 A.M.–8 P.M.; Wed.-Sat., 11:30 A.M.–9 P.M.;
Sun., 1 P.M.–6 P.M.

Jazz is a speciality here, with a basement loaded with jazz
collectibles. But Golden Disc's collection covers just about every
type of music except classical and rap. Vinyl and import CD's.

GRYPHON RECORDS
251 W. 72nd St., 2nd Fl., between Broadway and West End Ave. 874-1588
Mon.–Sat., 11 A.M.–7 P.M.; Sun., noon–6 P.M.

Gryphon is known near and far for its selection of rare albums. The
shop sells exclusively LP's, mainly out-of-print classical and opera,
but also classic Broadway, movie soundtracks, and jazz. It's also one
of the few stores specializing in personality vocals by singers like
Peggy Lee and Doris Day.

HMV
•Lexington Ave. at 86th St.   348-0800 Sun.–Thur., 10 A.M.–10 P.M.;
Fri.–Sat., 10 A.M.-11 P.M.
•Broadway at 72d St.   721-5900 Mon.–Sat., 9 A.M.–midnight;
Sun., 10 A.M.–11 P.M.
•Fifth Ave. at 46th St. 681-6700 Mon.-Fri., 9 A.M.–8 P.M.;
Sat., 10 A.M.–7 P.M.; Sun., 11 A.M.–7 P.M.
•Opening soon: Sixth Ave. at 34th St.

One of New York's three huge record department stores (J&R and
Tower are the others), HMV has branches as far afield as Dublin and
Tokyo. The stores carry an ernormous iventory of all types of music,
with the classical departments occupying spaces of their own (a
separate store at 72d St., and soundproof alcoves in the 46th and
86th St. branches). Among HMV's best features are its listening
stations, where you can try out an album before purchase. Prices
are competitive.

HOUSE OF OLDIES
35 Carmine St., near Sixth Ave.   243-0500
Mon.–Sat., 11 A.M.–7 P.M.

At House of Oldies you're almost guaranteed to find
what you're looking for, from rare to out-of-print
albums from the 50's through the late 80's. They have
LP's, 45's and, yes, even some 78's.

J&R MUSIC WORLD
23 Park Row, near City Hall   732-8600
Mon.–Sat., 9 A.M.–6:30 P.M.; Sun., 11 A.M.–6 P.M.

If it's in print, you'll probably find it at J&R, which has
a great stock of rock albums at extremely competitive prices. The
Jazz and Classical Annexes, separated by a few doors from the main
shop on Park Row, also maintain large inventories.

JAMMYLAND

60 E. 3rd St., between First and Second Aves.   614-0185
Tues.–Sun., noon–midnight

A mecca for world music, Jammyland has outstanding international collection—CD's and LP's from Greece, Egypt, Pakistan, Mali, and elsewhere, plus a slew of reggae and Caribbean music.

JAZZ RECORD CENTER

236 W. 26th St., Rm. 804, between Seventh and Eighth Aves.   675-4480
Tues.–Sat., 10 A.M.–6 P.M.; closed Sun. and Mon.

The Jazz Record Center is *the* New York shop for jazz albums, period. Vinyl LP's and second hand CD's are abundant here, and you'll also find books, videos, and magazines. Jazz lovers come just to hang out, chew the fat, and soak up the ambiance.

MIDNIGHT RECORDS

263 W. 23rd St., between Seventh and Eighth Aves.   675-2768
Tues.–Sat., noon–6 P.M; closed Sun. and Mon.

Midnight carries the whole spectrum of underground rock for the past 50 years. Vinyls, import CD's, blues, rockabilly, punk . . . you name it!

125TH ST. RECORD SHACK

274 W. 125th St., between Seventh and Eighth Aves.   866-1600
Mon.–Thur., 10 A.M.–8:30 P.M.; Fri.–Sat., 10 A.M.–9:30 P.M.;
Sun., 11 A.M.–5:30 P.M.

The Shack is a popular Harlem market for African, Afro-Caribbean, and the latest rap, along with current rock.

RECORD MART
Times Square subway station, near the N and R trains   840-0580
Mon.–Thur., 9 A.M.–8:30 P.M.; Fri., 9 A.M.–10:30 P.M.;
Sat., 10 A.M.–9:30 P.M.; Sun., noon–7:30 P.M.

It takes a token to shop here, but if you're into Latin or Afro-Caribbean music, it's worth the trip down into the subway. Record Mart has a remarkably extensive collection jam-packed into a small space.

REVOLVER RECORDS
43 W. 8th St., between Fifth and Sixth Aves.   982-6760
Sun.–Thur., 11 A.M.–10 P.M.; Fri.–Sat., 11 A.M.–midnight

Revolver specializes in rock bands from the 1960's, with special emphasis on the Beatles (recordings and memorabilia). It also has new and used CD's.

ROCK'S IN YOUR HEAD
157 Prince St., near W. Broadway   475-6729
Mon.-Thur., noon-9 P.M.; Fri.-Sat., noon-10 P.M.; Sun., noon-8 P.M.

This small SoHo shop features new and used underground rock, mostly CD's, but some LP's, too. Not a huge inventory, but there are a number of interesting items.

SAM GOODY
1211 Sixth Ave., at 48th St.   869-8860
Mon.–Fri., 9 A.M.–7 P.M.; Sat., 11 A.M.–6 P.M.; Sun., noon–5 P.M.

Another one of the large record chains (there are Sam Goodys all over town); this one is in the heart of Rockefeller Center. It carries the latest rock and pop, classical CD's, and some jazz, at decent prices.

SECOND COMING RECORDS
235 Sullivan St., near W. Third St.   228-1313
Mon.–Thur., 11 A.M.–8 P.M.; Fri.-Sat., 11 A.M.–11 P.M.; Sun., noon-8 P.M.

Used alternative rock albums, with the accent on hardcore punk and heavy metal.

SUBTERRANEAN RECORDS
5 Cornelia St., at W. Fourth St.   463-8900
Sun.–Thur., noon–7 P.M.; Fri.–Sat., noon–8 P.M.

It used to be known as Hideout Records, but the name's gone underground. Subterranean has a large selection of alternative, New York, and indie rock, as well as some jazz and R&B. Vinyl and CD's.

TOWER RECORDS
692 Broadway, at E. Fourth St. 505-1500 •2107 Broadway, at 74th St.
799-2500 Both stores open daily, 9 A.M.–midnight

An international chain of department store-style record shops, Tower even publishes its own magazine, "Pulse." The New York stores are enormous, with large inventories of classical, rock, jazz, country, show, world music, and more. Prices are competitive, and you'll almost always find something on sale. (The 74th St. store opened in March 1995, replacing the branch at Broadway and 66th St., where it had been a fixture for many years. There are also two somewhat smaller branches, at Third Ave. and 86th St., and in Trump Tower, Fifth Ave. at 57th St.)

TOWER RECORDS CLEARANCE OUTLET
20 E. Fourth St., at Lafayette St. 228-7317
Daily, 9 A.M.–midnight

Here's where to shop for bargains! Overstocks, cut-outs, and other CD's, LP's, cassettes, and even videos, from rock and jazz to classical and opera, at easy-to-handle prices. Almost all the merchandise is

brand new and unopened. (There is a small section of used LP's—
with some great stuff hiding in the bins.)

VENUS

13 St. Mark's Pl., between Second and Third Aves.   598-4459
Sun.–Thur., noon–8 P.M.; Fri.–Sat., noon–midnight

Venus has an excellent selection of 50's and 60's rock 'n' roll
originals and reissues, with lots of 45's. You'll also see current rock
imports, new and used CD's, and tapes from all eras and styles, at
prices cheaper than at many similar-size stores in town.

SHEET MUSIC AND BOOKS,
GIFTS, AND UNUSUAL ITEMS

Only those shops with regular hours are listed here. Some
organizations, like the New York Philharmonic
and   New   York   City   Opera,   also   sell
merchandise, but only at performances.

BROWN'S MUSIC CO.

61 W. 62nd St., at Broadway   541-6236
Mon.–Sat., 10 A.M.–7 P.M.

At this small shop across from Lincoln
Center you'll find classical and popular sheet
music, books about music, guitar picks,
violin strings, and other accessories. There is
also a small selection of gift items, including those
white plaster busts of composers that
remind me of my early piano lessons,
when 10 gold stars would earn me a statuette.

CARL FISCHER MUSIC STORE
62 Cooper Square, at Astor Pl.   677-0821   Mon.–Sat., 10 A.M.–5:45 P.M.

The retail outlet at this well-known music publishing house has one of the largest sheet music inventories in town. It's your basic old-fashioned music store with aisles and aisles of no-frills file cabinets crammed with all types of music. And if it's not in stock, the store will be happy to special order it for you. Fischer also sells some very pretty greeting cards.

JOSEPH PATELSON MUSIC HOUSE
160 W. 56th St., between Sixth and Seventh Aves. 582-5840
Mon.–Sat., 9 A.M.–6 P.M.

Patelson's is probably the first place music students, teachers, and professionals think of when they need sheet music. This store, which has been at the same location opposite Carnegie Hall's stage door since the 1940's, carries music for every instrument and voice, orchestral scores, and a good selection of music-related books. Patelson's also special orders.

JUILLIARD SCHOOL BOOK STORE
Upper level of the plaza at Alice Tully Hall,
Broadway at 65th St.   799-5000 ext. 237
Mon., Wed., Thur., 9:30 A.M.–7 P.M.; Tues., Fri., 9:30 A.M.–5:30 P.M.;
Sat., 10 A.M.–4:30 P.M.

In addition to its impressive selection of music-related books, the Juilliard Store is a marvelous source for sheet music. You'll also find college memorabilia: sweat shirts, pens, mugs, and the like with the school insignia.

METROPOLITAN OPERA SHOPS
•At the Metropolitan Opera House, Lincoln Center   580-4090
Mon.–Sat., 10 A.M.–10 P.M.; Sun., noon-5:30 P.M.
•835 Madison Ave., at 70th St.   734-8406
Mon.–Sat., 10 A.M.–6 P.M.; Sun., noon–5 P.M.

Looking for something related to opera? Search no more! The
Metropolitan Opera Shops carry the most comprehensive selection of
opera CD's, videos, and books imaginable, in addition to jewelry,
scarves, umbrellas, and an assortment of other wonderful items.

MUSIC INN
169 W. Fourth St., between Sixth and Seventh Aves.   243-5715
Tues.–Sat., 1 P.M.–7 P.M.; Mon., by appointment.

Crammed into a space the size of a walk-in closet, Music Inn has a
mind-boggling array of unusual instruments from around the world.
Every inch of space is covered with bells, lutes, African koras, Celtic
harps, Andean panpipes, and other uncommon items. To control the
number of customers (because the store is so small) there is a modest
entrance fee of $1, applicable toward purchase. Think of it as
admission to a small museum.

PERFORMING ARTS SHOP AT LINCOLN CENTER
Lower concourse of the Metropolitan Opera House   580-4356
Mon.–Sat., 10 A.M.–10 P.M.; Sun., noon–6 P.M.

Like the Metropolitan Opera Shops, this store carries CD's, tapes,
books, and all the associated musical paraphernalia, only here it's not
confined to opera. If you need a gift for a music lover, this shop is a
godsend. Down the hall there is a separate art gallery where you'll
find some wonderful paintings and posters.

RITA FORD MUSIC BOXES
19 E. 65th St., at Madison Ave.   535-6717
Mon.–Sat., 9 A.M.–5 P.M.

Rita Ford, who died in 1993 at the ripe old age of 92, was one of the world's authorities on music boxes. Over the years, her shop became a New York institution, attracting clients from around the world (the King of Saudi Arabia had made to order 20 matching boxes that play the Saudi national anthem). Her legacy lives on at the Madison Avenue shop where there is a fantastic collection of these charming toys for grown-ups: valuable antiques, unusual boxes, and more affordable new pieces. The store also does repairs and special orders.

CODA

You've been to the opera, you've gone to a jazz club; you're now taking trumpet lessons or singing in a chorus; you've found the perfect romantic spot to listen to music, and you know where to buy out-of-print rock albums. Still searching for something to do? Well, there are still plenty of places left to explore, things to see, sounds to hear. New York offers music lovers lots of interesting activities that are just a bit off the beaten path. Here are some to consider.

TOURS

CARNEGIE HALL
903-9790

Spend an hour exploring the world's most famous concert hall, learn about its history, and hear anecdotes about the musicians who helped make it what it is. Weekdays, except Wednesdays, at 11:30 A.M., 2 P.M., and 3 P.M. Tickets sold in the lobby, on the day of the tour. Adults, $6; students and seniors, $5; children under 12, $3. Also available for $27 is a "Tour and Tea," which includes the tour, followed by tea and savories at the Russian Tea Room next door.

HARLEM SPIRITUALS
757-0425

This company organizes a variety of unusual jaunts around Harlem, including a "Soul Food and Jazz" visit to a restaurant and jazz club, and "Harlem Gospel," which takes you to hear a church choir. They also venture into upper Manhattan and the Bronx, and multilingual tours are availabale. Prices vary.

LINCOLN CENTER TOURS
875-5350

Hour-long guided tours of Lincoln Center take you to three theaters: the Metropolitan Opera, New York State Theater, and Avery Fisher Hall. Experienced guides tell fascinating stories, and if you're lucky, you might get a glimpse of a rehearsal. Daily, from 10 A.M. to 5 P.M. Adults, $7.75; students and seniors, $6.75; 12 and under, $4.50. Reservations suggested.

MADISON SQUARE GARDEN BEHIND-THE-SCENES
465-5800

Visitors are guided through the cavernous sports and culture complex by experts who take them to the arena's luxury suites, on the stage and backstage at the Paramount, into the New York Knicks locker rooms and on the Garden Walk of Fame. Mon.–Fri., on the hour, 10 A.M.–2 P.M.; Sat., on the hour, 10 A.M.–1 P.M.; Sun., on the hour, 11 A.M.–1 P.M. Adults, $8; children under 12, $7.

MANDER PIPE ORGAN AT THE CHURCH OF ST. IGNATIUS LOYOLA

(see p. 104)

An organ tour? Well, not exactly. It's more like a personalized viewing. Malcolm Wechsler, a representative of Mander, the firm that built the fabulous new organ, will show you the instrument and even play it for you, for free. Call 203-348-8085.

METROPOLITAN OPERA GUILD BACKSTAGE TOURS

769-7020

Ever wonder how they build those lavish sets? Here's your chance to find out. You'll also see where the costumes and wigs are designed, as well as explore the dressing rooms and the multi-stage complex at the world's largest opera house. Tours are given September through June and last an hour and a half. Mon.–Fri. at 3:45 P.M.; Sat., 10 A.M. Adults, $8; students, $4. Reservations required.

NEW YORK CITY CULTURAL WALKING TOURS

979-2388

Alfred Pommer, a licensed guide and a veritable storehouse of information about the city, gives customized tours of Manhattan, focusing on history and architecture. While these tours are not specifically designed around music, Pommer does offer one of the theater district, called the Broadway Excursion, and he has lots of stories to tell about the Great White Way. $25 an hour for four or more people; $15 for three or less.

RADIO CITY MUSIC HALL GRAND TOUR

632-4041

Take a peek behind the scenes at this dazzling deco culture palace. You'll discover the secrets of one of the world's most technologically advanced stages, get a close-up look at the "Mighty Wurlitzer" organ, and maybe even meet a Rockette or two. Mon.–Sat.,

10 A.M.–5 P.M.; Sun., 11 A.M.–5 P.M. Tours depart every half hour. Adults, $11; children, $5.50.

ROCK AND ROLL TOURS OF NEW YORK
807-ROCK (7625)

The brochure says: "See where the stars of yesterday and today lived, wrote, performed, got signed, recorded, hung out, posed, partied and died." Except for their births, that about covers it! These two-hour bus tours begin and end at the Hard Rock Café (221 W. 57th St., near Seventh Ave.). Tickets are $25.

STEINWAY & SONS FACTORY TOUR
718-204-3127

The world's best-known pianos are built right here in Astoria, and now, in a free, two-hour guided tour, visitors to the 440,000 square-foot factory can watch as 300 craftsmen saw, bend, and sand the wood, put on the strings, and voice the instruments. You also go into the "Pounder Room," where a machine bangs on all 88 keys at once, 10,000 times—kind of like a crash test for pianos! Tours are usually held on the first Thursday of the month; you must reserve in advance.

MUSEUMS AND OTHER ATTRACTIONS

CARNEGIE HALL ROSE MUSEUM
247-7800

A small gallery on the second floor of Carnegie Hall, the Rose Musuem displays artifacts from the hall's first 100 years (program books, letters, ticket stubs, and what not). Every now and then there is a special exhibit about one of the celebrated performers who have appeared here over the years. Open free to the public. Hours: Daily, except Wednesdays, 11 A.M. – 4:30 P.M., and to concertgoers at concert time.

LAURA SPELLMAN ROCKEFELLER MEMORIAL CARILLON

At Riverside Church (see p. 108)   222-5900

For a smashing, 360-degree panoramic view of the city and the Hudson Valley, nothing beats the carillon tower at Riverside Church. This mammoth instrument is the world's biggest carillon, boasting the largest tuned bell (20 tons). If you climb the 392-foot tower during a recital, you get to watch Joseph Clair Davis, the resident carillonneur, in a booth playing the instrument, which he does on Sundays at 10:30 A.M., 12:30 P.M., and 3 P.M. Being inside the tower when the bells are ringing is an experience like no other! If you suffer from acrophobia, you can listen to the recitals from Grant's Tomb Park right across the street. The carillon is open Sundays, 12:30 P.M. – 4 P.M. Admission: $1.

METROPOLITAN MUSEUM OF ART INSTRUMENT COLLECTION

879-5500

The Met's collection is one of the finest in the country, with more than 5,000 instruments, 800 of which are on permanent display. Included is the oldest extant piano (built in 1720 by Cristofori), some rare Stradivari violins, and several Segovia guitars. There are two galleries, for Western and non-Western instruments respectively. Narrated audioguides with musical examples are available. Most of the instruments are playable, and can be heard in special concerts in the galleries, or in recordings.

MUSEUM OF THE AMERICAN PIANO

211 W. 58th St., near Broadway   246-4646
Subway: A, B, C, D, 1 or 9 to 59th St./Columbus Circle

It may seem odd that Kalman Detrich, a Hungarian immigrant, exhibits only American pianos at his shop/museum near Carnegie Hall. But Detrich began collecting American instruments years ago and ended up with so many he decided to open a small museum.

This humble gallery depicts the evolution of 19th-century
American-made pianos, some of which are on display, and visitors
get to hear them demonstrated. There are also photographs, old
booklets, piano keys, repair tools, and other memorabilia. Open by
appointment.

NEW YORK PUBLIC LIBRARY FOR THE PERFORMING ARTS
at Lincoln Center (see p. 49)   870-1600/1630

An invaluable resource for musicians, the library houses the world's
most extensive circulating, reference, and rare archival collections in
the arts. It has an impressive assortment of historic recordings,
videos, autograph manuscripts, sheet music, and other items. It's
also an active museum of sorts, with four galleries for both visiting
and permanent exhibits of art, photography, posters, and the like.
Recent shows have included "Come On and Hear: The Songs of
Irving Berlin," and "The Orchestra and the City: 150 Years of the
New York Philharmonic."

APPENDIX A

RADIO STATIONS AND MUSIC FORMATS

AM STATIONS:

WALK	1370	Adult Contemporary
WHLI	1100	Oldies, Big Band
WICC	600	Adult Contemporary
WLIB	1190	Black/Caribbean/Talk
WLIM	1580	Blues/Big Band/Talk
WMTR	1250	Pop Standards
WNJR	1430	Rhythm and Blues
WPAT	930	Easy Listening
WQEW	1560	Pop Standards/ Big Band
WRHD	1570	Country
WSKQ	620	Spanish Music/Talk
WWDJ	970	Christian Music
WWRL	1600	Gospel/Talk
WWRV	1330	Ethnic
WZRC	1480	Hard Rock

FM STATIONS:

WALK	97.5	Adult Contemporary
WAXQ	104.3	Rock
WBAB	102.3	Rock
WBAI	99.5	Mixed format
WBAZ	101.7	Light Contemporary
WBGO	88.3	Jazz
WBLI	106.1	Adult Contemporary
WBLS	107.5	Black/Urban Contemporary
WCBS	101.1	Oldies
WCWP	88.1	Mixed format
WDHA	105.5	Rock
WDRE	92.7	Progressive Rock
WEBE	107.9	Adult Contemporary
WEHM	96.7	Rock

WEZN	99.9	Easy Listening
WFAS	103.9	Adult Contemporary
WFDU	89.1	Mixed format
WFMU	91.1	Mixed format
WGSM	94.3	Easy Listening
WHFM	95.3	Adult Contemporary
WHTZ	100.3	Top 40
WHUD	100.7	Light Contemporary
WKCR	89.9	Mixed format (lots of jazz & avant-garde)
WKHL	96.7	Oldies
WKJY	98.3	Adult Contemporary
WLNG	92.1	Oldies/Adult Contemporary
WLTW	106.7	Light Contemporary
WMJC	94.3	Light Contemporary
WMXV	105.1	Adult Contemporary
WNEW	102.7	Rock
WNWK	105.9	Multi-ethnic
WNYC	93.9	Mixed format public radio/Classical
WPAT	93.1	Easy Listening
WPLJ	95.5	Top 40
WPLR	99.1	Rock
WPSC	88.7	Top 40
WQCD	101.9	Contemporary Jazz
WQHT	97.1	Top 40/Dance Music
WQXR	96.3	Classical
WRCN	103.9	Rock
WRGX	107.1	Rock
WRKS	98.7	Urban Contemporary
WRTN	93.5	Big Band/Nostalgia
WSKQ	97.9	Spanish Contemporary
WXRK	92.3	Classic Rock
WYNY	103.5	Country

APPENDIX B

ADDRESSES AND PHONE NUMBERS OF MAJOR CONCERT VENUES

AARON DAVIS HALL (p. 8)
at the City College of New York, Convent Ave. at 133d St., Manhattan 650-7100

ALICE TULLY HALL (p. 9)
at Lincoln Center
Broadway at 65th St., Manhattan 875-5050

AVERY FISHER HALL (p.10)
at Lincoln Center, Broadway at 65th St., Manhattan 875-5030

BROOKLYN ACADEMY OF MUSIC (p. 28)
30 Lafayette Ave., at Ashland Pl. 718-636-4100

CARNEGIE HALL & WEILL RECITAL HALL (p. 11) Seventh Ave. at 57th St., Manhattan 247-7800

CATHEDRAL OF ST. JOHN THE DIVINE (p. 103)
Amsterdam Ave. at 112th St., Manhattan 662-2133 or 307-7171

COLDEN CENTER FOR THE PERFORMING ARTS (p. 30)
at Queens College, Kissena Blvd. at the Long Island Expressway, Flushing 718-793-8080 or 718-997-ARTS (2787)

FLORENCE GOULD HALL (p. 13)
at the French Institute, 55 E. 59th St., near Madison Ave., Manhattan 355-6160

KATHRYN BACHE MILLER THEATRE (p. 14)
at Columbia University, Broadway at 116th St., Manhattan 854-7799

KAYE PLAYHOUSE (p. 15)
at Hunter College, 68th St., between Park and Lex. Aves., Manhattan 772-4448

LINCOLN CENTER FOR THE PERFORMING ARTS (p. 15)
North/South, from 66th St. to 62d St.; East/West from Columbus Ave./Broadway to Amsterdam Ave., Manhattan 875-5400

MADISON SQUARE GARDEN AND THE PARAMOUNT (p. 17)
Seventh Ave. at 33d St., Manhattan 465-MSG1 (6741)

MERKIN CONCERT HALL (p. 16)
129 W. 67th St., near Broadway, Manhattan 362-8719

METROPOLITAN MUSEUM OF ART (p. 17) Fifth Ave. at 82d St., Manhattan 570-3949

MILLER THEATER
(see Kathryn Bache Miller Theater)

92D ST. Y-TISCH CENTER FOR THE ARTS (p. 20) at Lexington Ave., Manhattan 415-5440

SAINT THOMAS CHURCH (p. 110)
Fifth Ave. at 53d St., Manhattan 757-7013

SYMPHONY SPACE (p. 22)
2537 Broadway, at 95th St., Manhattan 864-5400

TOWN HALL (p. 23)
123 W. 43d St., near 6th Ave., Manhattan 840-2824 or 997-6661

WEILL RECITAL HALL
(see Carnegie Hall)

INDEX

When more than one page number appears, the number in **bold** refers to the main listing in the book for that entry.

A.K.A.   146
AARON DAVIS HALL   8, 89, 238
ABSOLUTE ENSEMBLE   40
ACADEMY BOOK STORE   220
ACADEMY THEATRE   145
AFTER DINNER OPERA COMPANY   34, 79
ALGONQUIN HOTEL OAK ROOM, THE   74
ALICE TULLY HALL   9, 12, 44, 60, 71, 85, 183, 184, 188, 238
ALL SOULS UNITARIAN CHURCH   97
ALTERNATIVE MUSEUM   165
AMATEUR CHAMBER MUSIC PLAYERS   204
AMATO OPERA THEATRE   80
AMERICAN CHAMBER OPERA COMPANY   80
AMERICAN COMPOSERS ORCHESTRA   54
AMERICAN FEDERATION OF MUSICIANS, LOCAL 802   192
AMERICAN FESTIVAL OF MICROTONAL MUSIC   166
AMERICAN INSTITUTE OF GUITAR   43
AMERICAN LANDMARK FESTIVALS AT FEDERAL HALL   40
AMERICAN MUSEUM OF NATURAL HISTORY   153
AMERICAN OPERA PROJECTS   81
AMERICAN SYMPHONY ORCHESTRA   55, 183
AMERICAS SOCIETY, THE   159
AMOR ARTIS CHORUS AND ORCHESTRA   94
AMSTERDAM ROOM AT DOROT   41
AN DIE MUSIK   41
ANN GOODMAN RECITAL HALL   16

ANONYMOUS 4   109
APOLLO THEATRE   9
ARTEK   55
ARTISTS IN RADIO   41
ASCENSION MUSIC AT THE CHURCH OF THE ASCENSION   95
ASIA SOCIETY   153
ASSOCIATION FOR PUERTO RICAN– HISPANIC CULTURE   154
AUSTRIAN CULTURAL INSTITUTE   154
AVERY FISHER HALL   10, 19, 70, 238

BAM OUTSIDE: MUSIC AT METROTECH   123
BANG ON A CAN FESTIVAL   164, 166
BARGEMUSIC   74, 116
BATE RECORDS   220
BATTERY PARK CITY   123
BEACON THEATRE   146
BHARATIYA VIDYA BHAVAN, U.S.A.   154
BIG APPLE CHORUS   205
BIRDLAND   136
BITTER END, THE   146
BLARNEY STAR   154
BLEECKER BOB'S   221
BLOOMINGDALE HOUSE OF MUSIC   193
BLUE HILL TROUPE   205
BLUE NOTE, THE   136
BMCC DOWNTOWN SYMPHONY   206
BOROUGH OF MANHATTAN COMMUNITY COLLEGE   24, 206
BOTTOM LINE, THE   147
BOYS CHOIR OF HARLEM   8, 183
BRADLEY'S   136
BRANDENBURG OPERA   85

BRIDGEHAMPTON CHAMBER MUSIC IN NEW YORK 55

BRONX ARTS ENSEMBLE 27

BRONX HOUSE MUSIC SCHOOL 193

BRONX OPERA COMPANY 81

BRONX SYMPHONY ORCHESTRA 33

BROOKLYN ACADEMY OF MUSIC 28, 123, 238

BROOKLYN CENTER FOR THE PERFORMING ARTS 29

BROOKLYN CONSERVATORY OF MUSIC 193

BROOKLYN HEIGHTS ORCHESTRA 206

BROOKLYN MUSEUM 29, 66

BROOKLYN MUSIC SCHOOL 194

BROOKLYN NEIGHBORHOOD CHAMBER ORCHESTRA 56

BROOKLYN PHILHARMONIA CHORUS 207

BROOKLYN PHILHARMONIC ORCHESTRA 28

BROWN'S MUSIC CO. 227

BROWNIES 147

BROWNLEE OPERA THEATER 45

BRUNO WALTER AUDITORIUM 49

BRYANT PARK HALF PRICE TICKET BOOTH 37

BRYANT PARK YOUNG PERFORMERS SERIES 124

CABARET CONVENTION 137

CAFE CARLYLE AND BEMELMANS BAR 137

CAJUN CONNECTION 70

CAMI HALL 11

CANTERBURY CHORAL SOCIETY 106

CANTICUM NOVUM SINGERS 207

CARAMOOR FESTIVAL 133

CARIBBEAN CULTURAL CENTER 154

CARL FISCHER MUSIC STORE 228

CARNEGIE HALL 3, 10, 11, 97, 114, 119, 121, 137, 205, 215, 231, 238

CARNEGIE HALL NEIGHBORHOOD CONCERTS 42

CARNEGIE HALL ROSE MUSEUM 334

CATHEDRAL OF ST. JOHN THE DIVINE 20, 58, 84, 103, 117, 118, 120, 238

CBGB/OMFUG AND CBGB'S 313 GALLERY 147

CELEBRATE BROOKLYN 124

CENTER CIRCLE 70

CENTER FOR CONTEMPORARY OPERA 82

CENTERFOLD COFFEEHOUSE 42

CENTERSTAGE 125

CENTRAL CITY CHORUS 208

CENTRAL PARK SUMMERSTAGE 125

CENTRAL QUEENS Y PERFORMANCE SPACE 30

CENTRAL RESEARCH LIBRARY, THE 48

CHAMBER MUSIC SOCIETY OF LINCOLN CENTER 9, 12, 25, 71, 116, 184

CHAMBER MUSIC THROUGH THE AGES 32

CHANTICLEER 116

CHARLES IVES CENTER FOR THE ARTS 133

CHICAGO B.L.U.E.S. 148

CHILDREN'S ORCHESTRA SOCIETY 185

CHINA INSTITUTE OF AMERICA 154

CHORAL SYMPHONY SOCIETY AND CANTATA SINGERS 95

CHRIST AND ST. STEPHEN'S CHURCH 104

CHURCH OF ST. ANN AND THE HOLY TRINITY 104

CHURCH OF ST. IGNATIUS LOYOLA 104

CHURCH OF ST. LUKE IN THE FIELDS 218

CHURCH OF ST. MARY THE VIRGIN
105, 114, 177
CHURCH OF THE ASCENSION 95
CHURCH OF THE HEAVENLY REST 105
CHURCH OF THE HOLY TRINITY
(EPISCOPALIAN) 106
CITY CENTER 113
CITY COLLEGE OF NEW YORK 8, 175
CITY UNIVERSITY OF NEW YORK 39
CITY ISLAND CHAMBER ENSEMBLE
AT LE REFUGE INN 75
CLARION MUSIC SOCIETY 57
CLASSICAL MUSIC LOVERS'
EXCHANGE 71
CLASSICAL RECORD, A 220
CLOISTERS, THE 75, 121
COCONUTS MUSIC
AND MOVIES 221
COLDEN CENTER
FOR THE PERFORMING ARTS 30,
34, 59, 187, 189, 238
COLLEGE OF STATEN ISLAND
CENTER FOR THE ARTS 31
COLLEGIATE CHORALE 208
COLONY 221
COLUMBIA UNIVERSITY 14, 39, 158,
208, 238
COLUMBIA UNIVERSITY
ORCHESTRA 208
COMPOSERS CONCORDANCE 167
COMPOSERS' FORUM 167
CONCERT ROYAL 57, 110, 114
CONCORDIA ORCHESTRA 57, 114
CONGREGATION ANSCHE CHESED 82
CONSORTIUM SERIES 167
CONTEXT 168
CONTINUUM 168
COOLER, THE 148
COOPER-HEWITT NATIONAL
DESIGN MUSEUM 125
CORNERSTONE CHORALE 209
CORPUS CHRISTI CHURCH 106

COSMOPOLITAN SYMPHONY
ORCHESTRA 58
COTTON CLUB 138
CROSSTOWN ENSEMBLE 168

DA CAPO CHAMBER PLAYERS 169
DALCROZE SCHOOL OF MUSIC 194
DANCE THEATER WORKSHOP 169
DANNY'S SKYLIGHT ROOM
CABARET AND PIANO BAR 138
DESSOFF CHOIRS 209
DICAPO OPERA THEATRE 82
DILLER-QUAILE MUSIC SCHOOL 195
DOCTORS ORCHESTRAL SOCIETY 210
DONNELL LIBRARY CENTER 49
DORTHY DELSON KUHN MUSIC
INSTITUTE OF THE JEWISH
COMMUNITY CENTER 195
DOWNSTAIRS RECORDS 221
DOWNTOWN MUSIC
PRODUCTIONS 169

EARLY MUSIC FOUNDATION 58, 117
ECLECTIX CHAMBER ORCHESTRA 170
EIGHTY EIGHTS 139
ELYSIAN OPERA GROUP 92
EMPIRE STATE OPERA 82
ENCOMPASS MUSIC THEATRE 83
ENSEMBLE 21 170
ENSEMBLE FOR EARLY MUSIC 58, 117
ESSENTIAL MUSIC 170
ETHNIC FOLK ARTS CENTER 154
EXPERIMENTAL INTERMEDIA 171

FAMILY MUSIK 185
FAT TUESDAYS 139
FESTIVAL CHAMBER
MUSIC SOCIETY 71
FESTIVAL OF AMERICAN MUSIC
THEATRE 98
FEZ 148
FINYL VINYL 222

FIRST AVENUE   171
FIRST NIGHT NEW YORK   117
FLORENCE GOULD HALL   13, 57,
  187, 238
FLORENCE GOULD HALL
  CHAMBER PLAYERS   13
FLUSHING TOWN HALL   31
FOOTLIGHT RECORDS   222
FOREST HILLS
  SYMPHONY ORCHESTRA   210
FOUR NATIONS ENSEMBLE   59
FRENCH INSTITUTE-
  ALLIANCE FRANÇAISE   13
FRICK COLLECTION   42
FRIENDS AND ENEMIES
  OF NEW MUSIC   171

GAMELAN SON OF LION   172
GILBERT AND SULLIVAN
  SOCIETY OF NEW YORK   83
GOETHE HOUSE NEW YORK   155
GOLDEN DISC   222
GOLDEN FLEECE LTD.-
  COMPOSERS CHAMBER THEATRE   84
GOLDMAN MEMORIAL BAND   126
GOLIARD CONCERTS   59
GRACE RAINEY ROGERS AUDITORIUM
  (SEE METROPOLITAN MUSEUM OF ART)
GRAMERCY ARTS THEATRE   161
GRAMERCY BRASS   43
GRANDE BANDE   58
GREENWICH HOUSE
  MUSIC SCHOOL   195
GREENWICH VILLAGE ORCHESTRA   210
GREGG SMITH SINGERS   96
GROWING UP WITH OPERA   185
GRYPHON RECORDS   222
GUGGENHEIM MUSEUM   75
GUGGENHEIM MUSEUM SOHO   172
GUITAR AMONG OTHERS   43
GUITAR STAGE   43

HANDEL AND HAYDN
  SOCIETY OF BOSTON   114
HARLEM SCHOOL OF THE ARTS   196
HARLEM SPIRITUALS   232
HAYDN SEEK CONCERTS   186
HEAVENLY JAZZ   106
HEBREW UNION COLLEGE-JEWISH
  INSTITUTE OF RELIGION   107
HELLENIC CULTURAL CENTER   155
HENRY STREET SETTLEMENT   196
HIGHLIGHTS IN JAZZ   22
HISTORIC RICHMOND TOWN   155
HMV   223
HOLY TRINITY LUTHERAN CHURCH   107
HOSTOS CENTER FOR THE ARTS   32
HOT PROSPECTS   126
HOTEL WALES
  CHAMBER MUSIC SOIRÉES   44
HOUSE OF OLDIES   223
HUNTER COLLEGE   15, 60

I CANTORI DI NEW YORK   207
I GIULLARI DI PIAZZA   84, 117
IL PICCOLO TEATRO DELL'OPERA   84,
  115
INTERNATIONAL HOUSE
  OF NEW YORK   156
INTERNATIONAL OFFESTIVAL   173
INTERPRETATIONS SERIES   173
INTERSCHOOL ORCHESTRAS OF
  NEW YORK   186
IRIDIUM   139
IRISH ARTS CENTER   156
IRVING PLAZA   149
ITALIAN CULTURAL INSTITUTE   156

J&R MUSIC WORLD   223
JAMMYLAND   224
JAPAN SOCIETY   157
JAZZ AT LINCOLN CENTER   140
JAZZ AT NOON   140
JAZZ COMPOSER'S COLLECTIVE   141

JAZZ FOR YOUNG PEOPLE 140
JAZZ IN JULY 21
JAZZ INSTITUTE OF HARLEM 8
JAZZ LIVE 32
JAZZ RECORD CENTER 224
JAZZMOBILE 141
**JEWISH ASSOCIATION
FOR SERVICES FOR THE AGED** 197
JEWISH MUSEUM 56, 157
JONES BEACH 133
JOSEPH PATELSON MUSIC HOUSE 228
JUILLIARD OPERA CENTER 44
JUILLIARD SCHOOL, THE 44, 131, 197
JUILLIARD SCHOOL BOOK STORE 228
JULIUS GROSSMAN ORCHESTRA 126
JUPITER SYMPHONY 60
JVC JAZZ FESTIVAL 127

KATHRYN BACHE MILLER THEATRE 14, 65, 68, 98, 167, 176, 208, 238
KAYE PLAYHOUSE 15, 63, 116, 238
KIDSCLASSICS 187
**KINGSBOROUGH COMMUNITY
COLLEGE THEATER** 33
KITCHEN, THE 173
KLEZMATICS, THE 157
KNICKERBOCKER BAR AND GRILL 142
KNITTING FACTORY 142, 148
KOREAN CULTURAL SERVICE 157
KOSCIUSZKO FOUNDATION 60
KWANZAA 118

L'OPÉRA FRANÇAIS DE NEW YORK 86
**LA GRAN SCENA
OPERA COMPANY** 85
LA MAMA E.T.C. 174
**LAURA SPELLMAN ROCKEFELLER
MEMORIAL CARILLON** 235
LAVENDER LIGHT GOSPEL CHOIR 211
LE REFUGE INN 75
LEAGUE OF COMPOSERS/ISCM 174

LEFRAK CONCERT HALL 30
**LEHMAN CENTER
FOR THE PERFORMING ARTS** 33, 81
LIEDERKRANZ OPERA THEATRE 85
LIGHTHOUSE MUSIC SCHOOL 198
LIMELIGHT 149
LINCOLN CENTER FESTIVAL 127
**LINCOLN CENTER
FOR THE PERFORMING ARTS** 15
LINCOLN CENTER OFF STAGE 71
LINCOLN CENTER OUT-OF-DOORS 127
LIONHEART 96
LITTLE ORCHESTRA SOCIETY 60, 115, 118, 187, 212
LONGAR EBONY ENSEMBLE 61
LOTUS FINE ARTS CENTER 158
**LUCY MOSES SCHOOL FOR MUSIC
AND DANCE** 194, 198, 201
LYRIC THEATRE, LTD. 92
LYRICS AND LYRICISTS 21
LYRITAS PERFORMERS 92

MADISON SQUARE GARDEN 16, 232, 238
MAHRAJAN AL-FAN 29
MAISON FRANÇAISE 158
MAJESTIC THEATER 28
MANDER PIPE ORGAN 233
**MANHATTAN CHAMBER
ORCHESTRA** 61
MANHATTAN OPERA ASSOCIATION 86
MANHATTAN OPERA THEATRE 87
MANHATTAN SCHOOL OF MUSIC 45, 199
MANNES COLLEGE OF MUSIC 46, 144
MANNES OPERA ENSEMBLE 46
**MARTIN LUTHER KING JR.
CONCERT SERIES** 128
**MARYMOUNT MANHATTAN
COLLEGE** 39
MAXWELL'S 149
MCBURNEY YMCA 214

**MEASURED BREATHS
THEATRE COMPANY** 87

MERCURY LOUNGE 150

MERKIN CONCERT HALL 16, 50, 59, 64, 71, 72, 173, 181, 198, 238

METROPOLITAN GREEK CHORALE 211

METROPOLITAN MUSEUM OF ART 17, 63, 75, 76, 101, 116, 188, 235, 238

METROPOLITAN OPERA 8, 17, 36, 78, 111, 117, 233

METROPOLITAN OPERA GUILD 87, 185, 233

**METROPOLITAN OPERA
IN THE PARKS** 128

METROPOLITAN OPERA SHOPS 229

**METROPOLITAN SINGERS/
THE GREEK CHORAL SOCIETY** 211

MICHAEL'S PUB 143

MIDAMERICA PRODUCTIONS 62

MIDNIGHT RECORDS 224

MIDSUMMER NIGHT SWING 128

**MIDTOWN JAZZ AT MIDDAY
AND JAZZ VESPERS** 110

**MIND-BUILDERS CREATIVE ARTS
CENTER** 200

MOSTLY MOZART FESTIVAL 129

MUSEO DEL BARRIO 158

MUSEUM FOR AFRICAN ART 159

**MUSEUM OF MODERN ART SCULPTURE
GARDEN** 131

**MUSEUM OF THE AMERICAN
PIANO** 235

**MUSIC AND ART LOVERS
CLUB FOR SINGLES** 72

MUSIC BEFORE 1800 106

**MUSIC FOR HOMEMADE
INSTRUMENTS** 174

MUSIC FROM CHINA 159

MUSIC FROM JAPAN 159

MUSIC INN 229

MUSIC OF THE AMERICAS 159

MUSIC OF OUR TIME 12

MUSIC PROJECT, THE 46

**MUSIC TEACHERS
NATIONAL ASSOCIATION** 192

MUSIC UNDER CONSTRUCTION 175

MUSIC UNDER NEW YORK 47

**MUSICA SACRA
CHORUS AND ORCHESTRA** 97, 114

**MUSICA VIVA
CHORUS AND ORCHESTRA** 97

MUSICIAN'S CLUB OF NEW YORK 38

MUSICIANS FROM MARLBORO 17, 62

**MUSICIANS OF MELODIOUS
ACCORD** 98

MUSICIANS' ACCORD 175

N.Y.C. BALLET 119

N.Y.C. CULTURAL WALKING TOURS 233

N.Y.C. GAY MEN'S CHORUS 213

**N.Y.C. HOUSING AUTHORITY
SYMPHONY ORCHESTRA** 47

N.Y.C. LABOR CHORUS 214

N.Y.C. OPERA 19

**NATIONAL CHORALE AND NATIONAL
CHORAL COUNCIL** 98, 114, 115

**NATIONAL FEDERATION
OF MUSIC CLUBS** 192

**NATIONAL MUSEUM
OF THE AMERICAN INDIAN** 160

NAUMBURG ORCHESTRA 129

NEAR EASTERN MUSIC ENSEMBLE 160

**NEW AMERICAN
CHAMBER ORCHESTRA** 63

NEW AMSTERDAM SINGERS 212

**NEW AMSTERDAM
SYMPHONY ORCHESTRA** 212

NEW JUILLIARD ENSEMBLE 44

NEW MUSIC CONSORT 45

**NEW SCHOOL
FOR SOCIAL RESEARCH** 143

NEW SOUNDS LIVE 16

NEW YORK ALL-CITY HIGH SCHOOL
MUSIC PROGRAM   188
NEW YORK CHAMBER ENSEMBLE   63
NEW YORK CHAMBER SYMPHONY   20
NEW YORK CHORAL SOCIETY   213,
217
NEW YORK CONCERT SINGERS   99
NEW YORK CONSORTIUM
FOR NEW MUSIC   176
NEW YORK FESTIVAL OF SONG   99
NEW YORK GILBERT AND SULLIVAN
PLAYERS   88
NEW YORK GRAND OPERA   125, 129
NEW YORK HISTORICAL SOCIETY   48
NEW YORK MADRIGAL SINGERS   100
NEW YORK MANDOLIN
ORCHESTRA   214
NEW YORK NEW MUSIC ENSEMBLE   177
NEW YORK PHILHARMONIC   8, 10,
19, 36, 53, 64, 72, 103, 122,
128, 130, 164, 182
NEW YORK PHILHARMONIC
ENSEMBLES   64
NEW YORK PHILHARMONIC
PARKS CONCERTS   130
NEW YORK PHILHARMONIC
YOUNG PEOPLE'S CONCERTS   189
NEW YORK PHILOMUSICA
CHAMBER ENSEMBLE   64
NEW YORK PINEWOODS
FOLK MUSIC CLUB   160
NEW YORK POPS ORCHESTRA   64, 119
NEW YORK PRO ARTE
CHAMBER ORCHESTRA   65
NEW YORK PUBLIC LIBRARY   39, 48,
236
NEW YORK SOCIETY FOR ETHICAL
CULTURE   49
NEW YORK STRING ORCHESTRA
SEMINAR   119
NEW YORK UNIVERSITY   39, 158,
177, 181

NEW YORK VERISMO OPERA, INC.   92
NEW YORK VIRTUOSI X
CHAMBER SYMPHONY   65
NEW YORK VIRTUOSO SINGERS   100
NEW YORK YOUTH SYMPHONY   189
NEWBAND   175
NEXT STAGE COMPANY   177
NEXT WAVE FESTIVAL   28
NICHOLAS ROERICH MUSEUM   49
92ND STREET Y SCHOOL OF MUSIC   200
92ND STREET Y-TISCH CENTER FOR THE
ARTS (KAUFMANN CONCERT HALL)   20,
120, 185, 200, 238
NOONDAY CONCERTS   50
NORFOLK CHAMBER MUSIC
FESTIVAL   133
NORMAN J. SEAMAN
ENTERTAINMENT CLUB   38
NORTH/SOUTH CONSONANCE   178
NOT JUST JAZZ   24

OMEGA ENSEMBLE   50
125TH STREET RECORD SHACK   224
OPERA AT NOON   50
OPERA EBONY   8, 88
OPERA FESTIVAL OF NEW JERSEY   133
OPERA MANHATTAN   89
OPERA ORCHESTRA OF NEW YORK   89
OPERA QUOTANNIS   89
OPERASPECTIVES   90
ORATORIO SOCIETY OF NEW YORK   215
ORCHESTRA OF ST. LUKE'S/
ST. LUKE'S CHAMBER ENSEMBLE   66,
100, 110, 172, 184
ORPHEUS CHAMBER ORCHESTRA   66

PACE DOWNTOWN THEATER   21
PADDY REILLY'S   161
PALLADIUM   150
PARAMOUNT, THE   16, 117, 232,
238
PARK AVENUE SYNAGOGUE   107

PARNASSUS 178
PARTHENIA 58, 110
PAUL WINTER CONSORT 103, 120
PEOPLE'S SYMPHONY CONCERTS 50
PEOPLE'S VOICE CAFE 112
PERFORMANCE SPACE 122 (P.S. 122) 178
PERFORMING ARTS SHOP AT LINCOLN CENTER 229
PHILHARMONIA VIRTUOSI 67
PIERPONT MORGAN LIBRARY 67
PLANTING FIELDS ARBORETUM 133
POMERIUM 100
POSITIVE MUSIC 51
PRISM CHAMBER ORCHESTRA 179
PROSPECT PARK CONCERT GROVE 126

QUEENS COLLEGE 30
QUEENS OPERA ASSOCIATION 90
QUEENS SYMPHONY ORCHESTRA 34
QUEENSBOROUGH COMMUNITY COLLEGE 34
QUEENSBOROUGH ORCHESTRA 34
QUINTET OF THE AMERICAS 179

RADIO CITY MUSIC HALL 22, 120, 233
RAINBOW AND STARS 76
RECORD MART 225
REGINA OPERA COMANY 91
RENEE WEILER CONCERT HALL 195
REPERTORIO ESPAÑOL 161
REVOLVER RECORDS 225
RITA FORD MUSIC BOXES 230
RIVER MUSIC 130
RIVERDALE CHORAL SOCIETY 215
RIVERSIDE CHURCH 108, 120. 235
RIVERSIDE OPERA ENSEMBLE 91
RIVERSIDE SYMPHONY 68
ROCK AND ROLL TOURS OF NEW YORK 234
ROCK'S IN YOUR HEAD 225

ROCKEFELLER CENTER 130
ROSELAND BALLROOM 150
ROSEWOOD CHAMBER ENSEMBLE 51
ROTTENBERG CHORALE 198
ROULETTE 165, 179
RUSSIAN CHAMBER CHORUS OF NEW YORK 216
RUSSIAN EMIGRÉ CHOIR 101
RUSSIAN TEA ROOM 76

S.E.M. ENSEMBLE 180
S.O.B.'S 162
SAM GOODY 225
SARDI'S 140
SCHIMMEL CENTER FOR THE ARTS 21
SCHOMBURG CENTER FOR RESEARCH IN BLACK CULTURE 161
SCHOOL FOR STRINGS 210
SECOND COMING RECORDS 226
SEUFFERT BAND 131
SHOWBOAT BARGE AT THE HUDSON WATERFRONT MUSEUM 51
SINGERS FORUM 91
SMALL'S 143
SNUG HARBOR CULTURAL CENTER 35
SOHO CENTER FOR NEW OPERA 81
SONIC BOOM 176
SONIDOS DE LAS AMERICAS FESTIVAL 54
SOUTH STREET SEAPORT 120, 132
SPANISH INSTIUTE–CENTER FOR AMERICAN-SPANISH AFFAIRS 162
SPECIAL MUSIC SCHOOL OF AMERICA 201
SPECULUM MUSICAE 180
ST. BARTHOLOMEW'S CHURCH 108
ST. CECILIA CHORUS 120, 216
ST. GEORGE'S CHORAL SOCIETY 217
ST. JEAN BAPTISTE CHURCH 94
ST. MARK'S PARK 202
ST. MICHAEL'S CHURCH 109
ST. PATRICK'S CATHEDRAL 118

ST. PAUL'S CHAPEL 50
ST. PETER'S CHURCH
  AT THE CITICORP CENTER 110
ST. THOMAS CHURCH
  FIFTH AVENUE 57, 110, 114
STATEN ISLAND SYMPHONY 35
STEINWAY & SONS 234
STEINWAY HALL 52
STEPHEN WISE FREE SYNAGOGUE 111
STONEWALL CHORALE 216
SUBTERRANEAN RECORDS 226
SUMMERGARDEN 131
SUMMERPIER 132
SWEET ADELINE SOCIETY 215
SWEET BASIL 144
SWISS INSTITUE 162
SYLVAN WINDS 68
SYMPHONY SPACE 22, 46, 88,
  212, 238

TAIPEI THEATER 23
TALLIS SCHOLARS 120
TAVERN ON THE GREEN
  CHESTNUT ROOM 77
TEMPLE EMANU-EL 111
THALIA SPANISH THEATER 162
THAT! NEW MUSIC GROUP 180
THEATER DEVELOPMENT FUND
  (TDF) 37
THIASOS CAFE 162
THIRD STREET MUSIC SCHOOL
  SETTLEMENT 201
TOWER RECORDS 226
TOWN HALL 23, 51, 137, 238
TRAMPS 150
TRIBECA PERFORMING ARTS
  CENTER 24
TRINITY CHURCH 111
TURTLE BAY MUSIC SCHOOL 202

UKRAINIAN INSTITUTE 163
UPTOWN COFFEEHOUSE 163

VENUS 227
VIENNA CHOIR BOYS 121
VILLAGE LIGHT OPERA GROUP 217
VILLAGE VANGUARD 144
VINEYARD, THE 121
VIRGIN CONSORT 114
VISIONES 145

WALTER READE THEATER
  AT LINCOLN CENTER 24
WARMER BY THE STOVE 158
WASHINGTON SQUARE CHURCH 112
WASHINGTON SQUARE
  CONTEMPORARY MUSIC SOCIETY 181
WASHINGTON SQUARE
  MUSIC FESTIVAL 132
WAVE HILL 77
WAVERLY CONSORT 121
WEBSTER HALL 151
WEILL RECITAL HALL 11, 137, 238
WEST END GATE 145
WEST VILLAGE CHORALE 115, 217,
  218
WESTCHESTER PHILHARMONIC 73
WESTERN WIND, THE 116
WETLANDS 151
WILLIAMSON THEATER
  (SEE COLLEGE OF STATEN ISLAND)
WINTER GARDEN 25
WINTER STAR 121
WORLD FINANCIAL CENTER
  AT BATTERY PARK CITY 25, 132
WORLD MUSIC INSTITUTE 163
WORLD TRADE CENTER 125
WQXR CONCERT SERIES 132

YWCA ROOFTOP CONCERTS 131

ABOUT THE AUTHOR

Ira Rosenblum compiles and edits the music listings for *The New York Times*. A recipient of a Master of Music degree from the Juilliard School, he has written articles for *The New York Times* and other publications. In his spare time, he plays solo piano and performs in chamber music recitals.

ABOUT THE ILLUSTRATOR

Emily Lisker, whose illustrations have appeared in magazines and newspapers across the country, is currently working on her fourth children's book. She lives in Woonsocket, Rhode Island.